SPIRIT
OF
SASQUATCH

ERNEST SOLAR

This book is a work of fiction. Names, characters, places, businesses, and incidents either are products of the author's imagination or are used fictitiously. Any resemblance to actual events, locales or persons, living, dead, or undead is entirely coincidental and not intended by the author.

SPIRIT OF SASQUATCH

Cover design by Susan Wilson Designs
Front cover photograph by Ernest Solar

Manufactured in the United States of America

Paperback ISBN-13: 978-0-692-89219-0

For my Dad, who heard
Sookum first on Mallory Hill,
West Virginia during our first
father and son camp out.

AUTHOR'S NOTE

In this edition of *Spirit of Sasquatch*, I have chosen to use what I believe to be the correct grammatical representation when referring to the cryptozoological creature known as bigfoot or sasquatch by using a small *b* or *s* when referring to the creature. From a grammatical perspective, bigfoot and sasquatch should be written with a lowercase *b* or *s* because in theory there are multiple bigfoot and sasquatch living in the forests of North America. Similar to the thousands of bear, deer, moose, elk, and other wildlife creatures inhabiting the same forests of North America.

There would be two reasons why an author could legitimately use a capital *B* or *S* when referring to the creature. First, from a historical perspective, a capital letter would be appropriate if referring to the specific creature that left the prints found by Jim Crew near his bulldozer in 1957. Second, a capital letter would be necessary if the creature known as bigfoot is designated as a race or group of people (or hominids); such as, Americans or Homo Erectus. Many researchers would argue that the creature is a group of hominids; however, the scientific community has not yet officially accepted the existence of these creatures, therefore it is presumptuous of the amateur bigfoot research community to refer to these creatures as a hominid or animal.

As a writer, researcher, and educator, I feel it is important to incorporate the use of the lowercase distinction when referring to the creatures in general.

"They exist in another dimension from us but can appear in this dimension whenever they have a reason to."

~ *Ray Owen, son of a Dakota spiritual leader from Prairie Island Reservation in Minnesota*

PROLOGUE

"I speak of a time before the paleface came to take our land," said the ancient Native American Indian. The man's skin was dark and leathery from countless years out in the sun. Under his skin were the remnants of hard-earned muscle from living off of the land. Despite his age, the older man's hair was still jet black. It was pulled into a ponytail that hung to the middle of his back. He wore blue jeans, moccasins, and a worn cowhide leather vest. He sat cross-legged on a frayed, braided rug in a small hut in the desert. He was considered a great elder of his people, amongst the last.

"I speak of a time many moons before," he said as he looked up through the small opening in the roof of his hut, which allowed smoke from the fire to escape. Looking back into the small fire cooking his dinner, he said, "I had a different name then, not the name I have carried throughout my life. I was known as Little Otter." The man smiled at the thought. "I loved equally the forest trees and the water the river gave us." The elder man poked at the fire with a stick and chuckled to himself. "I was also small for my age."

"It was a time of the Sprouting Grass Moon. Our people had just moved from our winter camp. It was along the river, but near a place we called the Dark Rock." The man sprinkled some herbs over the meat cooking in the fire. "At a young age we were all taught to stay away from the Dark Rock. It was an evil place. Even during the day of the brightest sun, the forest around Dark Rock was always covered in shadows. At night, we would hear moans and howls from the forest near this forbidden place. Our mothers taught us to leave the forest and return to the river before the sunset to avoid the anger of our elder forest brothers that lived in the region."

The old Indian sat for a long time without talking. He simply stared at the fire, lost in a daze of a memory from long ago. Closing his eyes, he continued. "We knew of the paleface. Our elders had received word from Mother Earth that our time was coming to an end." The old man frowned. "Many of our tribal leaders did not believe Mother Earth. Many of our kind wanted to hide in the deep forest like our forest brothers of Dark Rock. In the end we did nothing. In the end the paleface came to us. First in ones and twos. Then in herds as great as the bison. I speak of the time before the herds."

"One paleface came. A trapper. He called himself Caven Hugh. He was not what the elders expected. He was a lean man with a thick beard and long, wild hair. He wore a lacing of bear claws around his neck and a cap of fur around his head. His clothes were similar to ours, but his leather vest sprouted fur around the collar. In some places, you couldn't tell where his beard ended and the animal fur began. He rode a horse but carried many more supplies than our own warriors would carry. I liked him.

"The paleface was trapping along the river. I saw him first. I brought him to our tribe. He stayed with us for many moons. While he was with us, he heard stories of our forest brothers who lived in the thicket of trees near Dark Rock. He questioned me often on the stories he heard. At first, I pretended to not know any of the stories. Then I became afraid that he would find someone else in the tribe to answer his questions. So, I started to share with him what I knew. He became determined to see one. I assured him that an arrow or knife would do no harm to the giants because of their size. He laughed and said that he had something stronger than an arrow or a knife. I knew he meant his rifle. Even though we hid in the deep forest away from the paleface many of our warriors had a rifle from trading with other tribes. I also knew they were useless against the giants near Dark Rock. I tried warning him that the giants were not real. This he did not understand. At the time I did not have the words to describe what I meant. I know the words now."

The Indian stared into the fire. "They are spirit walkers. I tried to explain this to the trapper. I do not think he understood what I meant." He sat in silence for a long time before continuing, "They are able to slip between our world and the spirit world. Similar to our medicine men. Caven did not understand this."

The fire popped and hissed. The old man cocked his head, then spoke to the flames in a long-forgotten mystic tongue. Moments passed before he spoke again. "He asked me to take him to the forest near Dark Rock. At first I refused. But again, I was fearful he would find another to show him. Many young boys of our tribe wanted the paleface's attention. I knew he favored me, and I did not want to lose that. Being a foolish young boy, I went against my mother's warning. I had heard whispers from the older warriors and mothers about a patch of blackberries near Dark Rock where our forest brothers were often seen. I took Caven there late one afternoon. I was scared, but brave. I suspected we would see a bear, not one of the hairy giants. I was wrong." The elder man paused and thought for a moment. "They are our forest brothers. Protectors of our Great Mother. I call them hairy giants, because they are." He pulled the stick from the fire and blew on the roasted meat. He pulled at the skin covering the meat with his teeth and the juices spilled over his chin. He bit into it and chewed while watching the fire dance.

A long while passed before he continued. "When we arrived, I felt eyes upon us. I believe Caven felt it also. I gathered my courage and crawled into the blackberry bushes. Caven waited among the trees with his rifle ready. I moved quickly and quietly through the underbrush and trees. I believed I was as quiet as our warriors." The elder man smiled to himself. "But they feel your presence even before you pass through the trees. I made my way to the Dark Rock. I touched the forbidden place. That is when it made itself known. He stepped from the trees." Saying this, he slowly shook his head while he chewed on the meat. "He stepped from a place beyond the trees. Larger than any creature I had ever seen in my young life. Covered in black hair darker than a new moon night. It hung long and matted from its arms and chest. I had seen bear. Bison. This thing was thicker and larger than the largest bear or bison ever brought to our camp. Its muscles and thickness made the trees seem to shrink in size. He was angry. I could see the anger in its eyes. In its face. I had no knife or bow." The elder man smiled and chuckled to himself. "I did what any brave warrior would do. I ran. It roared. I could feel the power behind its roar against my back as I ran through the darkened forest. I crashed through underbrush and branches. I never looked back, but I could feel him behind me. I could hear the thick branches it snapped off the trees as it ran me out of its home. The noise of its breathing and breaking branches consumed me. I crashed through the blackberry bushes. I never felt the thorns tear through my flesh. I was more scared of the hairy giant tearing my limbs off. I stumbled and rolled to the feet of my paleface friend Caven. I heard the report of his rifle but did not see what happened." The old Indian tossed the uneaten meat into the fire and picked up a long wooden pipe. He carefully packed it with tobacco. Lit the pipe and took a long puff.

He took another puff and slowly exhaled the smoke. "His retelling of the tale to the elder tribesmen gave me my new name. The one you know me by now, Rampaging Buffalo. In his telling of the tale he recounts waiting for me among the trees near the blackberry bushes. He waited a long time. Then he heard a scream unlike anything he had ever heard before. To him it sounded like the palefaces' Devil screaming. He felt the power of the shriek in his soul. He recounts that he loaded his rifle and raised it to his shoulder and waited. He said he heard what he thought was a rampaging buffalo crashing through the forest towards him. He said that he had faced buffalo before and was unafraid. But a buffalo is not what he saw. He watched my small body crash through the blackberries and he lowered his rifle to laugh, thinking it was I who caused all the noise. Then to his horror the hairy giant appeared and screamed at him. He quickly raised his rifle and fired. My paleface friend Caven said he could not have missed at that range. I believe him."

The elder man smoked on the pipe from a long minute before continuing. "He told the elders of the tribe that a bright light flashed before his eyes. Similar to a lightning flash. And the hairy giant was gone. Vanished before his eyes. I remember Caven cursing in words that were not familiar to me at the time. He grabbed the scruff of my neck like a dog and brought me to my feet. We both ran as swift as deer back to camp. Caven implored the elders of the tribe to explain to him what had happened. That is when we both learned that the hairy giants were spirit walkers. They are of flesh like you and I. Connected to the land and able to slip between our world and the spirit world. Our elders believe that is how they remain hidden from our eyes."

"Shortly after that meeting, my paleface friend Caven Hugh left in search of the hairy giants that could spirit walk. I believe my friend Caven has spirit walked with the hairy giants from Dark Rock."

The old man stared into the fire for a long time before he spoke again. "I am done speaking," said Rampaging Buffalo.

TRIBE

Chapter 1

Journal Notes from Abby Blackwood:

"He is both spirit and real being, but he can also glide through the forest, like a moose with big antlers, as though the trees weren't there... I know him as my brother..." –Quote by Oglala Lakota Medicine Man Pete Catches from an article titled "Attitudes Toward Bigfoot in Many North American Cultures," written by Gayle Highpine.

Trevor and I disagree.

Trevor believes bigfoot is a flesh and blood creature.

I believe the Big Man is both a spirit and a flesh-and-blood creature. A special type of "being."

Trevor agrees that bigfoot does contain an

intelligence superior to other animals of the forest. However, he does not believe the creature's intelligence is equal to our own.

Maybe it is because of my Native American heritage, compared to Trevor's Scottish heritage, but I believe that the Big Man brings messages and signs of trouble from Mother Earth, or in the Christian sense, God. (Oh, I'm sure that would tug at the priest's collars of my old Catholic school).

Trevor argues that bigfoot is a real physical creature because of signs that it eats, sleeps, marks its territory, and poops. He even agrees that the creature must practice family rituals of caring for its young.

I argue that the Big Man must take on the properties of our physical world when it is here. In the spirit world those human-like traits are not necessary.

I do see his point and understand his arguments. They are logical. It is easy to believe what you see and dismiss what cannot be seen or touched.

Believing stories from old men, about a time that has been lost, is a matter of faith. But I cannot dismiss the old stories of the Hopi, the Iroquois, the Sioux and countless other tribes spread across North America that speak of the Big Man as a spirit being capable of slipping through dimensions like the great medicine men of their tribes.

I understand how stories of old can be embellished or enhanced from one generation to the next. However, in Native American Indian cultures, the Big Man has consistently held a place of high regard in the spirit world, essential to human development and connected to Mother Earth, while also still being a physical creature that has been feared and respected by all tribes. Therefore, there must be an element of truth behind the old stories whispered by the elders of the tribes.

I must tend to my boys. They wait for dinner.

In closing, I love the words from Pete Catches, an Oglala Lakota Medicine Man. "I want him [the Big Man] to touch me, just a touch, a blessing, something I could bring home to my sons and grandchildren, that I was there, that I approached him, and he touched me."

That would truly be a blessing. I think.

Chapter 2

Trevor traced his fingers over the handwriting of his wife's words and imagined he could feel her own fingers as they moved across the page. It was the last journal entry she would write. He closed the leather-bound book and held it in his meaty hands. He looked at those hands. His lips twitched into a slight smile at the thought that Abby liked his hands. He argued they were rough and calloused. She would only squeeze them tighter and pull them to her chest, kissing each fingertip with tenderness.

Glancing up into the fire he quickly scanned the circle of men. He looked for any evidence of the men watching him. None were, except one. The newcomer, Jake. Jake gave Trevor a curt nod and said, "Blackwood." Trevor didn't know Jake's last name. In return he gave an equally curt nod. Something about Jake made Trevor nervous. Abby would say, as she often did, that anyone new made him nervous. He supposed she was right. He was naturally apprehensive. Then again, Jake seemed to take a liking to his elder boy, Darius.

Thinking of his son, Trevor stood and scanned the campsite for signs of his presence. Most of the other members of the expedition were still busying themselves with late morning activities getting ready for the day. He spotted Darius near the tent. Not seeing his younger son, Brock, he called to Darius in a tone that was more of a bark, "Darius, where's Brock?"

Darius looked up at his father and shrugged his shoulders. "He left before breakfast. Towards the river."

"Damn kid," growled Trevor as he dropped back into his seat and scanned the dense forest. To Trevor, he was comfortable in any forest. However, Brock was young and unfamiliar with the undergrowth, terrain, and wildlife of the Allegheny Mountains.

"What's wrong, T?" asked his longtime friend, Buzzy, who was sitting to his right.

"Boy ran off again," said Trevor as he gulped down his coffee.

Buzzy chuckled and shook his head. "Hell, if it was any other boy here outside of your two sons I'd be worried. Your boys? They're as competent as their old man."

Trevor wanted to smile at the thought but contained his emotions and pride. Abby and he insisted on teaching their boys how to survive in the woods alone. She argued it was part of their Native American heritage. He argued it was a necessity to be self-sufficient.

"He's like his mother," grumbled Trevor in what almost sounded like a curse.

Buzzy nodded his head in agreement. "Yeah, I can see that, and Darius is more like you. What's your point?"

Trevor shot his friend a hard look. He wanted to scream at him. Throttle him. Instead he took a slow deep breath. Since Abby disappeared, he had a difficult time controlling his anger. Especially towards Brock. He would like to think it wasn't intentional. He knew it was out of fear. Abby calmed him. She had been able to diffuse his anger with a touch of her slender hand. With her gone, his anger had likewise gone unchecked. He knew this. Darius knew this. His friends knew this. He closed his eyes and knew that Brock didn't understand his anger. Brock didn't understand his anger was based on fear. Fear of losing him like his mother.

Changing the subject, Trevor answered, "He's eleven." As if that statement answered all questions.

Buzzy smiled at Trevor. "Then be a dad and go look for him."

The words sounded so simple to him. Be a dad. He glanced at Darius and watched him for a moment. Then he looked into the fire. He was a dad. But he was not a good dad. He was rough on his boys. He didn't show them love, he showed them strength. It was their mother's duty to show them love. His to show power and determination. He could feel the anger inside of him rising as he stared into the fire. It was her job to love them and she left! He squeezed the journal in his hand tighter. It was her wish to be taken by those damn monsters. She abandoned them. She left her boys!

Trevor closed his eyes. He sighed out what he thought was a deep breath, but it came out as a growl. He loved his boys. They would come to understand that his harsh ways were the only way he could love them. They would understand when they were older.

Buzzy touched Trevor's arm. "Want him to go with you?"

Trevor looked down at his friend and snapped, "No."

He turned to leave when he noticed that Jake was gone. It caused him to pause. It bothered him that he didn't notice the man leaving the morning campfire. He scanned the campsite for the man but saw him nowhere. That gave him concern. He didn't understand why. He then walked to his son Darius and, without breaking his stride, tossed his wife's journal on his backpack and stated, "Stay here. I'm off to find your damn brother."

Chapter 3

Jake slipped from the morning campfire without notice, like the trained solider he was. Something about Trevor Blackwood's younger son, Brock, slipping away into the woods before breakfast made him curious. As he moved past his tent he opted to leave his daypack behind. He patted the hunting knife secured to his right thigh and passed through the underbrush as quietly as a mountain lion. He suspected he would be able to easily pick up the boy's trail to the river.

The first four days of the weeklong Bigfoot Research Expedition had passed without incident. Which was what Jake had expected. He was mildly surprised at who attended the expedition. Mostly wannabe outdoor enthusiasts accompanied by a sibling or spouse. The individuals on the expedition had limited knowledge of the outdoors and were mostly worker bees that spent the majority of their life behind a desk, looking at a computer screen. At times, the expedition members would hear a hoot of an owl at night, find a broken tree branch, or hear the rustle of leaves and excitedly exclaim a bigfoot was near.

However, there were a handful of members on the expedition

that were experienced woodsman with potentially real bigfoot encounters and that was why he was attending. The official expedition leader, Buzzy, his real name being David White, had a lot of book knowledge on the subject of bigfoot, but little fieldwork experience. Buzzy boasted that he had over twenty years of experience searching for evidence of bigfoot. He openly admitted that he had never seen one but was confident he would. Buzzy's friend, Wynn, was a pure Navajo. Jake knew that Wynn had not only seen a bigfoot, but suspected that he had probably wrestled one as well. Oftentimes during the expedition, Wynn would stare off into the trees with his hand over his chest, feeling the rhythmic beat of his heart. Jake knew those were times that Wynn felt that a bigfoot was near.

Prior to coming on the expedition Jake had read the government files on Buzzy and Wynn. They weren't considered a threat. Buzzy was seen as a novice. He had real facts based on documented research in paranormal and New Age books, but like the rest of the world, he doubted the veracity of the knowledge. Wynn, being a pureblood Indian, knew the truth. He had experienced the truth and it was well documented. However, sadly, old Indian tales and accounts are treated as myth and lore to be enjoyed, but not believed.

His real assignment was the Blackwoods. They were considered a threat. They had knowledge and experiences that threatened to expose the truth behind the bigfoot creature that inhabited the North American forests. His assignment was to monitor and assess the influence the Blackwoods had on the general topic of bigfoot and the potential threat of exposure. As far as Jake could currently assess, the only members of the expedition that gave any credence to Trevor Blackwood's stories were Buzzy and Wynn.

Jake could tell that Trevor didn't like or trust him. Oftentimes when Trevor was retelling one of his many encounters he would abruptly end the tale when Jake made his presence known to the group. Jake didn't care. He knew all about Trevor's experiences, including the abduction of his wife ten years earlier by what had been named the White One. That was why Trevor Blackwood was considered a threat. He had tangible proof and evidence of the existence of these creatures.

Thankfully, from a government perspective, Trevor came across as having too many screws loose to the average American citizen. Jake also knew that Trevor had questioned Buzzy on why he, Jake, was allowed to attend the expedition. Jake didn't know what answer Buzzy gave Trevor, though it didn't much matter. The truth was, unbeknownst to Buzzy, the expedition was secretly being funded by the United States Military. Therefore, it only took a telephone call from his commanding officer for Jake to join the expedition.

Jake picked up Brock's trail quickly and followed it to the river's edge. When he heard a young boy's voice scream "BANG!" he picked up his pace. He reached the thicket of rhododendron trees that lined the river and quietly picked his way through the tangle of branches. He paused when he heard a large splash. For a moment he feared the boy had fallen into the river. His fear of the boy drowning was quickly replaced with a mixture of adrenaline and anxiety when he slipped through the tangle of branches and saw the massive bigfoot creature standing just yards away from Brock. Upon seeing the creature, Jake felt a rush of heat course through his body. He momentarily froze in shock. No matter how many times he came face-to-face with these creatures it always took him a moment to regain his wits because their presence always felt unnatural to him. Through trained instinct his hand moved to his thigh to slip the hunting knife from its scabbard. He silently cursed himself for not having his side-arm.

The creature's head turned and looked in Jake's direction. Jake's blood went cold. He squeezed the handle of his hunting knife for strength. He glanced at the boy, who appeared unafraid. Then a gunshot off in the distance cracked through the silence of the forest. The bigfoot creature dropped to the ground in what looked like a push-up position. Brock followed the creature's example. Then Jake heard Trevor in the distance screaming, "BROCK!"

Jake knew this was his chance to earn Trevor Blackwood's trust by rescuing his son. He moved to push through the tangle of rhododendron branches and then stopped. He shook his head. He was directed to observe, not interfere. He heard Trevor's voice again and glanced behind him into the thick forest and knew the man was close. Jake looked back to the river's edge and saw that Brock and the creature were gone.

Chapter 4

Darius stared at his mother's journal as his dad stomped off into the forest looking for his younger brother. Any thought of guilt he may have been having for letting his brother run off into the woods alone disappeared from his mind when he saw the journal. His father had commanded both him and his brother to never touch the journal, let alone open it up and read it. Then again, his father demanded a lot of things. He quickly scanned the campsite to make sure his father was really gone and none of the other adults were watching him.

Darius knew and understood why his father was angry. He remembered bits and pieces of what happened the night his mother disappeared. His father repeatedly told anyone who would listen what had happened, though from the expressions on people's faces, Darius could tell no one believed him. His father usually ended the tale mumbling something about his wife leaving or abandoning their boys. In some sense, it was his father that abandoned and left his mom. At least that's what Darius thought in the small recesses of his heart.

As Darius held the journal in his hands he realized that he had never read it from cover to cover. He never had time. Usually he only had moments to flip through the pages and read snippets of words in his mother's delicate handwriting. In school, when he was younger, he had been determined to learn and understand cursive writing for the simple reason of being able to read his mother's handwriting in her journal. Sometimes at night he would lay in bed and wonder if his mom had other journals. A few times he snooped around the house looking for them. However, their father had taken most of their mother's belongings and stashed them somewhere out of sight or reach. It made Darius curious that their father had removed all of their mother's belongings, but left little things like the glass candy dish, her hiking boots, a picture by the front door, and her journal. It was like he wanted to erase every memory of her, but at the same time wanted her back. He knew his father read his wife's journal nightly. He suspected that his father had memorized every word she had ever written in the journal. To Darius, this was a clear sign that he missed her. Even though he never expressed that feeling out loud or to his sons. Instead, their father had become angry and borderline abusive.

Darius opened the journal and fanned through the pages. He liked seeing his mother's handwriting. He liked reading her words. He thought she had some interesting opinions and thoughts. The journal was mostly about bigfoot. Her research, her interpretations, her speculations. She also commented on his father's ideas. It was clear that both his mother and father had been interested in the bigfoot phenomenon from the beginning of their relationship. It was something they had shared. From what he had read in his mother's journal, it wasn't a matter of proving that bigfoot existed. They knew. They knew the creature was real. For his mother, at least, she wanted to be a part of the world that bigfoot inhabited. Darius wasn't sure what that meant, but he suspected it had something to do with his mother's Indian heritage.

Darius stopped at a page that caught his attention. One he hadn't read before. The top of the page read,

UFO connection—ridiculous!
Conspiracy theory—the Government knows!

Darius smiled. He had heard his father say the same thing around the campfire to what his father considered amateur bigfoot researchers. A little further down the page, Darius read:

Mind speak (telepathy)

Trevor also thinks this is ridiculous. He agrees that all animals have a form of communication among each other. He believes that bigfoots are capable of communicating with one another. I agree. There is enough evidence from Native American Indians and audio recordings of what has been termed "Samurai Chatter." The idea of bigfoots being able to communicate with one another with what has been determined as a language raises several questions related to intelligence, structural anatomy, culture, and societal structure. For example, if bigfoots are able to produce and communicate with a language, have they also developed other skills related to humans? Like family structure? Rituals? Burying their dead? Laws/rules? Simply, are they more than just an elusive animal in the forest?

But I digress from my original thought. Are bigfoots capable of communicating with humans (us) through telepathy, or what some have termed "mind speak"? Trevor says no. I'm on the fence with the idea. On the one hand, I do believe bigfoots are capable of producing infrasound. There is enough

evidence to prove that other animals in the wild use infrasound to hunt or monitor their territory. Therefore, if science has proven that other wild animals have this capability, reason would suggest so does bigfoot.

Are mind speak and Infrasound the same thing? I don't think so. There are enough stories to suggest they are two different skills used by bigfoots. Personally, I believe I have "felt" infrasound being used on me. However, I cannot prove it was from a bigfoot-type creature. It could have easily been from a mountain lion. I do clearly remember a time that Trevor and I crossed into a section of forest that "felt" and appeared darker than other sections of the forest. We ventured there because of the stick structures and tree markings we had discovered. However, upon entering, I quickly got the feeling that I walked into a "wall" of energy. I had the distinct feeling that we were not safe. We needed to stop. Turn around and leave. Trevor was reluctant to leave, but conceded to my feelings. I do not consider this "mind speak." What I felt was waves of energy pulsating against me, which must have activated my primal flight or fight response, which caused me to react. Trevor felt none of this. I often wonder if that is because he is not attuned to energy vibrations like I am? Or did the bigfoot creature not target him with the infrasound?

Again, I am off topic, sort of. In regards to "mind speak," I don't believe bigfoots are capable of telepathic speech. To me, that would fall under the same category as UFOs. However, I am open to the possibility that they are able to project images and possibly the sounds of fundamental words into a human's brain, depending on how attuned that individual is to the natural world. For example, Native Americans from years passed were probably able to communicate with bigfoots

through "mind speak" because they were one with the natural
world, unlike modern humans of today.

Darius scanned over his mother's words again. He was slightly confused at what she had written. He had heard of Samurai Chatter before. He knew it was believed by researchers to be a type of chatter or speech that bigfoot creatures use to communicate. He had never heard it himself, but he believed it was possible. His mother's suggestion of "mind speak" was something new, something that he had never heard his father or any other bigfoot researcher mention. The idea of bigfoot-type creatures being able to communicate with humans was a great idea. However, he didn't know of any other type of animal that could communicate with humans. If bigfoots could, did that make them more than an animal? And this idea of mind speak, being able to project images into a person's head, what did that mean? Like a picture?

A gunshot broke the silence of the morning. Darius glanced up from the journal and saw that everyone in the camp had stopped what they were doing. A feeling inside of him told him the gunshot came from his father's gun. He closed the journal and placed it back on his father's backpack exactly how he had found it. Then he picked up his rifle and followed the same path his father had taken when he went to look for his brother Brock.

Chapter 5

Brock had seen the bear prints the night before, not far from where he was camping with his brother and father. He tried to tell his dad, but he was too busy talking to the other men at the campfire. His brother, Darius, just ignored him. Brock wanted to follow the tracks but knew his father would get upset if he disappeared from camp so late in the evening. Instead, he planned on following the tracks in the morning. He woke early before everyone else. Darius questioned him, but put up no resistance when he slipped out of the tent.

He tracked the bear prints for what he guessed to be at least a half hour, though he couldn't be sure because he didn't have a watch with him. He also wasn't completely sure if he was still on the trail of the bear. He had lost the tracks shortly after he started following them. What he followed now was a game trail that cut through the underbrush and mature trees heading towards the river. To Brock it made sense that the bear would head towards the river. He was sure he would be able to find bear tracks in the soft mud and sand by the water's edge. He squeezed the long stick he was carrying in determination to find the bear.

The game trail led into a thicket of rhododendron trees that lined the river's edge. Brock belly-crawled down the embankment under the low branches to the river's edge as quietly as he could. Being an eleven year old boy with years of practice playing war with his friends, he was an expert at sneaking up on people. This was different, however. Now he was tracking and hunting like his father and brother. He was going to make his father proud by tracking down what he hoped to be a black bear. This was the first year he was allowed to tag along with what his father called an Expedition. His brother had been attending for years. That had always made Brock jealous. Brock was determined to make his father proud the first year he was able to attend. He would admit his father scared him. Once he overheard a teacher say to another teacher that his father was abrasive. Brock didn't know what abrasive meant. He assumed it had something to do with either the words his father used or the regular beatings he gave his sons for misbehaving. In either event, Brock was determined to do something on this expedition that would make his father not only proud, but brag about him.

Brock was certain that his father hadn't known that he had been paying attention as his father sat around the campfire and bragged about his adventures in the woods. Brock enjoyed hearing his father's stories, especially when he drank too much beer when sitting around the campfire. However, Brock didn't think his father's friends enjoyed the stories. To Brock it seemed like they were always laughing at him, which would eventually make him so angry that he would storm off into his camper alone.

Brock learned a lot from hearing those campfire stories. He learned how important it was to be quiet while in the forest. He learned how important it was to stay downwind from any creature he was tracking. Most important, he learned that hesitation was bad when it came to hunting. Brock was confident that he would not hesitate. He was determined to see the pride in his father's eyes for his accomplishment.

Brock reached the edge of the embankment that turned from wet clay to small pebbles and rocks. He looked up and to his surprise saw a black bear crouched by the river's edge. He momentarily froze in fear, and in that instant he felt his blood run cold through his body. The only thought that repeatedly ran through his mind was I found the bear! I found the bear!

He sat staring at the creature for a long time before he was able to command his body to move. He decided that it hurt too much to continue to crawl on his belly. He pushed himself up to his knees and crawled in the pebbles as quietly as he could. He cringed at the amount of noise he was making, afraid the bear would turn around and see him. He hoped the water rushing downstream would mask the sounds he was making. The pebbles hurt as they dug into his bare knees and shins. But he could tolerate a few moments of pain to hopefully see a smile on his father's face. Brock estimated that he was probably twenty feet away from the bear, which stood with its front paws in the water. He couldn't tell what it was doing. To Brock, it didn't matter because in a few moments it would be dead.

Brock lifted the heavy stick that he had quietly carried with him down the embankment and raised it to his chin like it was a hunting rifle. He closed his left eye and looked down the length of the wooden stick with his right eye. He lined up a notch on the stick to the middle of the bear's back. He let out a slow exhale. He tried to control the thin smile that was stretching his lips as he thought about the proud look on his father's face.

"BANG!" Brock screamed as loud as he could.

The yellow and black butterflies perched on the ground just yards away took to the air in a confused, tangling swirl. Several ducks quacked and flew across the river in retreat. The black bear slowly turned around and looked directly at Brock. Brock dropped the heavy stick to the ground in surprise. It was no bear. It was a creature he had never seen before. He froze in fear at what stared back at him.

The black creature charged Brock across the stones and pebbles in two quick leaps similar to a bear moving to attack. The creature stopped in front of Brock in a crouched position with its front paws hanging just inches off of the ground and less than a foot from him. The creature moved so fast that Brock sat frozen in place. The black creature opened its mouth and roared in Brock's face, "RAWWWWWRRRRRR!"

The scream ripped through Brock's body as the sound pushed him over on to his back. Brock pin wheeled his arms to catch himself but got distracted by his long hair blowing in the wind of the scream. It made him think of those television commercials where people stand in a gust of wind and their hair flies behind them or they end up flying away. For a moment he wondered if he would fly away before his body hit the ground. When he finally hit the dirt he lay stunned on the river's edge.

After a moment, Brock hesitantly sat up and leaned back on his elbows to look at the black creature. The black creature remained crouching in front of Brock, huffing and puffing in short ragged breaths. Brock blinked his eyes several times and bit his lower lip to try and control the tears that wanted to spill from his eyes. He wanted to turn and run back to his father as fast as he could. The memory of an angry dog snarling at him as it lunged for his forearm flashed through his mind. He remembered what his brother said after he was attacked by the dog, "Never show fear. All animals can sense fear." Unsure what to do, Brock tried to smile, raised his right hand just a little bit to wave, and said, "Hi."

The black creature pushed down on its front paws and leapt back about five feet to land in a crouched position again. Brock sat up fully and tilted his head to the side as an attempt to get a better understanding of what he was looking at. The creature mimicked Brock's head movement as if it were trying to figure out what Brock was. As his father would say, this creature's fur was as black as the ace of spades. But Brock thought the creature's fur looked more like his younger sister's matted hair after it had not been combed for days at a time.

The creature's eyes blinked at him several times. The eyes reminded him more of the eyes of a monkey he saw in a science film at school once. Brock opened his mouth to speak again, but stopped himself when the creature opened its mouth also. Brock was hoping it was going to speak and was disappointed when it closed its mouth. That was when he noticed that its mouth and nose were not the snout of a bear, but the shape of a man's. The creature's teeth were square like his father's and the nose was flat and wide like their neighbors who lived down the street.

"I don't think you're a bear," said Brock to the creature.

At hearing the sound of Brock's voice again the creature sniffed and grunted deep in its throat. It leaned forward a little bit as if to get a better look at Brock. Brock sat up and leaned his body to the side to look past the creature to the river bank where it had been sitting before he snuck up on it. The creature followed Brock's eyes and looked at the river bank and then back to Brock.

"What were you doing over there?" asked Brock.

The creature tilted its head to the side and narrowed its eyes but made no response. Brock looked down at the pebbles and stones that scattered in the sandbar underneath him. He found a flat, smooth stone about two sizes bigger than his thumbnail and picked it up. He held it out to the creature. "Were you skipping stones?"

The creature tilted its head to the other side as if it was trying to understand what Brock was saying. Brock pushed himself up to a standing position. The creature walked itself backwards in a crouch about a foot to keep its distance from Brock. Brock looked down at the front paws of the creature and noticed that they looked more like hands instead of paws. Brock smiled. "You have hands like me." Brock's smile broadened. "Bears don't have paws like you." The creature followed Brock's eye movement to its hands and it squeezed and flexed the digits of both hands.

Brock walked over to the water's edge where the creature had been and saw squiggles of lines in the sand. Brock smiled at the design and thought he would have probably done the same thing. He then realized his back was to the creature and his smile turned into a frown at the thought of his father yelling at him for turning his back on a wild creature. Impulsively, Brock spun around to face the creature. The creature was completely ignoring him. Instead it was pushing the big stick that Brock had used as his hunting rifle around on the ground with one of its hands. It then picked up the stick, sniffed it, then threw it on the ground. Brock liked that stick. He hoped the creature wouldn't break it.

"Hey," said Brock to get the creature's attention, "do you know how to skip stones? My papa taught me." Brock smiled at the thought of his grandfather and turned back to face the water. He held the smooth stone between his thumb and index finger, turned his body slightly to the side, and threw the pebble sidearm. The smooth stone skipped across the surface three times before falling into the water.

"Wow, did you see that?" asked Brock excitedly as he spun around to see if the creature was watching.

The creature tilted its head to the side and grunted out loud as if it was acknowledging Brock's question. Brock wondered where the grunt was coming from because he did not see the creature's mouth move. Maybe it was coming from its throat, thought Brock. The creature grunted a second time, then stood. Brock watched as the creature grew in front of him. He had to tilt his head back all the way just so he could see the creature's face. "Dang! You sure are tall," said Brock.

The creature ignored him and looked around. Then its eyes locked on to something to its right. It took two giant steps over to a boulder the size of the small refrigerator that Brock's father kept hidden in the garage and picked it up with one hand. It looked at Brock and threw the boulder sidearm towards the water. Brock felt the velocity of the boulder fly past him when the wind moved his hair. The boulder flew past where Brock's stone had fallen in the water and made a big splash. Brock tilted his head to the side and grunted in his throat the same way he thought the creature did to acknowledge how impressed he was. He looked at the creature and thought it was smiling at him.

Brock smiled. "Well, you didn't skip it, but that was still really cool." He bent down to pick up a larger stone and threw it as far as he could into the river. The rock splashed about a quarter of the way across the river. The creature moved behind Brock to pick up a boulder slightly smaller than the first one. The creature tossed it with ease and it sailed through the air across the river to land on the other side. Brock wheeled around and playfully said, "Hey, that's not fair."

The creature stood only a few feet from him. It looked down at him and snorted. Brock could see its nostrils flare and a mist of spray escape from its nose. Brock smiled and bent down to pick up another rock. Unexpectedly, the creature crouched down in front of Brock. It turned its upper body towards the tree line as if it heard something. That was when Brock noticed that the creature didn't have what appeared to be a neck. There were so many muscles on the creature that it had to turn is entire upper body in order to turn its head in the direction it wanted to see.

Then they heard a gunshot. A real gunshot. The creature dropped to its belly in a push-up position. Brock mimicked the creature and fell to his stomach. The creature's eyes continued to scan the tree line. A short distance away they heard a man's voice screaming for Brock.

"Brock!"

Brock perked up and tore his eyes away from the creature. He knew that voice. It was his father. He looked toward the tree line in fear of seeing his father crashing through the branches toward them.

"Brock! Dammit, boy, where the hell are you?" screamed Brock's father again.

Brock leaned closer to the creature and whispered, "I'm Brock."

The creature's eyes looked at him briefly and then darted back to the tree line. That was when Brock realized that if his father found him next to this creature he would shoot and kill it. The feeling of dread that this creature could die because of him, filled Brock so completely that tears started to spill from his eyes. The creature looked at Brock again as if it knew what Brock was thinking.

Brock made eye contact with the creature. "You have to go," he whispered.

The creature softly grunted. It nodded its head toward a large boulder just a few feet from them. Brock looked over to the boulder. To Brock it looked like the air around the boulder was shimmering with lines of light. It reminded him of those times he would look at the road during the hot summer days and see the heat lifting off the black pavement.

"Dammit, boy, when I find you I'm going to give you a lickin'!" screamed Brock's father as his voice got closer to the river. Brock shuddered at the thought of getting a lickin' from his father. He thought about the last one he got. He had to stay home from school for two weeks just so the sheriff wouldn't come to their house. Brock could feel the creature looking at him. He couldn't bring himself to make eye contact again because of the thought of his father beating him still lingering in his thoughts.

Before Brock could react, the creature wrapped one arm around him and pulled him close to its body. The next instant the creature leapt from the ground towards the boulder. Once at the boulder, Brock heard his father crashing through the rhododendron trees to the river bank. Still holding Brock, the creature stepped into the shimmering light. At that moment all color in the world faded away.

Brock looked back and saw his father standing by the water's edge. It was as if he was watching his father act in a black and white movie. His father circled in place as if he was looking for something on the ground and then screamed for Brock. Brock could barely hear his father because his voice had begun to muffle, as if he was far away or something was blocking the sound from reaching him. Then the creature forced his head and face into its matted black hair. Brock began to feel dizzy and then he passed out.

Chapter 6

Darius pushed through the rhododendron branches to the river's edge. He paused to watch his dad carefully dig out a plaster cast of a footprint near the water. He suspected that his dad heard him return to the river with the supplies he requested. He took a moment to look around. It was pretty. He would never say that to his dad. For his dad, expedition trips were not about beauty or nature. They were about tracking and finding bigfoot. Darius shook his head. No, he thought, it's an obsession. Finding bigfoot had become an obsession for his dad in an attempt to prove that his wife really was stolen by a bigfoot. He looked over at his dad, who was still intently examining the plaster cast of the print. Darius also believed his dad's anger and obsession with bigfoot creatures was because his dad felt guilty for leaving his wife behind the night she disappeared. He felt sorry for the man.

When Darius was younger he blamed his dad for abandoning his mother. However, as he got older, he realized that his dad hadn't abandoned her. His father had acted in the best interest of the family in a moment of crisis. In order to save him and his brother, he had to leave his wife behind. Darius never let himself wonder what would have happened if his father had tried to save his mother. Over the years, as Darius got older, he wondered if all of their hunting and camping trips were fueled by the guilt of leaving her. Later, after his dad's failed second marriage and the birth of his younger sister, Darius realized his dad's guilt had turned into an obsession. His dad never hid the fact that he believed a bigfoot creature stole his wife. He was so adamant about it that his second wife left him and his friends ridiculed him. Though, to his dad's credit, he never wavered in his conviction.

Darius was used to being ignored by his dad. He knew, however, that his dad needed him. He took care of his father after he got drunk at campfires and had to be guided back to their tent or camper. He also took care of his younger brother Brock. He tried to shield his brother from their father's anger and guilt, which was not easy. If asked, Darius would admit that he did a better job of shielding his brother from the story of their mother's disappearance and bigfoot tales than any beating his brother might receive.

As he stood there watching his dad, he nervously waited for his dad to lash out at him for Brock's disappearance. In the scheme of things, it wasn't his fault that his brother went missing. At the same time it was, because it was always his responsibility. Darius was sick with worry about his brother. As the hours ticked away without any trace of Brock, the fear of losing his brother escalated. Every member of the expedition had been scouring the forest for the young boy since his disappearance. His dad had stayed by the river searching for clues. He was eerily quiet and contemplative, which made Darius even more worried. He would rather have his father scream and yell in a tantrum. Darius was used to that response.

Even though Brock was eleven years old, Darius was confident that his brother could find his way back to base camp. His dad had taught them both at a young age how to survive and navigate the thick forest for an extended period of time. Darius knew that the knowledge of how to survive in the wilderness stemmed from his mother. He vaguely remembered her teaching him how to gather edible roots when he was younger. He also knew it was her idea because of her journal. His dad agreed with her that knowledge of the forest and nature was more important than anything they could be taught from books or in school. What made Darius nervous was if Brock had confronted a bear or a mountain lion. He knew for a fact that the only thing Brock had with him when he left camp was the clothes on his back and a walking stick. Finding Brock's walking stick by the river's edge didn't settle well with Darius. At least if his brother had his walking stick he had some defense against a predator.

Darius remembered Brock awakening early that morning. When Darius questioned his brother on what he was doing up early he mumbled something about making their father proud and tracking a bear. At the time, Darius thought his little brother was kidding and went back to sleep. When their dad had gone out looking for Brock, Darius knew his dad was worried that Brock had been gone for so long. Trekking off into the forest by yourself was expected and encouraged by their dad. Though, his dad expected them to be gone for only short periods of time. Darius knew their dad would be able to pick up Brock's tracks quickly. Darius's dad was known as one of the best trackers this side of the Rockies.

Sure enough, Dad found Brock's tracks. They led to the river's edge. According to the story his dad told him hours earlier, Brock crept through the rhododendron bushes. Kneeled. Something large charged him. He fell backwards. Dropped his walking stick. Stood up. The large creature jumped backwards. Brock walked to the river's edge. The large creature investigated the walking stick. Two large boulders were removed from the water's edge. Both the large creature and Brock lay on the ground. Any trace of Brock then disappeared.

Then the large creature rapidly moved to the massive boulder near the river's edge and his father lost the creature's trail.

Darius was able to follow most of his dad's story by the evidence of tracks in the sand and pebbles next to the river. To a person unfamiliar with tracking animals, the ground would simply looked scuffed up. Even for Darius, the footprint his dad was casting seemed to be a stretch of the imagination for him. His dad, however, was convinced it was a bigfoot track.

Before Darius moved to join his father he noticed two large deadfall trees by the boulder where his father found the alleged bigfoot print. It looked as if the two deadfall trees were placed in an X formation above the boulder. What grabbed his attention was that he had seen a similar drawing in his mother's journal. However, he couldn't remember what she said about the X formation of the trees in relation to bigfoot. He made a mental note to himself that he would have to check next time he was alone with the journal.

"Darius, come look at this," said his dad, breaking Darius out of his thoughts. Before Darius could take a step, his dad called out, "Watch that cast. It's a knuckle print."

Darius looked down next to his right foot and saw another dried cast on the ground. He moved over to his dad, who handed him the cast of the footprint. He pointed to an indentation of a ridge on the foot. "See here, a midtarsal break. Not human and not bear." His dad then hurried over to the knuckle print. "When I shot at him, he dropped to a push-up position on his knuckles here," his dad squatted down and showed Darius. "Brock must have been lying on the ground next to him." Darius could see his brother's small hand prints. His dad then hurried over to a massive boulder half in the water, half on land. His dad squatted next to the boulder and outlined what he believed to be a footprint. Darius didn't see it. "It stepped here and then nothing." His dad looked across the river. "I believe the damn bastard took Brock and crossed the river when it heard me coming." Darius followed his gaze across the river. It's possible, he thought. For a seven-to-eight-foot bigfoot creature, the water was maybe only thigh deep.

Darius asked, "But wouldn't you have heard Brock screaming for help?"

His dad didn't look at him and didn't say anything for a long time. "Not if he was unconscious."

True, thought Darius. "I need to check the other side of the river again. Maybe further upstream or downstream. The creature had to move back on land," reasoned his dad out loud, more to himself than Darius.

Darius hesitated, then said, "Dad, you can't. The rangers will be here soon and they are going to want to talk to you."

His dad's head dropped slightly and Darius heard a loud exhale. Darius knew from experience that the longer his dad waited to track Brock the slimmer the chances of finding him grew. To his dad the park rangers were only going to be a hindrance.

Darius continued, "When I went back to get more supplies, I was told that one of the group members hiked out to contact the park rangers when they heard Brock went missing. Buzzy, Wynn, and the new guy Jake are still looking for Brock." He paused, still waiting for his dad to explode in anger. "The park rangers are going to wanna talk to you," repeated Darius.

"Sonsofbitches," groaned his dad as he slowly shook his head. He turned around to face Darius. "Those idiots can't interfere; we'll lose the track."

Darius knew his dad was referring to the park rangers.

"Where did the others from the expedition track?"

Darius shrugged, "I'm not sure," before nodding toward the river, "I think Jake has been out searching on the other side."

"Hmpf. I don't trust him," mumbled Darius's dad more to himself than Darius as he turned to look across the river again.

Hesitantly, Darius said, "Dad, maybe we shouldn't mention that you think bigfoot took Brock. And maybe we should hide these casts." As soon as the words left his mouth Darius regretted saying them out loud. This was his dad. He believed him. At the same time, he knew the park rangers wouldn't. He was just trying to protect his dad from being ridiculed.

His dad spun on him faster than Darius thought was possible. He grabbed him by his jacket and threw him violently to the ground. Darius cradled the cast of the footprint to his chest and prayed it would not break as he hit the ground. His father towered over him like a wild beast, foaming at the mouth, and screamed, "DO YOU THINK I CARE WHAT THOSE BASTARDS THINK? THOSE MONSTERS TOOK YOUR MOTHER AND NOW YOUR BROTHER! THOSE STUPID SONSOFBITCHES KNOW THESE MONSTERS ARE REAL AND ARE HIDING IT! IF THEY INTERFERE WE'LL LOSE HIM!"

"I know, Dad," whispered Darius.

His dad stood over him panting. The anger slowly drained from his face. He dropped to his knees next to Darius and rested his hand on Darius's leg. He closed his eyes for a long time without opening them. Darius pushed up to a seated position and leaned the side of his body against his dad's. He could tell that his dad was trying not to cry. His dad mumbled, "Why do these monsters keep taking everything from me?"

Darius rested the plaster footprint on his lap. He wrapped his arms around his dad to hug him. He whispered to him, "We'll find him."

His dad opened his teary eyes and looked at him. "You tell the rangers whatever you have to," finished Darius.

Chapter 7

Jake rammed the bow of the canoe against the sandbar on the other side of the river. He jumped out and pulled the boat all the way onto shore. Hearing the approaching helicopter he hurriedly looked for some bushes to hide the canoe.

"Damn," he muttered to himself as he spied a low clump of bushes about fifty yards away. He dropped his backpack with a shrug, grabbed the bow of the canoe, and dragged the boat to the bushes. He was able to hide the boat, grab his backpack, and duck behind some rocks before the police helicopter flew over the river. At the same time, park rangers emerged from the tree line across the river to where Brock had disappeared. He stayed long enough to watch the rangers wrap yellow tape around trees and rocks to block off the beach were Brock went missing.

Pointless, he thought to himself as he stealthy moved from his position by the river's edge. He checked his watch and estimated he had about six hours until nightfall. He determined he would lay low until then, canoe upstream to his rendezvous point with his partner, and evacuate the area. When Darius asked him to check the other side of the river for tracks he readily agreed. Jake knew there weren't going to be tracks on the other side of the river, so he didn't bother looking. He agreed in order to avoid any engagement with the park rangers or local police. When it came to these types of investigations, the rangers and police were just as clueless as the rest of the general public. In his opinion, if possible, it was always best to fade away and not be questioned. It was easier to just disappear.

Jake found a large tree with thick foliage cover about three hundred yards downstream from his canoe. He climbed the tree and found a good crook of a branch to hole up in for the day. He pulled out his binoculars. From this position he had a good view of the activity across the river with the park rangers. The police helicopter passed over his position several more times, but he was confident that the tree foliage hid him from sight. He watched for a bit to ensure the rangers stayed on the opposite side of the river. After a short time he rested against the trunk of the tree and looked around at the canopy of leaves.

It wasn't a jungle, but he wondered if his own father had a chance to sit in the canopy of trees when he was in Vietnam. He thought about his father a lot when he was in the forest or the mountains. He never met the man. Just heard stories from his mother before she passed away. As far as his mother knew, and the official word from the United States Government, his father was killed by friendly fire during the Vietnam War. As a kid growing up, that was hard to handle. Instead he used to tell his friends that his father was killed saving prisoners of war in the deep jungles of Vietnam. That sounded more impressive than getting killed by friendly fire. He even maintained that story when he joined the Army himself at eighteen. Except he told it less and less, because he could tell by the looks of senior officers they didn't believe him.

It wasn't until after his second tour in Afghanistan that he learned the truth about his father's death in Vietnam. It was the night his mother had passed away. He was sitting at a bar in Fayetteville, an Army town, drinking alone. He was an only child. His mother never remarried or had any other kids. He was alone in the world. An elderly man, Jake guessed he was in his seventies, sat at the bar next to him. Per his training, he glanced at the man for a moment to assess if he was a threat. For an older man, Jake was impressed how thick and muscular the man was. Jake could tell that the muscles under the aged skin were solid with a strength that would probably surprise him. From the man's clean shaven face and buzz cut he assumed the older man had been in the military his entire life. Jake smiled to himself. He was sure the old man could still put up a good fight if he needed too.

The older man ordered a shot of whiskey. The bartender poured the shot and asked Jake if he needed a refill. Jake waved her away.

"Nice ass on that one," grunted the old man. "Only reason why I come around this place."

Jake glanced over at the bartender and guessed she was in her mid-thirties. Probably the wife or girlfriend of an Army grunt stuck in this town while her significant other was off saving the world somewhere. It was clear that she enjoyed the attention from the men in the room. "I like her rack," countered Jake.

The older man looked over at the woman. Grunted. "Not bad, but I'm an ass man myself."

Jake looked at her bottom one more time before returning his gaze to the gold liquid of beer in his glass. The older man elbowed Jake in the shoulder. "Name's Whiskey."

Jake stifled a laugh and stuck his hand out. "Jake."

Whiskey gave a strong returning handshake that impressed Jake. He then turned his attention back to his beer. He wasn't really in the mood for conversation. Lost in thought about his mother,

Jake vaguely heard Whiskey say something to him. The older man elbowed him a second time. Jake looked at him with a mixture of annoyance and curiosity.

"Diddja hear me, boy?" asked Whiskey.

Jake shook his head. "No, sorry."

Whiskey grunted. Slammed the shot glass on the bar. The bartender came back with the bottle and filled the glass with a smile. She left again. Jake watched Whiskey pick up the shot glass and look into the brown liquid. Nonchalantly, the old man said, "Your father wasn't killed by friendly fire."

Jake remembered staring at the man for a long time before the words penetrated his brain and made any sense to him. During that time Whiskey got another refill of his shot glass. "Excuse me?" was all Jake could manage out of his mouth.

Whiskey held the shot glass inches from his mouth while he talked. "It wasn't friendly fire. We were on a recon mission deep in the jungle. Our commander had gotten word there was a camp of Charlies twenty miles to our south with possible POWs. We spent three days trudging through that bullshit looking for that camp." The old man put the shot glass down and then picked it back up again. "The entire time we all felt we were being watched, but we pushed on. The thought of those bastards holding our brothers prisoners was bullshit to us." The old man put the glass down and muttered, more to himself than to Jake, "We never found them."

Jake sat in silence for a long time waiting for the old jarhead to continue his story. The old man threw the shot back and slammed the glass on the bar again. The bartender refilled the glass and walked off. The old man stared at her ass and said, "It was the night of the third day. We made camp on top of a ridge. Our platoon spread out. We had sentries posted." The old man looked towards the ceiling of the bar as if it was the night sky. "It was a full moon." He sipped the liquid from the shot glass. "I was with your father. Shortly after midnight, something started to throw rocks at us. Your father and I. The whole platoon. The greenies—you know the, newbies—thought it was the locals. Our commander, your father, and I knew it wasn't the locals." He paused. "It was the Batutut. The hairy little bastards," said Whiskey as he sipped the whiskey again. "We called them Rock Apes."

Confused, Jake asked, "What?" Turning to the old man, he said, "What the hell is a Batutut or a Rock Ape?"

Whiskey shot Jake a look that told him that the old man wasn't used to being interrupted. "Shut up and let me finish," said the old man with a tone of authority.

Recognizing that the older man's words were more of an order than a suggestion, Jake sat in silence as the old soldier continued to tell him an unbelievable tale about his father. Whiskey continued, "The greenies popped off a couple shots into the dark. That didn't help the situation." Whiskey paused and stared at the bottles against the wall behind the bar. Jake could tell that the man was reliving the experience in his mind. Whiskey shook his head and continued, "The ugly, smelly bastards got the better of me. One of them charged me like a linebacker and laid my ass out. It picked up your father and broke his back over its knee and tossed him away like garbage. I lit the asshole up with my Colt!" The old man shook his head. "I know I hit the bastard with at least eight slugs. We never found the body." Whiskey finished his shot and the bartender moved to refill his drink. He waved her away. "We made a tight circle with your father in the center. We waited the night out and then EVACed ASAP at daybreak," finished Whiskey.

Jake remembered sitting there staring at that old man for the longest time, unable to find his voice to ask any questions. A part of him felt like he was waking up from a bad dream. He wanted to ask questions. But the words were stuck in his throat.

Whiskey continued, "The Batutut are similar to our North American Great Ape, but smaller in stature. However, equally as nasty and elusive. I broke curfew…"

"Wait a second," said Jake as he found his voice and cut the old man off, "are you saying my father was killed by a bigfoot?"

Whiskey nodded his head yes.

Feeling anger rise to his cheeks, Jake had to control himself from exploding on the man, "Bullshit!"

Half chuckling to himself, Whiskey said, "Not any more bullshit than the report you filed three months back about spotting a bigfoot-type creature with your infrared scope in the Afghan Mountains."

Feeling like a fool, Jake pushed away from the bar to leave. He was sure that one of his buddies from the platoon was playing a sick joke on him. It pissed him off even more that they were doing it on the night his mother died. Before he could move away from the bar, the old man clamped his hand down on Jake's wrist. The old man's grip was like iron, strong and firm. It was full of determination. "I stopped caring a long time ago if anyone believes me. In time you will too." Whiskey paused and then continued, "In three days a gentleman will approach you with a new assignment. As your new commanding officer, I strongly suggest you accept." The man let go of Jake's wrist.

Jake readjusted his position in the tree. That was six months ago. Sure enough, he met Mr. Smith three days later after his conversation with Whiskey. He was in the mess hall eating breakfast when Mr. Smith, a tall, lean, African-American man wearing a three-piece suit came and sat across from him at the table. Jake looked at him and then back to his food. "You were told I would approach you in three days," said the man. Jake looked up at him and said, "I'm tired of this bullshit. I'm tempted to break your neck if you continue with this game."

Jake remembered the man's smile. "No bullshit. I'm for real," said the man. He stuck out his hand. "I'm Mr. Smith." Jake stared at his hand for the longest time before he finally shook it. Mr. Smith wiped his hand clean. "What the old man told you is true. We may bullshit the rest of the world, but never each other. They are real, and they do exist."

Jake looked around the mess hall to make sure no one was listening in on their conversation, "You mean bigfoot?"

Mr. Smith nodded his head in agreement. "Yes, the North American Great Ape and all of his cousins around the world."

Jake leaned back on the bench. "Bullshit," he spat.

Mr. Smith exhaled a deep sigh and closed his eyes. Jake watched the man for a long time before returning to his breakfast. "What you saw in the Afghan Mountains was a Barmanou. Translated from Sanskrit means, it means 'Man of the Forest.' Just as your father was killed by a Batutut or a Rock Ape, these—"

Jake threw his fork against his tray of food and barked at Mr. Smith, "Enough, asshole! My father…"

Mr. Smith held up his hand to silence Jake. "It doesn't matter how your father died or what you want to believe. You, my friend, don't have a choice. Your report of the Barmanou got the attention of our commander. You can believe or not believe what you want. But in the end you are a soldier of the United States Army. You will follow orders or be dishonorably discharged. Are we clear?"

Jake wanted to reach across the table and break Mr. Smith's neck. His rage boiled inside of him so hot he was positive that fire was shooting out of his eyes. His hands trembled and he forced them into clenched fists to control his rage. Mr. Smith continued, "Now, my last partner went AWOL. I need you to infiltrate an expedition party west of the Rockies and determine the extent of their knowledge on the subject. If they are a threat, eliminate them."

"What?" asked Jake. His mind swirled with misunderstanding and questions. "What are you talking about?"

Mr. Smith sighed and rubbed his hand over his scalp. "What do you not get?"

"Everything," barked Jake.

Mr. Smith leaned forward and gestured his hand back and forth between him and Jake. "You and I are partners." He pointed at Jake. "You are my field guy. Understand?"

"Field guy?" asked Jake.

"Yes, the one that goes in the field and does the grunt work," answered Mr. Smith.

"Why me? Why not you?" asked Jake.

A hearty laugh broke out of Mr. Smith's mouth. "Oh that's rich! I have a family. A wife and three kids. My ass ain't steppin' foot in any forest. Me," he pointed to himself, "I'm a city boy."

Jake remembered looking at his cold, runny scrambled eggs and couldn't understand a word that Mr. Smith was saying. Everything was happening so fast. He felt as if his whole world had been turned inside out from his asshole. Mr. Smith continued, "You are expendable. No family. No connections. If you go AWOL, no loss on our part. No messy cover-up." He paused for a long time before he continued. Jake understood what the man was saying. He had no ties to the world. If he vanished, no one would miss him. Mr. Smith pushed a sealed envelope across the table to Jake. "This man's wife was kidnapped by an alleged bigfoot about ten years ago. He has become a thorn in our side. He needs to be monitored. If he can prove they exist he is to be quieted. If he can't prove they are real we continue to let him look and sound like a fool."

Jake stared at the envelope.

"A bigfoot?" asked Jake.

Mr. Smith nodded his head yes. "According to our sources, a huge white one. Nasty booger, that one."

Mr. Smith pushed up from the table and Jake could feel him staring down at him. "Jake, one more thing," said Mr. Smith.

Jake looked up at him.

"Grow a beard."

Jake squinted his eyes together. "Why?"

"Prerequisite to being a mountain man," said Mr. Smith. He then turned and disappeared out the mess hall door.

Jake scratched at his freshly grown beard. He wasn't used to the long hair either. However, he did enjoy his time in the mountains. He looked to the west and saw the sun dipping below the mountains. Using his binoculars he checked the beach upriver. No activity. He descended the tree.

Jake waited an hour past sunset before pushing off in his canoe. He quietly paddled across the river to the police tape. The forest was quiet. He suspected a search for the boy would begin in the morning. They wouldn't find him anywhere near here. From what he had learned in the past six months, these creatures could travel far very quickly. The missing boy and the bigfoot that took him were probably two or three mountain ranges away by this time. He turned his canoe in the water and started to slowly paddle upstream to meet his partner at the extraction point.

Three strokes upstream, Jake heard the distinct sound of a shotgun being pumped. He looked to his right and saw Trevor Blackwood standing on the shore of the river with a shotgun pointed directly at him. He made eye contact with the man. "I know who you are," spat Trevor. "Stay the hell away from me and my boy, you hear?"

Jake nodded his head once in acknowledgement.

Trevor jerked his head up river to give Jake permission to continue on his way. Jake suspected the man never lowered the shotgun until he was out of sight. Mr. Smith was right. Trevor Blackwood was a thorn in their sides.

Chapter 8

Sookum. The thought popped into Brock's head, which caused him to wake from his restless sleep. He rolled over on the bed of dead pine needles to rest on his right side. He kept his eyes closed, not wanting to wake up yet. Hoping that his father did not notice him move. He wanted a few more minutes to think about his dream. He tried to contain the smile that wanted to stretch across his lips, but he was pretty sure he was giving himself away as he lay there pretending to sleep. He knew he gave himself away when a giggle slipped out because he heard his father moving behind him. He squeezed his lips shut and waited for his father to shake him awake. But the shake never came. So he figured he had a few more minutes to himself. He giggled again when he remembered how funny it was that Sookum threw the boulder into the river when he was trying to skip it.

Sookum? he thought.

Brock's eyes popped open at the thought of the name Sookum. He didn't remember the creature telling him his name was Sookum. But somehow Brock knew. Actually, the more he thought about it, he didn't remember the creature even telling him he was a he. Then again, it was pretty obvious. The creature had the same boy parts he had, so it must be a boy. But how did he know his name was Sookum? Maybe at some point in his dream the creature had told him, but he couldn't remember. In either event, the more he thought about it, the more he agreed that the creature did look like a Sookum. Personally, he didn't think he looked like a Brock. But he knew he didn't have a choice in the matter. His father had named him. He asked his father once why he had picked the name Brock. His old man laughed and said, "Because it was the name of the town where you were born." Which confused Brock, because one time he looked up the town of Brock and there was no hospital located there. But maybe he was born in a different state. He was too afraid to ask his father if that was the case. One time he asked his father what his mother wanted to name him. His father spanked him for that one. That night while he was crying in bed, his older brother lay next to him and comforted him and advised him to never ask about their mother again. Brock never asked again. The more he thought about it, he didn't even know his mother's name. She felt like a mystery to him.

Brock wiped the water that was forming in his eyes and focused on the wall in front of him. It was wood. No. Bark. He reached out and touched the rough surface of bark and a piece fell away from his hand. He quickly retracted his hand to his chest. Nothing happened. He leaned his head forward just a little bit to peer out the hole and saw the undergrowth of a forest floor and small saplings growing off in the distance. Confused, he rolled onto his back on the dry pine needles and found himself looking at the trunk of a tree that must have fallen at some point in its life. He looked to his left and saw another wall of bark. He grasped at the ground and clutched the pine needles and brought them to his face to get a better look. He dropped the pine needles and sat up as much as he could under the fallen tree. Down by his feet on his left he saw an opening. He wiggled around under the tree trunk so he could crawl out of the shelter head first.

He poked his head out the entrance of the crude structure and blinked his eyes several times to adjust to the bright sun. He then stood and looked back at the entrance. He was right. He was lying under a fallen tree. But he wasn't sure how he had gotten there. What happen to his father's tent? What happened to the camp?

Brock looked around and noticed he was standing in a small clearing surrounded by a thick wall of brambles as tall as he was. He walked over to the brambles to see if there was a way he could crawl through them or push them out of the way. But the thorns were at least an inch long and he couldn't even see where the brambles ended. Among the brambles, Brock spied a patch of blackberries. His stomach rumbled and growled at the sight of food. He gently reached out and picked a handful of berries.

As he ate the berries he scratched his head in confusion and walked back to the crude tree shelter. Finishing the small clump of blackberries, he climbed on top of the fallen tree trunk and looked up towards the couple of trees that were still standing inside the bramble patch. They were tall and thick. He guessed they were at least a hundred years old. There were no branches for him to climb for at least fifty feet.

He jumped down off the tree trunk and landed on his feet. As he did, the creature Sookum landed in front of him in a crouch, as silent as a bird. At a crouch Sookum was as tall as Brock. He sat there for a moment with the fingertips from his right hand barely touching the dirt. Brock did not move. He had become too afraid to move. Brock started to slowly realize that Sookum was not a dream. Sookum had taken him when they heard his father calling for him. He was alone.

Sookum leaned forward slightly and sniffed in Brock's direction. Brock watched as the nostrils on the creature's flat nose twitched with each sniff. Sookum moved slightly closer to Brock as it sniffed him from head to toe. He then tilted his head to the side and looked past Brock to the bedding structure.

Brock followed the creature's eyes and saw what it was looking at the fallen tree with the bed of pine needles. A little bit of the fear he was feeling dissipated and he asked, "Did you make that?"

At the sound of Brock's voice, Sookum snapped his head back to face Brock again. That was when Brock noticed the streak of gray mixed throughout its jet black hair, crossing from the left side of its forehead at an angle down across its right eye ending at its cheek bone. Sookum's eyes widened and Brock noticed how yellow his eyes were as he watched him. Sookum's lips spread slightly, almost in a smile, and Brock could see its grayish white teeth. Brock leaned forward slightly to whisper, "Are you Sookum?"

The creature stood to his full height and towered over Brock. Brock had to take a step back and tilt his head completely back in order to see Sookum's face. Sookum stared down at him. Brock turned and scrambled up the fallen tree and stood facing Sookum. This allowed him to look Sookum in the eye without breaking his neck. Sookum stepped forward and stood less than a foot from Brock. Brock smiled and laughed out loud. "You are real!" he said, laughing. "I can't believe you are real! I thought you were just a dream!"

Sookum tilted its head to the right and then back to center. Then it huffed.

Brock fell silent.

Sookum leaned a little closer again and huffed louder, "HUFF!" The sound came from its throat. Brock could feel the force of exhaled air blast against his face as Sookum's breath escaped its nostrils.

Brock imitated the huff back to Sookum as best as he could, "Hufff!"

Sookum's whole upper body moved back slightly from the waist and then leaned in towards Brock. The creature let out a roar so powerful that the vibrations knocked Brock off the fallen tree on to his back.

After Brock hit the ground it took him a few seconds to figure out what had just happened. When he did he was instantly afraid. He shook his head and tried to pull himself away from the fallen tree as best as he could lying on his back. He could see Sookum leaning over the fallen tree looking at him. Brock was about to turn on to his hands and knees to crawl through the thick brambles when they both heard a soft "Whoop."

Brock froze.

Sookum perked up and looked around. It let out an equally soft, "Whoop." It then reached over the fallen tree, extending its hand toward Brock. Brock looked at the long muscular arm covered in black hair and could not comprehend why its hairless hand and fingers were motioning for him to come.

Sookum grunted one more time and jammed its hand towards Brock. Brock sat there frozen, unable to comprehend what was happening. Sookum glanced up towards the forest and pulled its arm back. It stepped away from the fallen tree and disappeared from view. Then Brock heard a thumping sound behind him. With each thump the ground under him shook his body as if he was being shaken in an earthquake. He tried to scramble to his feet to see what was making the noise. The vibration of the ground prevented him from being able to stand on his feet. He pushed himself against the bark that was leaning against the fallen tree and hoped whatever was making the thumping sound would pass without noticing him. He was not so lucky.

In horror Brock watched a creature similar to Sookum walk through the brambles directly towards him. The creature was twice as big as Sookum in size and height. Brock watched in shock as the brambles slid away from the creature's white hair. He couldn't understand how the brambles were not snagging or getting tangled in the creature's long hair. When he cleared the brambles, the creature stopped in front of Brock. It reached down and clamped its massive hand over Brock's small head. Palming the boy's head it lifted him off the ground. Brock's feet dangled in the air. He immediately threw both hands up and clawed at the creature's long white matted hair to try and get a grip to hoist himself up to release the pressure on his skull. His hands kept slipping off the creature's hair, as if its hair was coated in some sort of oil that prevented him from grabbing it. He didn't remember Sookum's hair feeling that way. The pain from the grip around his head was beyond bearable. Brock had never felt so much pain before in his life. Tears flooded his eyes and spilled down his face uncontrollably. The creature pulled Brock up to its eye level. Brock blinked through his tears and saw the pure hatred in the creature's dark red eyes. Brock peed his pants in fear. For a moment the creature watched Brock's urine drip down his leg in a sort of satisfaction.

Behind him, Brock thought he heard Sookum growl. The creature that was holding him focused its attention past Brock to Sookum. Then it tossed Brock to the side into the bramble thorns. The shock of the pain around his scalp being released blocked out the pain of the hundreds of brambles that stabbed into his flesh. He rolled out of the brambles on to his stomach and pushed to his knees. As he did, Sookum leapt over the fallen tree to stand in front of the much larger white creature. The larger creature immediately backhanded Sookum across the face. As Sookum's face was turned away from the larger creature it quickly made eye contact with Brock. Sookum turned back to face the larger creature and screamed louder than anything Brock had ever heard before in his life. The sound was so deafening he clamped his hands over his ears to try and block the noise. The larger creature turned towards Brock and leapt towards him to grab him again. Brock flinched in fear. Sookum stepped forward and shoved the larger creature with both hands. The larger creature lost its balance and fell to the ground. It rolled and came back up in a crouch facing Sookum. It sprang at Sookum and knocked him in the chest. They both crashed through the fallen tree. Brock kept his hands over his ears and leaned forward, burying his face in his legs.

The sound of the two creatures fighting was more than Brock could bear. He cried uncontrollably and rocked back and forth on his knees. The sounds reminded him of all those times his father and brother had fought because his brother was protecting him. He loved his brother. He wished his brother was with him right now. He needed his brother's strength. He wished he was as strong as his brother.

Brock was not sure how much time had passed since the noise of the fighting stopped. He wondered if he had cried himself to sleep while the two creatures were fighting. He slowly pulled his hands away from his ears and confirmed that he did not hear any more growls or screams. He opened his eyes and saw Sookum crouching in front of him. Its left eye was swollen shut and blood was caked in its black hair on its right shoulder. But that did not stop Brock from propelling himself into Sookum's arms. He couldn't wrap his small arms around Sookum, but he tried. He burst into tears again, this time from happiness, and tried to press himself into Sookum.

Sookum wrapped his left arm around Brock for a moment and let out a long, slow, deep exhale. Brock smiled and felt safe. Sookum stood and Brock let go of his grasp. This time when Sookum offered his hand, Brock took it. Sookum picked him up and swung Brock around on to his back. Brock squeezed his knees into Sookum's side and draped his arms over the massive creature's shoulders and grasped his long hair to hold on. Sookum flinched a little but moved off into the bramble. As Sookum moved into the brambles, Brock felt the hair on the creature become oily and slick. He watched as the thorns slipped off of Sookum and his own legs. Sookum whooped once and they both heard a responding whoop not far off in the distance.

Chapter 9

Trevor sat in the kitchen with a large map spread across the table. He took a long drink from his bottle of beer. He ran his hand through his thinning hair and exhaled loudly. He glanced down the hall to Brock's dark room and gave his head a slight shake. He then looked up towards Darius's room in the loft and assumed that his oldest son was asleep. Lastly, he looked at the picture of his daughter on the coffee table. Leaving his drink on the table, he walked over to the bookshelf and pulled down a copy of the book The Night Circus, by Erin Morgenstern, Abby's favorite book. Opening the front cover he pulled out a picture of his wife. He rubbed his calloused thumb over the image of her face. I miss you, he thought.

Still holding Abby's picture, he looked out the window into the dark night. Why, God? Why do you keep taking everything away from me? First Abby. Now Brock. Am I being punished for something I did wrong in this life? Or in a past life?

The night seemed to grow darker around him. He waited for the answers. But from experience with similar one-sided conversations he knew the answers would never come. Turning from the window,

Trevor moved back to the kitchen table and sat down with a heavy sigh. He finished his beer in a long drink and pushed the empty bottle to the table's edge with the other bottles. He placed the picture of Abby on top of the map and said out loud, "Abby, how am I supposed to find him? What if you are right and bigfoot can slip through portals to a different dimension?" He paused for a long time before speaking again. Then in a low voice he continued, "Brock could be anywhere." After another long pause, his voice dropped to almost a whisper. "You could be anywhere."

He spread his hands over the map as if to press out the folded creases. He touched each blue dot on the map that represented a bigfoot sighting. He then reached across the table for a red pen and removed the cap. Locating his previous expedition trip where Brock had disappeared a week earlier, he pressed the tip of the pen to the map. Recapping the pen, he touched a second red mark on the map and whispered out loud, "Why did you disappear, Abby? Did you not love me? Why leave me and the boys?"

Pressing his finger harder into the map and table, a spark of anger surged through Trevor's mind. "Did you send those damn creatures after our boy?" Almost growling, he hissed through clench teeth, "You leaving wasn't good enough?"

Trevor wanted to be angry. Being angry was easier for him to understand than the pain of missing someone he loved. He dropped his head and sighed. But sometimes missing the woman he loves is a stronger emotion than the manufactured pain he could so easily manifest. He stretched his left arm across the map on the table and rested his head on his arm. His eyelids grew heavy with fatigue. With his right hand he slowly traced Abby's face in the picture until he fell asleep.

Chapter 10

Darius quietly pushed away from his desk when he heard his dad talking to himself. He closed his leather journal and tip-toed out to the loft. When he discovered his mother's journal a few years earlier, he started to keep his own. When he was younger he usually wrote about silly things that happened to him throughout the day or random thoughts that popped into his head. In the past year, his random words turned into an inner dialogue of his thoughts. He never wrote in the journal around his dad or Brock. He kept it a secret.

Quietly, Darius opened his door and moved into the shadows of the loft. He sat near the stairs leading down to the main level and waited. It was common for his father to stay up late drinking alone. He usually passed out on the couch or half-laying on the kitchen table. Darius never helped his father to bed. Instead, he would clean up any mess his father may have left and cover him with a blanket. The next morning his dad would never say anything to him and Darius never talked about what he did. Darius took care of his dad and that was understood between the two of them.

Darius never tried to hear his father's words. Usually he couldn't because the man was often half-drunk and mumbling. But he guessed they usually had to do with his mother and her disappearance. Darius knew from the past couple of nights it was about his brother Brock. The previous night had been particularly bad when his dad smashed all of the beer bottles with the handle of his hunting knife.

The quietness from the kitchen snapped Darius out of his thoughts. Moving out of the shadows, he looked over the railing and could tell that his father was asleep. Slowly, he tiptoed down the wooden stairs. Quietly, he placed the empty beer bottles in the trash. He draped a blanket over his dad's shoulders and then gently pulled the picture of his mother from under his dad's fingers. He peered at the picture. His mother had such a beautiful smile, he thought. Placing the picture back into his mother's favorite novel, he returned the book to the shelf. He slipped the book next to his dad's favorite book, The Hobbit. Darius glanced back at his dad sleeping on the table and gave him a sad smile.

Darius avoided the first step of the stairs and climbed back into the loft to his room. Standing over his desk, he opened his journal to the sketch he had been working on. He added some finishing touches to the trees with the pencil. Then under the sketch he wrote the letter X with a question mark.

Darius closed the journal and slipped it under the pile of junk papers in his desk drawer before going to sleep.

Chapter 11

Journal Notes from Abby Blackwood:

Four Groups of bigfoot in North America

Several bigfoot researchers have suggested that there are four types of bigfoot creatures in North America. In some research circles, to avoid being ridiculed, I suspect, they are referred to as the North American Great Ape.

My belief is similar to the Native American Indians. bigfoot is more than an ape and more than human. Because of their spiritual nature with Mother Earth, they transcend human capabilities; therefore, they fall into the realm of something greater than human. In private, I would dare say that bigfoots may be an offshoot of a type of fairy. However, I fear individuals would classify bigfoot incorrectly and attribute their abilities to the supernatural. Their gifts are not supernatural, but evolutional changes in order to adapt to their environment and their one and only predator, humans.

If I was anyone of influence I would suggest a change

in the classification of the four types of bigfoot creatures in North America. By the way, I do not like the term "type" or "species." I understand that species is a technical scientific term. But trying to understand these creatures from a scientific paradigm is and will be nearly impossible. To understand these creatures, a person must look upon bigfoot from a spiritual perspective. And NOT from a religious view. Hence the reason why Native American Indians, especially shamans, are capable of understanding these creatures better than any other human group on the planet. Native American Indian medicine men/women and shamans understand the spiritual connection between our own existence and the invisible threads that intertwine and bind our world with the seen and unseen world of nature and Mother Earth.

Therefore, since there are multiple groups of humans on our planet, I propose there are four different GROUPS of bigfoot in North America. They would be:

Group 1—Northwest Pacific: Similar to Patty from the Patterson-Gimlin film. Usually move bipedal. However, some reports of Group 1's in Eastern North America will and are capable of moving on all fours. (I suspect this is because the forests on the east coast are less dense; therefore, the Eastern cousin must move on all fours to remain elusive as compared to the Pacific cousin.)

Group 2—Ancient Ones: Smaller in stature, with more human-like features. Often confused in mythology with "wood nymphs" or "wood fairies."

Group 3—Skunk Ape" Similar to an orangutan/gorilla, however, equally as large as the Group 1s. Distinguishing characteristic—repulsive odor.

Group 4—Dogman: Extremely dangerous

Chapter 12

Brock sat cross-legged in the mud by the stream. He momentarily shielded his eyes from the morning sun reflecting off the water and noticed his hands. They were filthy and caked with dirt. He leaned forward and dipped both hands into the cold water. Rubbing his hands together he tried to wash the dirt away. It didn't work. Pulling them from the water, he turned his hands over and wondered if his skin was stained. He wiped them on his tattered jeans that were equally dirty. Leaning forward, he peered at his reflection in the water and didn't recognize himself. His hair hung down past his chin in a matted mess and his face was covered with dirt. He dipped both hands into the water again as if making a cup and was about to splash the water on his face when he heard a noise. He looked up and saw Sookum move out of the brambles to the stream. Sookum kneeled down and rested one large hand in the mud. He then leaned forward and drank directly from the stream.

When Sookum finished drinking, he looked up at Brock. Brock thought he smiled at him. Sookum grunted and nodded his head towards him. He looked down at his cupped hands and drank the water as opposed to splashing it on his face. As he drank he wondered how long he had been in the woods with Sookum. A month? Maybe longer? He wasn't sure. The thought got cut short in his mind by an uncontrollable itch on his scalp. He dropped his hands. The excess water splashed back into the stream and he scratched at his scalp like a dog with fleas. Something was biting him and it hurt. He glanced at his fingernails and saw blood.

Sookum grunted and moved across the stream to squat down next to Brock. The large creature roughly grabbed Brock by the shoulder and pulled him closer. Brock had no choice. He felt something scrap against his scalp. He winced in pain. Sookum's large hand moved in front of his face and was holding a black bug on his dark, tapered fingernails. Brock focused more on Sookum's fingernails then the bug. His fingernails weren't claws. They were nails, but tapered to a point. Sookum flicked the bug away and went back to digging through Brock's hair. Brock flinched each time Sookum combed through his matted hair. It hurt. But at the same time he felt relief from whatever bugs Sookum was removing from his scalp.

Brock and Sookum heard a soft grunt from their left. Sookum stopped. Brock looked to his left and watched as three more creatures similar to Sookum stepped out of the tree line to the stream. Brock had sensed that he and Sookum were not alone. There had been many nights and mornings that Brock had heard noises in the woods and Sookum would disappear for long periods of time. At first he assumed Sookum was gathering food for them. However, as time passed and he became more familiar with the sounds of the forest, Brock realized Sookum was being called away. Several times Brock had heard Sookum respond to different sounds with either a whoop, a grunt, or a chatter.

There were a few times that Brock thought he saw glimpses of similar creatures to Sookum on the edge of his vision moving through the forest. At first, he didn't want to believe what he saw was real because he was afraid they would be like the White One that had attacked him. But at the same time, if what he saw was real, maybe they hadn't shown themselves until now because they were afraid of Sookum. Now seeing the three standing before him, he wasn't sure how he felt. A part of him wanted Sookum to be the only one. As if Sookum was his own, private, imaginary friend. The other part of him didn't want Sookum to be alone.

The smallest of the three was slightly taller than Brock and covered in blonde hair. In a way, Brock thought she was beautiful. He knew she was a female by her breasts, which caused him to quickly look away out of embarrassment. However, curiosity got the better of him and he glanced back at her through his matted hair. Seeing the blonde creature again, he couldn't help but smile. She smiled back at him and then kneeled by the stream to drink.

The largest of the three creatures was equally as big as Sookum and was covered in auburn hair. She too had breasts. She moved over to Sookum. Brock had to tilt his head all the way back in order to look up at her. She shook her head and grunted as she playfully pushed Sookum away. Brock thought he heard what sounded like a half grunt, half chuckle come from Sookum as he moved away toward the third creature.

The third creature had jet black hair and was slightly hunched over. As it moved towards Sookum and Brock, it used its hands on the ground similar to a gorilla. When it reached Sookum, it stood on its legs and embraced Sookum. It was easily a head shorter than Sookum. It moved passed Brock, carrying with it a wave of stench. Brock shot both of his hands to his face, covering his nose and mouth, and involuntarily let out an "Aughhh." He instantly felt sick to his stomach. At the sound of his voice, all of the creatures stopped and looked at him. The creature with the jet-black hair grunted a laugh and moved to the other side of the stream.

The creature with auburn hair squatted down behind Brock and started to pick at his scalp. He flinched. Not because it hurt, but because he was afraid. The creature stopped and grunted. It waited a few seconds and then started to pick at his scalp again. Brock felt the relief of the bugs being removed from his scalp and realized the creature with the red hair was much better at grooming than Sookum. He looked around the streambed and watched as Sookum and the other two creatures cleaned themselves. After the creature with the red hair removed all of the bugs from his scalp, she meticulously started to untangle his long dirty hair.

Chapter 13

Jake stared up at the X-like structure in front of him in the stream valley. He scratched at his beard and picked out a piece of bramble that had been lodged in his facial hair. Absentmindedly, he flicked the bramble away. He sniffed his armpit and shook his head. He stunk. He tried to think of how long he had been out in the field. Three months? He thought. He shrugged his shoulders and walked around the X-structure. The tree holding up the top part of the X was alive. He could tell the live tree strained against the weight of the two dead trees against it. By evidence of the moss and vine coverage, the X-structure had been in place for a number of years. Which didn't surprise Jake; the location was isolated and free of human contamination.

Jake noted that the trunks and root systems of the two dead trees that formed the X were nowhere near the structure. It was clear that they had been carried to this location. Which would be an impressive task, considering they were as thick as him and longer than sixty-feet. Jake concluded there was no way this structure happened by chance. He had seen similar structures in various other forests across North America. Per field reports from other agents in the field, these

X-structures were constructed by bigfoot creatures. In the same reports, the purpose of the structures was currently unknown.

Jake took a step back from the structure and noted the surrounding area was clear of undergrowth. He suspected this was evidence that the structure was still being visited or used by bigfoot creatures. Moving towards the stream, he walked along the edge searching for any sign of bigfoot activity. Even though the creatures were extremely elusive, they periodically left evidence by choice or by circumstance.

Reaching a large oak tree that had fallen across the stream, he noticed a slight disturbance in the mud. He moved down from the bank of the stream and squatted under the fallen oak tree. He smiled at his discovery. Two handprints. One massive. One smaller. Jake stretched out his own left hand and placed it over the massive hand print in the air. The handprint was at least twice as big as Jake's hand. Which Jake thought was impressive, because he thought his own hand was meaty and thick. Moving his right hand over the smaller print, he noticed that it was half the size of his. Pulling his hand away he whispered to himself, "Son of a bitch, the kid's alive."

There was no empirical evidence suggesting the smaller handprint belonged to the kid, who went missing a year ago during his first assignment. It was more of a gut feeling. He pulled out a digital camera and a tape measure to document the evidence. He then pulled out an older-model Polaroid camera and snapped a single picture. The instant picture slowly ejected from the camera. Jake shook the picture until it developed and the two handprints were clear. He then used his boot to scratch the two handprints out of the mud.

Jake moved to the other side of the stream and climbed to the top of the ridge along a game trail. At the top of the ridge he found evidence of a latrine, an area where an animal will leave several deposits of scat to mark its territory. By the size of the scat, Jake concluded it was left by a bigfoot. He wasn't surprised by its location, considering it gave the creature a perfect vantage of the stream valley below. Moving further along the game trail, he came to a thick maple tree. He pulled out a pen and wrote a simple note on the back of the Polaroid picture. Placing the picture in his last envelope that he would normally use to send reports to Mr. Smith, he pinned it to the maple tree with one of his black throwing knives.

Looking around the isolated forest, Jake was confident that the Blackwoods would find the picture. He had been keeping track of the Blackwoods since Brock went missing. Jake's commanding officer, Whiskey, still considered them a threat to national security. Jake, on the other hand, classified the father and son as fanatical, but a non-threat. Jake's partner, Mr. Smith, argued that the Blackwoods had accumulated a substantial amount of evidence proving the existence of bigfoot in North America. Jake agreed, but he countered that the Blackwoods were a non-threat because of their obsession with finding Brock and Abby Blackwood. Pushing the black throwing knife deeper into the tree, Jake hoped that Darius would be the one to find the picture. He then sniffed his armpit again and groaned, "I need a shower."

Chapter 14

Darius stood on the deadfall, straddling the scat. He squatted down over it. He slowly scanned the forest for any movement. It was quiet. He only heard the distinct rustle of a squirrel through the leaves. The game trail he had been following led down to the stream below. In the distance he could see a large oak tree that had fallen across the water. It was a natural bridge he would use to cross. To his immediate right was an old barbed wire fence which he thought was interesting considering how deep they were in the forest. He guessed it was from a ranch long forgotten to time. The game trail split off across the wire fence. He could see deer tracks in the mud as they skittered down the steep slope. The tracks weren't what grabbed his attention. It was the stick twisted in the barbed wire fence. Something took a tree branch as thick as his arms and as long as his legs and had interwoven the branch between the strands of wire. And then turned the branch in order to twist the four wires together, collapsing the fence, making it safe to step over. He guessed by the new growth of vines over the fence and along the game trail leading away from the twisted fence it had been done years ago. Still, it was curious.

Darius stood from his squatted position and saw a bone in the crook of the tree directly in front of him. He moved to the tree and reached his arm up to the crook. He couldn't reach it with his arm outstretched despite his height of six feet. The bone was at least nine feet high in the tree. Curious, he thought. He glanced down the game trail and saw the markings of what appeared to be a deer that had rubbed against a tree trunk. He moved down the trail to the damaged tree. From the top of the ridge he heard his companions.

Darius glanced back up the game trail and watched as three men crested the ridge. Two of the men stopped at the scat and squatted down to examine it. The third man turned in a slow circle as he surveyed the area. The third man's gaze, his father's, rested upon the twisted barbed wire fence. He tilted his head to the side and then glanced down towards Darius. Darius could tell by the expression on his face that he thought it was curious as well. It gave Darius a sense of pride.

On scouting and hunting trips like these his dad always took up the rear. The other two men were brothers. They had hired Darius and his dad to take them on a hunting trip as a bonding adventure among brothers. Darius agreed, of course. It was how he and his dad put food on the table and paid their bills. When his dad had started the business just under two years ago, he had asked his long-time friend, Buzzy, to help. Buzzy helped for little over a year, until Darius had turned eighteen. When Darius became a legal adult his dad insisted that he become the face and voice of the business. He advertised in all of the hunting magazines and the Internet as the most authentic hunting experience in North America. The selling point of the hunting experience was the primitive approach Darius and his father used during the expeditions. The hunters were not allowed to bring any form of firearms. They were only permitted to bring one of three weapons: a bow, spear, or a knife. A majority of the time the client would bring a recurve bow. However, the two brothers with them carried spears and were dressed like Native American Indians. Darius's dad thought they were idiots. Darius didn't care. Their money would keep them afloat for at least three months.

They were five days into a ten-day trip. The two brothers had seen at least a dozen different deer in those five days. However, their spears missed each time no matter how close they approached. If the brothers had had a recurve bow, they would have killed at least half as many as they saw. Then again, Darius would have only agreed to a three day trip as opposed to a ten day trip. For Darius and his dad, these trips weren't about hunters being successful in killing whatever animal they tracked. These trips were an excuse for the two of them to look for Darius's younger brother Brock.

Even though Brock had been missing for a little over a year, his father was confident that his younger son was still alive. For reasons unknown to Darius, he felt the same way. In his heart he believed that his mother was still alive too. Darius had no reason to believe his brother was in this particular forest. But that didn't matter, because his father believed Brock could be in any forest across North America. One of them, Darius or his father, were in the woods at all times looking and searching. He looked up at his father and wanted to smile. He loved his dad. He suspected his dad loved him also, though he couldn't recall ever hearing the man say the words out loud.

The younger of the two brothers came running down the game trail toward Darius with a huge smile on his face. His charge down the trail caused every bird hiding in the undergrowth to take flight. Which in turn alerted any animals in the area that something large was moving into their territory. Darius closed his eyes and envisioned punching the man in the face.

"Dude, did you see the size of that scat up there on that log?"

gasped the younger brother.

Darius hated being called "Dude." Darius simply grunted an acknowledgement because he was afraid if he opened his mouth to form words, they would be offensive.

The man asked, "Was that from a bear?"

Darius shook his head. "No, something larger."

The man looked back towards his older brother, who was coming down the game trail a tad quieter than his sibling, and then back to Darius. "A moose?"

Darius agreed with his father in that moment that the man standing in front of him was an idiot. "Moose don't live in this part of North America."

The man looked confused.

Darius's father walked past the three of them and simply stated, "A sasquatch."

The two brothers looked at each other. The younger one had a smile that stretched across his face in excitement. The older brother looked skeptical and asked, "Is he serious?"

Darius wanted to smile and turn the conversation into a joke. However, he couldn't. The signs were too compelling. He simply shrugged and followed his dad down to the stream. At the stream his father waited by the downed oak tree. As Darius approached, his dad shook his head and muttered, "Idiots."

Darius patted his dad on the back and climbed up on to the thick dead tree. As he walked across the log he looked down into the stream. After crossing the stream he glanced back and watched as the two brothers wandered through the trees of the stream valley looking for tracks. The game trail led up a steep incline to a ridge. He followed the trail to the top. Along the way he saw several more signs that piqued his curiosity. At the top of ridge he found another deadfall tree with several piles of scat. Large piles of scat. By what he saw they were left at different times. By the smell, at least one pile was only half a day old. He stood on the log and looked down into the stream valley. From this position he could see both directions of the stream and the entire valley below. A great vantage point if a bigfoot was hunting or scouting. As he swept the valley for any sign of game he saw a curious structure directly across from his position. Two large dead trees leaned against one living tree to make a large X. He knew it was possible that the structure happened by accident with the trees falling into place. He had seen it before. However, from his position, it appeared the two dead trees were placed against the living tree to purposefully make the X-structure. Similar to a sketch he had seen in his mother's journal years ago. The two trees were at least thirty feet long and as thick as his own body. No single human or group of humans could maneuver those dead trees into that position to form an X. It was possible that something human-like could have made the structure with the trees. However, in the forest things can look deceiving. He whistled to get his father's attention. He pointed to the structure. His father nodded once and moved to investigate. The two brothers were a distance away and oblivious to their surroundings.

Darius moved up the game trail over the ridge and out of sight from the other three men. In a tree directly in front of him he saw a weathered envelope pinned to the trunk with a black throwing knife. He stopped in his tracks and looked around. He glanced back down along the game trail and knew his father was busy. Darius was alone. He quickly moved to the tree with the envelope. From what he could tell, the throwing knife and envelope had been there for a few months. He pulled the knife from the tree and dropped it into one of his cargo pockets to hide it from his father. He glanced back behind him to guarantee he was still alone. He moved further up the game trail to what appeared to be a meadow with tall grass the color of gold.

Darius crossed the tree line into the field. The game trail was gone. He moved into the tall grass and squatted down out of sight. He waited and listened. He heard nothing. Pulling his own knife from his pocket he slit opened the envelope. He pulled out a picture. The picture was of two handprints in mud by a stream. One massive and one small. Darius brushed his thumb over the smaller handprint in the picture. He suspected the stream was the one he had just crossed. He flipped over the picture and saw a handwritten note on the back.

He's alive.

Jake

Chapter 15

Jake sat at the bar and stared into his drink as he swirled the liquid. The bartender walked by. He watched her pass. He momentarily wondered if it was the same woman that served him the last time he was in this bar almost two years ago. He shrugged. He couldn't remember. It didn't matter. He sipped at the liquid in his glass. Staring up at the television, he absentmindedly scratched at his beard. The bartender walked past again and he glanced at her. Even if she was the same woman, there is no way she would recognize me with his tangle of hair, he thought.

Jake felt movement to his left. He dropped his right hand to palm one of his throwing knives. His own movement was slight and went unnoticed. A lean black man with a bald head, dressed to play golf, sat next to Jake. Mr. Smith dropped a folder on to the bar and pushed it towards Jake. Jake let the knife slip back into its sheath.

"Let's get something straight," hissed Mr. Smith. "I do the communicating. Not you." The man turned and glowered at Jake, "You are supposed to stay in those godforsaken woods until I call for you."

Jake held the man's gaze for a long time before the bartender broke the uncomfortable silence.

"What can I get you?" asked the woman.

Mr. Smith broke his gaze away from Jake. He flashed her a sweet smile that visibly calmed the woman's nerves. "Scotch on the rocks."

The bartender moved away to make the drink.

Mr. Smith pushed the folder closer to Jake for him to open it. Jake refused. He knew what was in the folder. He had sent it to Mr. Smith.

"What the hell is this?" asked Mr. Smith.

The bartender returned with the drink and then left.

Mr. Smith took a long drink. The glass crashed down to the bar. "We have proof they exist. Or did you not get that memo during your briefing?"

Jake raised the glass to his lips. He closed his eyes. He took a slow deep breath to calm his nerves. Then he drank. Gently placing the glass on the bar, he said, "That folder is more than proof of their existences." Jake pushed the folder back to Mr. Smith. "That folder contains the link we need to track the tribe that is associated with the White One."

Mr. Smith looked to his left and then to his right, beyond Jake, before speaking. "Are you serious? Is that what this is about?"

Jake turned and looked at Mr. Smith. "I was briefed that the White One is our main priority."

Mr. Smith pressed the palms of his hands against the bar, pushed himself an arm's length away, and barked out a laugh. "Oh, don't tell me about my job. I am well aware of the priorities. But let's be honest with each other. This has nothing to do with the White One. It's about that damn boy!" Mr. Smith looked towards the ceiling in thought. "What was his name again? Brandon? Bradley? Bec—"

"Brock," growled Jake with annoyance.

Mr. Smith shot forward toward Jake. His finger jabbed into Jake's shoulder and he growled, "Of course his damn name is Brock! I never forget!"

Jake glanced down at Mr. Smith's finger pushing into his shoulder. He glanced at Mr. Smith's other hand that was hidden inside of his suit jacket, resting on the handle of a concealed pistol. "That's right, asshole. I have no problem putting a hole the size of the Grand Canyon through your thick skull in the middle of this rat-hole," hissed Mr. Smith. Dropping his finger, he straightened. "Remember, you are replaceable."

The bartender interrupted again, "Can I get you two another round?"

Mr. Smith flashed his smile at her. "That would be great doll."

The woman's smile stretched across her face as she moved away to make two more drinks.

Mr. Smith straightened his suit jacket. Picking up his drink, he said, "I get that you feel guilty about this kid. But I'm telling you, let it go. If he's not dead already, he will be soon. He's officially a missing person."

The bartender placed two new drinks in front of Jake and Mr. Smith. With an exaggerated frown, she interjected, "Oh, a missing person? Those pictures on the milk bottles are so sad." Jake looked at her without comment. Mr. Smith nodded in agreement. Her frown turned right side up into a huge grin. She walked away to help another customer. Mr. Smith shook his head as she walked away. "If her ass didn't make up for her brain, she would be worthless."

Jake's right hand fingered the hilt of his knife. One quick stab between the ribs and no one would be the wiser. Mr. Smith pulled a piece of paper from the inside pocket of his jacket. He dropped it on the folder in front of Jake.

"Here's a new recruit for the Unit," said Mr. Smith. "Since you are in town, go pick him up. Brief him and take him with you for a few months on a field assignment." Mr. Smith paused as the bartender walked past. "When you think he is ready, send him on his own and discretely track him." He paused again and glanced down at his drink before finishing, "I assume you will be able to determine if he is a risk to our Unit or not. If he is, silence him."

Jake looked at Mr. Smith.

"Yes, we did the same to you," Mr. Smith sipped his drink, "Please don't let me think you were dumb enough to think you were the only field agent? The only difference is the Commander didn't think you needed to be babysat for the first few months. But I insisted that we track you to ensure you were not a risk to national security." He tapped the paper in front of Jake. "This guy," he shook his head, "I don't know, he might be too gung-ho." Mr. Smith finished his drink. "His last commander called him Butcher. Butch for short. He's a trained sniper. Rumor has it, he was on a top secret mission in Siberia. Reasons unknown. I don't even have clearance that high." Mr. Smith lifted his glass and noticed it was empty. "When he was extracted he was found among the remains of four large, hairy children that had been butchered to death." He pushed the empty glass to the edge of the bar. He stood. "They weren't children. They were young Almas." Mr. Smith paused and smiled. Sarcastically, he finished, "You know, Russia's version of bigfoot."

Jake looked at Mr. Smith with a spark of anger rising up through him. He hissed between clenched teeth, "I know what an Alma is, asshole."

Mr. Smith lips spread into a charismatic grin. "We don't need this guy butchering bigfoots in our national parks. Understand?" asked Mr. Smith.

Jake barked out a laugh and threw back the rest of his drink. Looking straight ahead as he placed the glass delicately on the bar, he said, just as sarcastically as Mr. Smith, "Don't we want them butchered?"

Jake could feel Mr. Smith's eyes burning into the side of his face. He turned to look at his partner. Mr. Smith blinked and his eyes matched the smile that spread across his face. "Remember, our job is to protect. Only our commander has the authority to eliminate." He paused, and then as an afterthought said, "If they are a threat, of course."

Jake gave a nod of his head in acknowledgement. He knew the rules of engagement. He just liked to annoy his partner for the pleasure.

"Which brings me to the last thing. Find the White One. The Commander wants him taken down."

Mr. Smith paused again and Jake knew his partner was waiting for some type of reaction. He continued to just look at the man. Mr. Smith half-laughed as he slapped Jake on the back, "You seem to be the commander's golden boy, and capable of the job." He laughed, "Good luck with that."

Jake hissed through his teeth, "Don't ever touch me again, prick."

Mr. Smith eyed Jake for a moment. He then slapped the bar to get the bartender's attention. When she looked at him, he said out loud, "My friend here will cover me." The bartender smiled and moved to the cash register.

Mr. Smith moved close to Jake and whispered, "I have the power to make you disappear forever." He then turned and walked out of the bar.

Chapter 16

An image of a tree flashed in Brock's mind. Followed by the deep husky voice of Sookum, "Be a tree." The deep husky voice that Brock heard in his head was not actually Sookum's voice. He knew it was the voice he imagined Sookum's to be if the creature spoke words. When Sookum did communicate with Brock, it was with images that appeared in his mind. The words and voice Brock associated with the images were his own translation of Sookum's projected images. The images were brief and scattered. Brock interpreted the images as best he could. Sometimes he was wrong. But there was no mistaking the meaning behind the image of the tree.

Brock froze in place and did not move. This was their code for hiding. Usually it was because a deer was near and Sookum was going to make his move to catch and kill it. Brock was hoping that was the case. He was especially hungry that afternoon. In the back of his mind, though, he suspected something else, not a deer but something frightening. The image of the tree had flashed in his mind so quickly. The voice in his head sounded urgent, not cautious.

Brock looked towards Sookum, who was across the field near

the tree line. He wondered why Sookum didn't just turn and walk into the trees. With Sookum's long legs he could be among the trees and gone from sight in less than a second. Instead Sookum squatted down and became a bush. Not a literal bush, but at the same time, from a distance, it was extremely hard to distinguish Sookum from the bush that was just a few yards to his right. Brock always wondered how Sookum did it.

The image of the tree flashed in his head again with much more urgency. Brock looked around and saw that there was no place for him to hide. He was out in the open in the field with just the tall grass and wildflowers. He squatted down in place and braced himself for being in this position for a long time. It was times like this that he was thankful his father used to make him sit or lie still for long periods of time. He wanted to smile at the thought of his father, but happiness was not an emotion he usually attached to memories of his father. Fear dominated his thoughts of his father instead. He remembered those times that his father would offer to pay him money if he could sit or lay still for five minutes, ten minutes, or even an hour. To his father's astonishment and anger, Brock would succeed. His father always paid him what he promised, plus a spank or two on his bum. During times like this when he had to remain still for long periods of time, Brock was thankful for that practice with his father.

Of course, out here in the forest, time meant nothing. Brock had lost the sense of time so long ago that he almost forgot what the concept of time was. When he did think about it, usually when he was waiting to fall asleep, he tried to remember how old he was. He knew he was eleven years old when he first met Sookum. He certainly did not feel eleven anymore. He felt older now, maybe fourteen? But that didn't make sense. That would mean that he had been living in the forest with Sookum and his tribe for at least three years. Three years was a long time. At the same time he would spend an entire night tracking and hunting deer with Sookum and that time passed quickly. So maybe it had been three years. To be honest, he didn't care.

Life in the forest with Sookum was completely different than life with his father. With Sookum he felt safe and protected. With his father he lived in constant fear. He missed his brother. But missing his brother didn't match the fear he had of his father. Brock closed his eyes for a moment and wondered if his father or brother had ever gone looking for him? The thought made him sad; therefore, he tried to never think about it. Times like this, when he had a moment to think, he wondered. He wondered if he was missed. At that same moment he heard a voice off to his right breaking through the tree line into the field.

"Oh my God, look at all the wildflowers," said a high-pitched female voice. The woman's voice cut through the silence of the forest like a knife through warm butter. Brock's eyes snapped open, the birds stopped singing, and the bees stopped humming. Brock started to stand from his crouched position, but the image of the tree slammed into his mind so forcefully he almost fell over backwards.

Brock looked towards the clump of bushes that he knew was Sookum. The creature's eyes flashed at him to remain still. Brock looked back towards the woman. He leaned forward slightly on his hands to try and get a better look at her. She stood maybe a head taller than him. She had light-colored hair that was pulled back away from her face with some type of cloth wrapped around her forehead. She wore shorts and a tank top. She unclipped a belt around her waist to shrug the backpack off her shoulders to fall upon the ground. She stretched her arms over her head and twisted at the waist. She turned back towards the tree line and at that moment a man stepped through the trees.

The man was larger than she. He was thick and muscular, with a large stomach. He had jet-black hair sprinkled with streaks of gray. His beard looked ragged and unkempt. He stopped in front of the woman and reached into a pocket of his shorts. He pulled out a handful of something and pushed it into his mouth. Brock guessed it was some type of food by the way he was chewing. The man smiled at the woman. She leaned forward and kissed him on the lips.

"Isn't it pretty?" she asked.

The man casually looked around the field and smiled in acknowledgement. When his gaze passed by, Brock was tempted to stand up. But he didn't. He knew if he did Sookum would be upset. Sookum wouldn't hurt him. He was not afraid of Sookum, but he also knew that Sookum was in charge. In the past whenever he did something against what Sookum wanted, Sookum would give him what Brock called a lion roar. Sookum's lion roar was so loud and so intense that it often knocked Brock to the ground and made his insides shake. He figured that Sookum's lion roar would probably make a lion piss itself.

Brock watched as the man looked towards Sookum. The man stopped and leaned in Sookum's direction. Brock could tell that the man questioned what he saw. Brock knew this from experience. The first time he saw Sookum hide as a bush his brain was completely confused. He would look at the bush and see a bush, but at the same time his mind, or maybe his sixth sense, was telling him it was something different. Eventually over time and practice his mind could distinguish between a bush and Sookum. It even worked when he saw Sookum's tribe-mates. They were a little bit harder to distinguish in the forest because he was not used to seeing them as much as he saw Sookum. Brock suspected that his time in the forest with Sookum had enhanced his ability to see what was hidden in the forest.

The man motioned towards the woman who was drinking out of

a container. "Lilly, get your pack on. We should go."

The woman, Lilly, stopped drinking and looked at him, confused. "Why? This is a perfect spot to camp for the night."

The man looked back towards Sookum and shook his head no. "I don't have a good feeling about this place." He paused and then looked back at Lilly. "Let's find another spot."

Lilly frowned, "What's wrong, Nathan?"

Nathan looked back towards Sookum, "I feel like we're being watched."

At that moment Brock heard a soft wood knock and the chatter of a squirrel off to his left. He didn't have to look. He knew it was one of Sookum's tribe-mates announcing its position to Sookum. They did this often when they hunted deer. He knew at least one more, if not two, would be getting in position to herd whatever they were hunting towards Sookum. But this behavior confused him, because there was no deer, just this man and woman.

Nathan turned back towards Lilly and picked up her pack. With more urgency and fear in his voice, he commanded Lilly, "Put your pack on, we're leaving now!"

Lilly reluctantly grabbed her pack from Nathan. "You don't have to be a dick about it."

"Come on, Lilly, let's go," urged Nathan.

"Honestly, Nathan, what's wrong with you? There is nothing out here for miles. We're all alone," said Lilly as she slung her pack on.

Nathan looked back towards Sookum and shook his head no. "No, Lilly, we're not alone." He grabbed her hand and pulled her towards the tree line.

Brock watched as they disappeared into the tree line of the forest. Some time passed before Sookum stood from his position. To Brock's left he saw movement as Sookum's tribe-mate with the auburn-colored hair, who Brock called Red, stepped out from behind a thick tree. The third creature, who he called Skunk because it stank so badly, dropped out of a tree that the couple had just passed under. It looked at Sookum, then faded into the forest in the same direction as the couple.

Sookum whooped once and moved towards Brock. Brock looked in his direction and watched as the massive creature moved towards him with an elegance that he knew no other creature in the forest could match. To his left he heard Red whoop in acknowledgement. He didn't bother to look in her direction because he knew she was already gone. Sookum stood in front of Brock and looked down at him. The creature's face almost looked sad. Brock tilted his head to the side and wondered why. An image of his father with a gun shooting a bear flashed through his mind. Sookum grunted. Brock looked towards the direction of the fleeing couple.

He looked back towards Sookum and pushed his open palm against the creature's muscular chest. He whispered, "Yes, humans are dangerous."

Sookum grunted and moved off into the forest in the opposite direction of the fleeing couple. Brock watched him fade into the trees. He walked over to where the couple had broken through the tree line and squatted down in the dirt. He traced the outline of their boot prints. He looked down at his own bare feet. The boots he wore when he first met Sookum had worn away and fallen off of his feet before the last winter. He looked at his bare legs and chest. He couldn't remember when he had lost his clothes. He stood and ran his hands through his matted black hair. Movement from the tree line caught his attention. He watched Skunk move towards him. Skunk grunted what Brock took as a greeting as it walked past him. To Brock it almost seemed like Skunk was smiling. Brock looked toward the trees again. Humans were dangerous. His father was dangerous. He turned and followed Skunk up the mountain slop

Chapter 17

B rock crouched down on the thick branch in the tree. His movement caused the leaves on the tree to shake. He hoped the movement of the leaves wouldn't give away his hiding spot. The giant black bear underneath him continued to lumber in its slow gait, sniffing the ground. Brock assumed the bear was sniffing for the blackberries that were just a few yards away that he had been snacking on. If it was not for the chattering of a squirrel to warn anything around that the black bear was coming, he may have been caught off guard. But he doubted it. Sookum had taught him well.

He found himself missing Sookum during these times. It was not often, but there were times that Sookum and his tribe-mates would go away for a few days. During those times he was not allowed to join them. Brock never asked where they went. He assumed if they wanted him to know they would bring him. A part of him was glad that they never brought him, because of the shimmer jump. That's what he called it, not them. All he knew was that it made him sick every time they brought him on a shimmer jump.

Brock called it a shimmer jump because whenever they bedded down for a period of time it was always near a spot where the air seemed to shimmer. The few times Sookum carried him through the shimmering air the world would lose all color and sound. If he didn't pass out from the jump, seconds later they would emerge in another part of the forest, he assumed miles away from where they were originally. He preferred to pass out, because if he didn't he always vomited. He hated throwing up.

A tribe-mate was always tasked to stay near the spot of air that shimmered, as if to guard the space. When Brock was first with Sookum and his tribe-mates, he started to call the creature who guarded the spot Shimmer. She never strayed far from the shimmering air and never went on hunts with the other tribe-mates. Out of all the tribe mates, Shimmer was probably the closest to his age. She was smaller than all of the other creatures and had long, blonde-colored hair that covered her entire body, including the breasts she was developing. Even though her breasts were covered in long hair they were still noticeable. It took a long time for Brock to get used to looking at Red and Shimmer without being embarrassed.

Brock quietly adjusted his position on the branch because the thought of Shimmer made him feel funny. Especially down in the pit of his stomach and groin. He often wondered who would pair with Shimmer. He wondered if he was even a choice. He knew he was different than the other creatures. But he had the same man parts as Sookum and Skunk, so he knew it was possible. However, something felt wrong when he thought about pairing with Shimmer. He gave his head a quick shake to try and push the image of Shimmer's breasts out of his mind.

Other times when he was alone he found himself thinking of that woman Lilly he saw in the woods many moon cycles back. He remembered her bare arms and legs. He remembered her long hair and curve of her face. He especially remembered the curve of her breasts. He smiled to himself at that thought. He doubted Lilly had hair on her breasts like Shimmer. Brock shifted his weight on the tree branch at the comforting feeling growing in his groin at the thought of Lilly's breasts. He smiled and concluded that he preferred hairless breasts; he assumed Lilly's were hairless.

The black bear underneath Brock stopped its slow lumber and sniffed at the air in aggravation. Brock grunted under his breath in frustration at his clumsiness for losing his concentration and moving the tree branch that gave away his position. The tree he climbed to hide from the bear would be considered a mature tree among its peers. Its roots were deep, its lower branches thick, and its canopy among the elders. But its trunk was no thicker than Brock's body. It was sturdy and strong, but would never withstand an angry shake from a mature black bear. Brock estimated the bear weighed as much as Sookum, at least eight hundred pounds. The bear probably stood as tall as Sookum if it reared on its hind legs.

Brock closed his eyes and tried to calm his breathing. He was scared. He wished Sookum or one of their tribe-mates was near for him to call. But when they jumped through the shimmer they were unable to hear his loudest whoops. Instead of a whoop to try and frighten the bear off, he tried a low quiet growl. Brock had seen Sookum do this on several occasions when they hunted deer. Sookum would growl from his throat in an almost imperceptible tone to Brock, but the deer would freeze in place. Brock suspected the deer froze in fear because Sookum had done the same thing to him the one time he thought about fleeing from Sookum. He was unable to move. He actually fell to his knees crying because he was so afraid. Instead of Skunk stepping from his hiding place to break his leg like he did to the deer, Red came over, picked him up and cuddled him until he fell asleep. He never tried to escape again. Brock shook his head. Escape? Why had he tried to escape in the first place? That was dumb. He loved Sookum and his tribe-mates.

The combination of the bear's roar and the vibration of the entire forest shaking broke Brock out of his reverie. Brock reached back and grabbed the trunk of the tree to prevent himself from falling off the branch on top of the bear. The bear reared up on its hind legs again and roared at a deafening pitch in the direction of the blackberry bushes. The vibration of the forest stopped when Numyc crashed through the forest brush and stopped in front of the giant black bear.

"Oh shit," whispered Brock.

Numyc was the giant white-haired creature that Sookum had protected him from the morning after his first shimmer jump. This was the giant creature that had palmed his small head like a basketball and lifted him off the ground. The same giant creature that haunted his dreams. The same giant beast that Brock believed would have eaten him if Sookum had not interfered. Brock had seen him before, but always from a distance and always with Sookum or the tribe-mates nearby. Never alone and never trapped. Brock wished he was near a shimmer spot so he could jump to wherever. Jump far away from Numyc. He would gladly deal with a day of violent vomiting just to get away from this devil of the forest.

Brock watched as the black bear reared up on its hind legs and revealed a small cub. The cub glanced at its mother and tried to imitate her, but fell forward and rolled towards Numyc. Numyc stood at least a head taller than the bear and weighed at least two hundred pounds more. The bear was a solid mass of bone and fat. Numyc was solid muscle. The black bear snorted in what Brock thought was an attempt to distract Numyc from noticing the cub. Numyc glanced at the mother bear and then down at the cub. Then Numyc moved faster than Brock thought was possible and lifted the small, brown squirming cub to its giant mouth and took a bite out of its throat. The squeal of the cub pierced Brock's ears and then abruptly ended.

Numyc spat out the bear cub flesh at his feet and then nonchalantly tossed the limp body at the mother bear's legs. When the dead cub hit the ground the bear dropped to all four paws and sniffed at the baby. Brock watched and felt as if time slowed almost to a halt. He could hear each sniff of the bear. He could feel the dirt on his nose as the bear nudged the baby. He could taste the iron in the blood that dripped from the cub's neck as the bear's tongue gingerly licked at her baby.

Time abruptly sped forward as the giant bear reared back on its hind legs and roared with its full anguish. The roar was sorrowful and desperate. The bear lunged at Numyc in anger, stumbling forward with its massive weight balanced on its two hind legs and let its full weight crash into Numyc. The bear's two front paws swatted at Numyc. One paw struck Numyc in the face, dragging a claw across his cheek. The force of the blow and the bear's full body weight crashed into Numyc and forced him to stumble backwards. Numyc grabbed the front shoulders of the bear and effortlessly tossed the bear to the side as if he was playing with a rowdy puppy. The bear rolled to its feet, attacked again with a powerful roar. The bear's mouth was open with its massive teeth in an attempt to tear Numyc apart. Numyc batted the bear's bite away with an open palm strike. The bear stumbled and then swung its massive head and shoulders back towards Numyc, striking him in the legs. Numyc reached down and wrapped an arm around the bear's neck and tossed it to the side again. The bear rolled into the trunk of the tree were Brock was perched. The blow to the tree shook Brock from his branch. He slipped from the branch, but caught himself, his body and legs dangling just above the bear.

Numyc saw Brock drop and hang from the tree branch. Their eyes met. Brock could feel the evil hatred penetrating from Numyc's dark red eyes. Numyc lunged for Brock over the bear's body. Brock hoisted himself back up on to the tree branch. Numyc's giant hands just missed Brock's legs. The bear saw an opportunity and clamped its powerful jaw on Numyc's ankle. Numyc howled in pain so loud that Brock went temporarily deaf. He watched in horror as Numyc reached down and grabbed the bear by the scruff of the neck. He tore the bear's bite from his ankle, leaving several canine teeth embedded in flesh of his leg. He pulled the bear's head to his eye level as its body struggled to its rear legs. Numyc punched the bear in the snout. The force of Numyc's fist crushed the bear's snout into its skull, immediately killing the animal. Numyc dropped the bear's limp, useless body to the ground without a thought.

Numyc immediately turned its attention to Brock in the tree. The giant creature lunged forward and struck the tree with both hands. The trunk of the tree snapped at the base and fell away from Numyc. Brock lost his balance. He crashed to the ground, several feet away from the dead bear. He scrambled to his feet with all the intention of making a run for it, but knowing he would never outrun Numyc. Instead, Brock screamed a siren howl as loud as he could. It was the type of call that Sookum and his tribe-mates only used if they were in distress or danger. Brock called it a siren howl because to him it sounded like the siren of an emergency vehicle. He was in distress now. Numyc stopped in his tracks and sneered at Brock. Brock took in a deep breath and screamed again at the top of lungs. He prayed that his tiny voice would carry over the mountains to wherever Sookum and his tribe mates had gone.

Numyc took a quick, giant step forward and grabbed Brock by the top of his head. Brock closed his eyes and waited for it all to end. He knew this was what Numyc wanted to do to him since he first came to be with Sookum. For whatever reason, Numyc hated Brock's kind. He hated humans. Brock could feel the pressure of each of Numyc's massive fingers on his skull. He could feel his skull press tighter against his brain. He knew his feet were at least four feet off the ground. Brock struggled and kicked at Numyc, hoping to strike the creature in the face with his feet. He tugged and pulled at the long white hair that hung from Numyc's massive arm. Brock tried anything to get Numyc to release his head. He wasn't ready to die yet. Brock knew that Numyc was enjoying the opportunity to finally kill him, but he didn't want to make it easy for the creature.

Just as Brock's vision was about to go black from the pressure on his head, Brock and Numyc both heard a loud, "Harrumph." Brock struggled to open his eyes and looked past Numyc's massive shoulder and head to see Sookum, Red, and Shimmer emerge from the trees. Brock could not help but smile that his tribe had heard him. Numyc slowly turned his head and upper body toward the three creatures standing behind him. He nonchalantly dropped Brock. Brock braced for the ground to rush up and meet him, but instead Skunk caught him and righted him to his feet. Skunk quickly pushed Brock behind him to be a shield while still holding on to him. Blood rushed back into his head and Brock struggled to remain conscious. Skunk slowly pushed Brock back towards the thick brush without making a noise.

Numyc took two quick steps towards Sookum and screamed, "Grawarrgh!"

Sookum stood his ground and a low growl from his throat reverberated through Numyc and the surrounding forest. Numyc huffed a disgruntled growl and turned to crash through the forest. He disappeared from sight.

As soon as Brock saw Numyc disappear into the forest his legs gave out from under him. He sank to the ground behind Skunk. Skunk turned around and grinned down at him, showing his teeth and bobbing his head up and down in excitement. Despite the horrible smell of Skunk, Brock smiled back and passed out.

Chapter 18

J ake strapped his gear to the thick bough of the tree for the night. He leaned against the trunk and adjusted his back until he was comfortable. He peered down through the branches at Butch from the height of the tree. He had a perfect view of the man. Butch was in a small clearing with a fire burning. He was unaware of Jake's presence.

For three months, as part of Butch's training, the two of them had been tracking bigfoot creatures in various forest regions throughout the country. Butch was told the purpose of the assignment was to become familiar with the operations of the Unit. Jake knew the true purpose of the assignment was for him to evaluate the effectiveness of Butch as a field agent. When the initial three-month assignment was completed, Butch would be assigned to monitor a remote forest in the Northeast, where there were several reports of a Type Four bigfoot creature, also known as a Dogman. Unknown to Butch, Jake's assignment was to covertly track and monitor Butch's activities during this period to determine if the newcomer was a stable asset while on his own. At the conclusion of tonight's observation, Jake would report to Whiskey that Butch was stable. The man was eccentric, but then again, they all were in their own way.

Jake watched as Butch pulled something out of his pack. He knew it was the man's comic book. Butch always carried a couple in his pack and would reread them each night. It sparked Jake to start carrying a paperback book in his own pack. However, he never opened it. He leaned his head back and stared towards the stars. He smiled as a shooting star streaked pass. He glanced down at Butch, who was engrossed in his comic books. He wondered if the man was intrigued by anything in nature. Or curious in general. The only things the man seemed to show any passion about were reading comic books and hunting bigfoot. Hunting bigfoot was never a topic they discussed. It was understood. It was what they did. However, by Butch's actions, Jake had deduced that Butch enjoyed the endeavor. It seemed to Jake as if Butch thought it was his destiny in some ways.

During the past six months Jake had learned that nothing frightened Butch. He never flinched at a sound or a confrontation with a wild animal. Jake had watched Butch stand his ground to a grizzly bear. Even Jake had enough sense to back down from that standoff. Butch just stood there and mumbled to himself until the massive bear became bored and shuffled off. That particular encounter was the epitome of stupidity; however, it also earned Jake's respect.

The only concern Jake had in regards to Butch was his lack of people skills. He would never be a Mr. Smith. He would never be able to infiltrate a hunting party to assess a hunter's knowledge of the subject. They would need to keep him in the field at all times. Preferably the deepest forest they could find away from civilization. Jake had no problem being away from other humans. However, it was a bit unnerving to spend three months with someone and barely speak a handful of words to them each day.

Jake was also going to have to report the encounter that occurred about four months back. He found a set of tracks in a remote part of the forest. Butch took the lead on following the tracks. They both suspected there was more than one bigfoot associated with the tracks. He also suspected that he and Butch were not the only ones tracking the creatures. Jake found signs of at least two other humans. Jake and Butch tracked the creatures for days. Butch didn't sleep during that entire time.

Then early one evening, Butch caught sight of a bigfoot. Butch reported it was a large female with dark red hair. Jake suspected she was acting as a sentry for the rest of the tribe as they rested. A tribe was usually limited to four or five of the bigfoot creatures. He hardly ever found evidence of more than that.

When Butch saw the sentry he circled around the creature and tried to find higher ground. He eventually scaled a large tree and remained stationary. They held their position at a distance and maintained surveillance. Their main directive in the forest was always to track and observe bigfoot creatures. They only engaged the creatures if they were ordered to kill one for the purpose of public safety.

Late in the evening the large red female bigfoot creature alerted her tribe-mates to some danger with a series of wood knocks and whistles that broke the silence of the night. Her warnings were immediately answered. Jake knew the creatures becoming alerted was not because of him or Butch. Before the tribe evacuated from the area, Jake thought he heard the scattering of at least four large bipedal creatures moving through the forest in their general vicinity. He also thought he heard smaller bipedal creatures moving in the underbrush. The next morning he confirmed at least two humans were in the vicinity the night before, based on the boot tracks he found. As usual the creatures vanished and he found no evidence of their existence except for one partial print.

Jake was concerned about the other humans in the forest that night. He knew that he and Butch had maintained their positions in observation. The other humans caused the bigfoot creatures to scatter and vanish that night. What concerned him more, however, was that the other humans were experienced bigfoot trackers. Not amateur bigfoot researchers stumbling through the forest at night. He had been around enough researchers of both kinds to tell the difference. Plus, only experienced bigfoot researchers would trek this deep into the forest looking for proof. Jake suspected it was Darius and his father. However, he would leave that speculation out of his report.

Butch snuffed the fire out. The forest fell into complete darkness. Jake smiled and stared up at the stars in the night sky.

Chapter 19

Darius gradually rose to his feet, lifting his chin so the artificial light bathed his skin as he stretched his arms over his head. He twisted from side to side to work out the kinks in his muscles from sitting for too long. He looked down at his journal and flipped it closed. In the corner of his eye he saw a flash of light from the bedroom window. Absentmindedly, he dropped his journal in the open desk drawer and pushed it closed with his knee. He went to the window and pulled down one of the blind flats with his fingers. The light he saw was coming from his father. Darius glanced at the red neon numbers of his alarm clock and saw that it was a few minutes past nine. The sun had set about an hour earlier. His dad was late checking the infrared lasers around their property.

The log cabin and property they owned had been a part of the Blackwood family for at least four generations. His dad had inherited the homestead from his father and Darius had every reason to believe the same would happen with him. They owned roughly seventy-five acres in the middle of nowhere on the side of a forgotten mountain. Darius remembered hearing stories that originally they owned thousands of acres when his second great-grandfather and great-grandfather owned the land. He always wondered what happened with his grandfather and why he sold off so much of the property. His own father didn't know the answer. Darius also knew that much of the original property was home to the local Indian tribe. As a kid he found many arrow heads and fragments of pottery along the creek beds that crisscrossed the mountain.

During his grandfather's time, approximately a half-acre of land around the house was cleared of all the trees. Surrounding the cleared yard was a thick line of mature trees that buffered their home from the dense forest. The remaining acres they owned were a thick forest of mature trees. It was easy for a person to walk two or three feet beyond the tree line and vanish from sight.

The forest itself was alive with a variety of wildlife. It wasn't uncommon for Darius and his dad to find evidence of bears, mountain lions, coyotes, and deer during most seasons of the year. However, for short periods in early fall and late spring the deer slept closer to the house, the bears and mountain lions went into hiding, and the coyotes were more vocal. This was also the same time that they would hear screams and whoops during the night, see rocks thrown at the house, and find an occasional tree structure or footprint. Darius knew these were signs of bigfoot activity. On a few occasions they even heard the creature slap the side of the house or scratch its claws along the length of an outside wall. Darius suspected that their property was part of the bigfoots' migratory territory. Of course his dad believed otherwise. He was convinced they lived among the seventy-five acres they owned.

Prior to Brock going missing, Darius's father was tolerant of the sounds and intrusions from the bigfoot creatures. His father enjoyed obsessively documenting the evidence they found on the property. He would routinely capture the screams and howls with a parabolic microphone, cast the prints, and photograph the tree structures.

After Brock went missing, his father's behavior changed drastically. The man almost became terrified of the bigfoot creatures being so close to their home.

As Darius watched the light in the forest from Trevor's flashlight weave through the trees, he finally understood the man's drastic change in behavior. From what Darius gathered from his mother's journal, she was the true believer. Darius suspected it was her Native American heritage that gave her so much confidence in her belief. Trevor, on the other hand, was a skeptic. However, because he loved Abby so much, he would go anywhere with her. Even to look for the elusive bigfoot. When she was abducted, his dad's curiosity turned to an obsession. An obsession to learn and understand the creature's behavior in an effort to find her. With Brock's disappearance he became fearful. Fearful that they weren't safe. That either one of them could be snatched or killed at any moment.

Before Brock's disappearance Trevor started to suspect from numerous eyewitness testimonies that bigfoot creatures detested the game trail cameras that hunters used in the forest. Often times hunters would find the game trail cameras crushed, torn off the tree, or facing the wrong direction. Trevor also learned from homeowners who deployed game trail cameras on their property because of recent bigfoot activity around their home would report a cessation of activity immediately after setting up the cameras around their home. However, the bigfoot activity would return if the homeowner removed the game trail cameras. Under further investigation Trevor found that almost all of the game trail cameras in these testimonies used infrared technology.

Darius moved from his room to the loft so he could continue to watch his dad check the infrared lasers in the back of the house. Based on what they had learned from eyewitness interviews, Trevor suspected that bigfoot creatures could detect infrared light and therefore avoid being caught on film. In the bigfoot research community, this idea wasn't so farfetched. There was a faction of researchers who believed bigfoot possessed supernatural abilities, which his dad thought was ridiculous. However, there were creatures in the world that were able to see or detect infrared light. Therefore, the idea of bigfoot creatures having the same ability was not so farfetched.

Instead of using infrared game trail cameras, Trevor used infrared lasers. The man strategically placed infrared lasers along the perimeter of trees that surrounded the house. In essence, putting up an invisible fence to keep bigfoot out of the yard, as opposed to keeping a dog in the yard. The lasers were approximately six feet off the ground and powered by an electrical source attached to the house. Every night his dad checked each laser to make sure they were in good working order. Since the installation of the lasers, the bigfoot activity around the house had dramatically decreased. Occasionally they would hear a scream or a howl. They still found tree structures and prints. But the clawing and slapping of the house ceased.

At first some of the lasers had been crushed by rocks, or a fallen tree, or some other interference would disrupt the infrared light. Trevor quickly realized he couldn't hide the source of the lasers, because in theory a bigfoot creature would be able to find the source of the infrared light and disable it. In response, his dad had to create an intricate maze of infrared light to keep the creatures at bay, but also protect the lasers. A few of his strategies were to vary the heights of the lasers, crisscross the infrared light, and have at least one infrared light illuminating the source of any of the lasers. Darius had to admit, it was an ingeniously convoluted mess.

His dad stepped out of the tree line and turned off his flashlight. He looked up at Darius through the loft window and nodded his head. Then walked off. Darius smiled. *The man never misses anything.*

Chapter 20

Sookum and Brock sat underneath a large fir tree on the edge of a small valley. They watched a snare that Brock had built by the small stream that ran through the valley from the ridge to the north. His father had taught him how to make snares when he was just a little boy. His father always said that he needed to be prepared in case he was ever on his own. At the time the logic never made any sense to him. Right now he was thankful for being forced to learn how to survive on his own in the forest. Not that he needed to survive in the sense his father had taught him. His tribe-mates provided all the food and shelter he needed to be comfortable. Brock stopped questioning his comrades long ago when Red, Shimmer, or Skunk would bring clothing or food items to him from their nightly excursions. He was grateful for the shorts and pants or the winter jackets that were brought to him, but he always felt slightly guilty that some hiker or camper was missing their clothes or food. They never brought a sleeping bag or tent. It was always small items that he could wear. Never carry. Brock learned early on it was because they were always on the move, or needed to be able to relocate within seconds for their own safety. And they never brought anything that could make a fire. In the beginning that was all Brock ever thought about. Making a fire. To stay warm. To cook his meat. He asked once. Sookum became angry. He tore up the camp and disappeared for three days. When he returned Brock never asked again. He learned how to eat his portion of the raw meat, which he evidently learned was actually the liver of deer or elk. They ate other foods as well. Berries, roots, fish, and some bugs. But liver was always their first choice. They ate smaller game like rabbit, squirrels, or fox during hunting season. Usually during those times they kept to the thicker forest and higher elevations to stay away from the hunters. Occasionally, they would hear gunfire. Sookum would become alert. Skunk would vanish. Red and Shimmer would prepare to depart.

The gunfire would trigger Brock's memories of his father and brother. There were times he missed his father, but not many. In the beginning Brock never missed him. Now he found himself missing him more and more. Then he would remember how mean and harsh his father was to him. How the man would push him around and yell at him. Then he would no longer miss him. He wondered if he found himself missing him more now because he was forgetting how mean and nasty he was? His brother, he always missed.

Sookum grunted and lightly pushed Brock on the shoulder, which knocked him over. Brock thought he heard Sookum grunt a chuckle as he moved from a seated position to a crouch. Brock rolled to his feet and rushed toward Sookum, striking him with both arms and trying to knock him over. The creature did not even move. Brock smiled and crouched down next to him to see under the branches of the fir tree to the snare.

A large field rabbit moved down the game trail to the water's edge. Brock had set the snare a good distance away from the small stream because he knew any creature that would come along the trail would be more cautious near the water. The snare was an easy design. He had used the drawstring from a sweatshirt that Skunk had brought him for the loop. Then he pulled down a tree limb from a nearby tree and anchored it to the ground with the loop in the middle of the game trail. He knew it was a long shot to catch anything. He also knew it was pointless because any of his tribe-mates could catch anything without the help of a snare. But for some reason Sookum liked him to make the snares. Sookum would sit with him until something stumbled into the trap or they had to move on. Brock liked these times. They were peaceful and comforting.

The rabbit stopped periodically to sniff at the wind that moved the grass. Then it hopped a few more paces before stopping again. Brock settled back down against the sticks that were arranged against the trunk of the tree like a recliner to wait. He knew it would take the rabbit a long time to reach the snare and it was only two or three hops away from the trap. Rabbits were cautious. Sookum growled a low and quiet "Huurrr." Brock glanced toward the rabbit and saw that its ears were perked. It heard or felt something. Something was wrong. The rabbit's ears twitched and then it darted down the game trail toward the snare. As the rabbit hopped through the snare the tree branch snapped upwards and the drawstring tightened around the rabbit's neck. The rabbit hung from the tree branch with its four legs struggling to find purchase.

Sookum crawled out from under the fir tree with Brock behind him. When Brock emerged and stood up, Sookum put his arm out to the side to stop him. Brock stopped. Brock could hear a low "Hhrrraaa" vibrating from Sookum's chest. Brock could feel that the air had changed. There was a new energy in the valley. Something was different. Something was in the valley with them. Brock pushed a thought towards Sookum: "Be a tree?" Sookum's fingers twitched on Brock's chest as a sign to remain still. Then at that moment, a tall, dark creature stepped out from behind the tree with the snare. This creature was as tall as Sookum, but leaner. It did not have the same muscle mass as the rest of Sookum or the tribe. The hair was a sleek fur that clung tightly to the lean shape of the creature. It appeared as if its knees were bent in the opposite direction of his and Sookum's. But in reality, what Brock thought were its knees were its ankles because it was standing on its toes. Then Brock noticed its face. Its mouth and nose was a snout like a dog. Its ears were slightly pointed upwards on the side of its head. Brock could see its fangs and teeth as the mouth of the snout opened and closed as if it was trying to speak.

Brock wondered, "Is that a werewolf?" He thought it to himself more than asking Sookum through their mind speak. But Sookum answered, "No. Us."

Brock looked at Sookum and then back to the creature. "Us?" he questioned.

The creature reached out and grabbed the struggling rabbit with its five-fingered hand by the head. The other hand ripped the body of the rabbit away from the head. The blood from the rabbit poured down the creature's hand. It licked the blood. It took a bite out of the body of the rabbit. Blood spurted and sprayed across the face of the creature. It then looked up and tossed the rabbit's head towards Sookum and Brock. The head bounced within a foot from them. When Brock looked up toward the creature again, it was gone. Sookum stared at the rabbit's head for a long time before moving off to leave.

Chapter 21

The longer Jake stayed in the field the more he started to despise the city. The concrete hurt his feet. The lights were too bright. The noise hurt his ears and the cars appeared to be angry. He sighed audibly and closed his eyes against the oncoming wind though the car window. He had finished his assignment of monitoring Butch and had met his partner, Mr. Smith, for a new assignment. He opened his eyes and watched the suburban homes and townhomes fade into rolling hills and low mountains. At least I'm not in New York City, thought Jake. The thought of walking through the streets of an enormous city like New York gave him anxiety. At least this assignment would be quick and then he could return to the field.

Jake had finished his surveillance of Butch and submitted his report to Whiskey. Jake concluded that Butch was several degrees off-center, but his intentions were in the right place. In the report to Whiskey, Jake noted that Butch was dangerous if he was not kept on a tight leash. In general, Jake liked Butch. He enjoyed his time in the woods with him. The man had good skills and proved he was capable of taking care of himself. Jake thought Butch was slightly obsessed with the idea of tracking and potentially hunting bigfoot creatures, which he included in the report because he knew similar agencies were against their assets in the field being overly excited about their job. To Jake, it seemed that the only thing that kept Butch centered was the fact that the man believed he was the human incarnation of the superhero Wolverine. He chose to leave that part out of the official report. In the end, Jake concluded that if he needed a partner in the field, he would want Butch as his backup. To Jake, that was the most important trait a man could have.

He glanced over at the driver's seat and watched Mr. Smith sing along with the song on the radio. He didn't like Mr. Smith. The man just rubbed him the wrong way. He could tell that other people liked him. He was extremely personable and friendly. But Jake could tell that Mr. Smith was hiding something behind his broad grin and flashy white teeth.

Mr. Smith turned the wheel of the nondescript rent-a-car and pulled onto a single-track dirt road. Jake watched the trees that lined the road and noted how they were less trimmed the further they traveled down the road. Typical, he thought. A majority of the time these visits were in rural areas off of the beaten path. The roads were often riddled with potholes that could swallow a car and tree boughs as thick as tree trunks. They always made these visits in pairs, never alone. More for protection as opposed to intimidation. The people they visited were often hard-nosed, down to earth individuals that had a grit about them that was to be admired. They were individuals that scraped the earth and society to get by in the world. From Jake's experience, they were the type of people you didn't mess with. In their own way they were unpredictable and dangerous. They often didn't care what people thought or said about them.

Mr. Smith reached over and snapped off the radio. Without

looking at Jake he said, "Remember, I do the talking."

A few choice words passed through Jake's head, but he chose to keep his mouth shut. They pulled into a gravel driveway that led to a doublewide trailer precariously perched on the slope of a steep hill. The immediate front and side yards were littered with old cars, trucks, and trailers in various states of disrepair. Behind the doublewide trailer and surrounding the yard the forest was thick with mature trees. Through those trees Jake spied several four-person tents and generators. Each generator had a thick black cord running up the mountain slope and one towards the doublewide trailer.

As the car came to a stop in front of an old trailer from an eighteen-wheeler perched on cinderblocks, a gruff middle-aged man with a large belly dropped down from the trailer. Casually, the man picked up an axe that was leaning against the bed of a truck as if he was going to go chop wood. From the doublewide trailer a middle-aged woman with an equally large belly emerged from the front door and walked down towards the man. Mr. Smith popped out of the car like he was a salesman. Jake was a bit more cautious. Still surveying the area, he noticed the woman was carrying something behind her back. The middle-aged man propped the axe over his shoulder as if a friend just stopped by for a visit. The bulge in the man's lower lip hinted at tobacco. Jake felt the pistol in the shoulder holster under his jacket as he stepped out of the car. He made the choice to stay behind the open car door.

Mr. Smith moved to the front of the car and quickly flashed the man and woman a badge. "Hello there, I'm Mr. Smith, and this is my partner Jake," he said without glancing at Jake, but motioning towards him with his right hand. "We're from the Department of the Interior and wanted to ask you some questions."

The man spat on the ground in front of Mr. Smith.

He's going to get himself killed one of these days, thought Jake.

The woman spoke up first. "About what?" she said in a southern drawl. Mr. Smith answered the woman while still watching the man,

"The bear you two were talking about in town."

The man spat on the ground a second time in front of Mr. Smith. Jake discretely moved his hand to his pistol.

"It ain't no bear," said the woman

Mr. Smith flashed his white teeth and broad smile. "Oh yes, it was," he said as he still watched the man.

The woman barked, "I tell you, it ain't no bear. It was one of them bigfoot creatures you seen on TV."

"Shut it, woman!" snapped the man as he spat on the ground again.

Mr. Smith's smile stretched further across his face. "Like I said, let's talk about this bear you saw."

The man chuckled once and then scraped at one of the spit spots in the dirt in front of him. He looked back up at Mr. Smith with a smile that Jake knew was dangerous.

"My woman," said the man as he nodded towards her, "said it wasn't a bear."

Still smiling, Mr. Smith said, "It was a bear."

The man laughed harder this time. "What the hell is this? You tryin' to tell me we didn't see what we saw? Who the hell are you?"

"It was a bear," said Mr. Smith as he toed a black cable that stretched from a nearby generator with the tip of his shiny dress shoes.

The man spat on the ground again and took a step closer to Mr. Smith. "Who the hell do you think you are, coming to my house and telling me what I saw?" The man moved closer to Mr. Smith, obviously trying to intimidate him. "It was a damn bigfoot we saw and you or your stupid thug aren't going to tell us different," snapped the man.

Jake had to stifle a chuckle. That was a new one. Him being called a thug.

Mr. Smith's smile dropped. "You saw a bear." He then turned his back on the man and moved back to the driver's door of the car. The man dropped the axe into both hands and spun the handle as he stepped closer to Mr. Smith's back. The woman pulled out a small pistol from behind her back. Jake withdrew his own gun but held it behind the car door. Yup, he's going to get himself killed one of these days, Jake thought.

The man motioned the axe towards Mr. Smith back and glanced over at Jake. "You can't tell me what I saw, you sonofabitch!"

Before opening the car door, Mr. Smith looked around the man's property and up into the forest. He then turned back to the man and smiled. "It would be a shame for the ATF to find your dope fields or the FBI to get wind of the power you're siphoning off the grid." He then opened the car door and stepped in.

Jake watched the comprehension dawn on the man's face. The head of the axe slowly rested on the ground. The man spat in the dirt again. Jake dropped into his own seat and pulled the door closed. As Mr. Smith started the engine and reversed out of the driveway, Jake heard the woman yell at the man, "Those assholes can't threaten us."

The man snapped at the woman, "Shut up! We saw a bear, you hear?"

Jake looked over at Mr. Smith and thought, There's no doubt that he's good at his job.

Chapter 22

When Brock and Sookum returned to camp that night after the encounter with the Dogman creature, the mood of the tribe changed. Sookum talked with each member of the tribe in private. He first spoke with Red, then Skunk, and finally Shimmer. Shimmer moved off towards the deadwood trees that formed an X that indicated the entrance to the shimmering light. Brock sensed they were all sad, which was a new experience for him because he had never seen his tribe-mates sullen. Over the time he had been with them they were usually happy and playful. Once he saw his tribe fearful because they were being hunted. A few times he had seen them angry, which was scary because they became violent, but never towards him. Never like his father. When they were angry his tribe-mates would howl and scream, throw rocks, and knock down trees. In time their anger would pass, just like anyone else.

Brock could tell by Shimmer's actions that they were getting ready to move again. Skunk offered Brock some food, but he declined. He suspected they would be traveling through the shimmering light before dawn. He didn't want food in his stomach because he would only throw it back up after moving through the shimmering light. The night passed without incident, and before the sunrays of dawn crested the mountain tops, Sookum gave the signal for them to depart.

As the tribe prepared to leave through the shimmering light, Brock moved closer to Shimmer. She reached out and held both of his hands and smiled. She then turned and stepped through the shimmering light. She vanished from sight. Brock felt Sookum move to stand behind him. He turned to face his giant friend and expected to ride on Sookum's back through the portal. Sookum nodded his head towards the shimmering light and gave a soft grunt that Brock understood was permission for him to step through the portal alone. Brock turned towards the shimmering light and took a deep breath. He had been through the shimmering light several times before, but never alone. He was always carried through by Sookum, or in an emergency he rode on the back of one of his tribe-mates. This time he was given permission to go on his own. He was both excited and scared. He hesitated and then took a step toward the shimmering light of the portal.

Brock bravely stepped through the shimmering light and watched as the world lost all color and sound. He could see Shimmer standing before him as if she was waiting for him. When she saw Brock she turned and walked towards a shimmering purple light. She stepped through and vanished. Brock glanced around and saw a rainbow of shimmering lights all around him. He wondered if each light was a different door or portal to another area. He stepped towards a red shimmering light and reached out towards it. Sookum's massive hand rested on his shoulder. Brock glanced toward Sookum. Sookum motioned towards the purple light that Shimmer had passed through. Brock stepped through the light into a field of golden grass encircled by a thick forest of shimmering trees. The sky was a hue of deep purple and a million silver stars sprinkled the sky.

Sookum stepped behind him from the shimmering light and playfully shoved Brock as a way of congratulating him on his first journey. That was when Brock's stomach protested and he buckled over and violently vomited on the ground. His whole body convulsed as the spasms took over. He dropped to his knees and wished the spasms would stop. He vaguely felt a hand on his back and heard a soft female voice say, "Chew on this." It pushed what felt like bark into his mouth. "It helps with the sickness."

Brock chewed on the bark and felt the sickness immediately fade away. He felt two hands help him to his feet. He opened his tear-stained eyes and saw another pair of hairless feet in front of his own. He lifted his head, and through his long, black, matted hair he thought he saw the outline of an older human woman standing in front of him. The woman reached up and brushed the hair from his eyes and smiled.

"Hi, Brock, it's about time Sookum brought you," said the woman.

Chapter 23

"My name is Abigale, but you can call me Abby," said the woman as she sat across from Brock and handed him a bowl of hot broth.

Brock looked at the contents of the bowl and waved his hand over the hot liquid. The steam stung his bare skin but he did not flinch. It had been so long since he felt something hot that was food or liquid that he was somewhat in shock. Memories of other hot food and liquids flooded his mind. He remembered hot cocoa. The marshmallows floating on the surface. The hot cheese on pizza. Hot salty French fries and a cold milkshake with his brother at the local fast food place down the street from their home. Brock shook his head and pushed it back towards the woman. The woman cupped his hand and the bowl with both of hers, pushing the bowl of hot liquid back to him.

"Please, Brock, eat," she insisted.

Brock tentatively took a sip and could taste the deer meat in the broth and a hint of mint. Abigale said, "The mint will help with your sickness."

Brock mumbled under his breath as he took another sip of the broth. "I hate the sickness."

"We all do," confirmed Abigale as she ladled a portion of the broth into a second bowl and took a sip.

Brock watched her and waited until she finished her sip and asked, "We?"

Abigale looked at him and smiled in a way that, rather than reassuring him, suggested that she felt sorry for him. Instead of answering Brock's question, she said, "You really have been disconnected for a long time."

Brock put his bowl down and felt a surge of irritation beginning to surface. He tried to control the sound of his voice to not give away that he was not in the mood to try and figure out what was going on. "What does that mean?"

Abigale reached out and touched Brock's forearm to try and reassure him. To calm him. Brock retracted his arm and avoided her touch. Abigale eyed him a long time before speaking again.

"Do you know how old you are?" asked Abigale.

Brock looked away and shook his head. He did not. He thought maybe he was thirteen or fourteen, but he was not sure.

"I was eleven." He looked up at Abigale, "When I met Sookum."

Abigale's green eyes warmed and she smiled. "You are older than eleven now." She looked him up and down and continued, "I would say you are closer to fifteen."

Brock straightened his back and pulled his shoulders back. I'm a teenager, he thought to himself. His brother was an older teenager when he left. His little sister would be about ten now. Then his smile faded. Being a teenager with his tribe mates meant nothing.

Abigale broke his train of thought and asked, "Have you seen others like us?"

Brock narrowed his eyes, "You mean humans in general or us

who live with our tribes?"

"People," Abigale smiled, "or humans, as you like to call them."

Brock nodded his head in acknowledgement. "Yes, from time to time we would see a hunter, or hiker, or camper. One time I think we saw the military."

Abigale watched him from across the small fire and asked, "Why didn't you ever go with them?"

"Who?" asked Brock in confusion.

"The people? The hiker? Or hunter? Or whoever?"

Brock narrowed his eyes. "Why would I? I don't know them. They could be dangerous."

"Hmmmm," said Abigale.

Brock took a longer sip of the broth and admitted that the mint was helping the sickness pass. He looked up and saw Abigale watching him. At first he did not realize it, but it was nice to see another person. He wondered why, because he had seen other people over the years. But this was different. She was a tribe-mate. Not a person. He asked, "How long have you been with them?"

"You mean the First People?" asked Abigale.

"First People?" asked Brock in confusion.

"They go by many names. But they prefer First People or Ancient Ones," answered Abigale. She took a drink of her broth. "About fourteen years."

"Fourteen years?"

Abigale nodded her head yes and a strand of black and gray hair fell across her right eye. She brushed it behind her ear. "Yes, I chose to be with them."

Brock tilted his head to the side in confusion. "Chose?"

"Yes. Didn't you? I assumed you did," said Abigale with a look of panic in her eyes.

Brock shook his head no but then stopped himself and

wondered. Did he? That entire day was still a blur to him. He could not quite remember what happened. He closed his eyes to think back. His eyelids involuntarily tightened when he recalled his father's angry voice threatening to give him a lickin'. He opened his eyes and looked at Abigale. "No, Sookum rescued me." He paused. "That's why I never went with the people I saw. I never wanted to go back."

Chapter 24

For being an older woman, Brock found Abigale attractive. When the thought first hit him, he corrected himself and redefined her as pretty in a sisterly or motherly way. She insistently pressured him to call her Abby, but he did not like shortening her name. To him Abigale sounded natural. More respectful. In the short time he had been at the camp he could tell that she was respected by all of the First People and their own kind. She was constantly engaged in a conversation or activity with someone or something. Except when she was with him. During those times they were never interrupted.

Abigale was slightly shorter than him with long black and gray hair that fell to her waist. She wore leather skins from deer and elk that she had learned how to make over the years. Her body was lean, and her green eyes always held his attention. There were times he felt that he could not look away when she spoke to him. He also learned that she was part Native American Indian on her mother's side, which he found fascinating. But he was not sure which was more interesting, the stories of Abigale's mother or the stories about her mother's tribe. When he heard the stories, it felt more like he was hearing stories about his own grandmother, which was impossible because his father had reminded him several times that he had no other family outside of his father, brother, and sister.

One morning Abigale came to Sookum's section of the camp and found Brock being instructed by Skunk on how to sneak up on someone without being heard. Shimmer was the intended target. However, when Abigale arrived, Shimmer stomped off with a huff.

Abigale pushed a pair of deerskin leather pants into Brock's hands. "I think she is smitten with you."

Brock looked over to Shimmer stalking off and caught her glancing back in their direction. Brock shook his head. "I don't think so."

Abigale smiled. "I know."

Brock held up the pants to admire them. "Thanks, but you didn't have to."

Abigale turned to walk off. "Yes I did. You can't go walking around in those hiking pants that are too big for you and reek of people."

Brock glanced down at the pants he was wearing and then to Skunk. "How can anything smell me over him?" he asked playfully.

Skunk grunted and mock charged at Brock before leaping up into a nearby tree and disappearing. Brock caught up with Abigale and matched her stride as she walked through the camp. For a long time they did not talk. He just observed all the activity around him. As they walked he saw four different types of First People scattered across the field of golden grass. Over near the cliff wall with the cave entrance that protected the shimmer portal were Skunk's original tribe. They tended to stay isolated from the rest of the First People because of their body odor. Abigale explained to Brock that all the First People had the ability to emit a strong body odor as a protection mechanism like a skunk. But Skunk's tribe never practiced discretion in masking their smell. They emitted it proudly, which isolated them from everyone else. She also shared with him that Skunk and Sookum had been best friends since being newlings.

Sookum and Red were mates and from the same tribe. They differed slightly from Shimmer's tribe in the respect that their heads sat upon their shoulders with the appearance of not having a neck and their heads were shaped more like a cone, while Shimmer's head was more rounded like his own and had a slightly longer neck. Since Abigale had pointed it out to him he could see the difference. Brock could also tell that Shimmer's tribe were in general more attractive and appealing to the eye than Sookum's tribe. But he could also tell how easy it would be to confuse the two tribes. Abigale also alluded to the fact that Shimmer's tribe tended to be more sexually active than the other tribes, which contributed to the large number of mixed male and female humans among their tribe. Brock asked why and the explanation Abigale gave was that Shimmer's tribe were often mistaken as the mystical wood nymphs spoken in ancient myths around the world. Abigale also told him that Shimmer's tribe considered themselves the Ancient Ones and controlled the shimmer portals.

The fourth tribe, the creatures with the dog faces, kept near the tree line. Brock frequently watched the Dogman creatures darting in and out of the woods in what appeared to be a spastic frenzy. When they walked near the Dogman tribe's territory all the creatures would stop their activity and silently watch them. The feeling made Brock feel incredibly uncomfortable. He also noticed that several deer hung from the branches of the trees as if they were stocking up for a feast. Abigale corrected him and informed Brock that they constantly ate, so the deer he saw today would not be the same deer tomorrow. When Brock commented how many deer were in the tree she simply answered, "Better than us." That was when he noticed that no humans were among the Dogman creatures. When Brock questioned Abigale she was more open with her answer and hinted that the myth of werewolves originated because of the Dogman creatures, and they were also responsible for humans believing that First People are cannibals.

Abigale climbed up a part of the cliff wall near the cave entrance and nodded towards a large boulder. "Go change."

Brock did not question her. He went behind the boulder and changed into the deerskin pants. When he returned, Abigale was leaning against the cliff wall and staring up into the drifting clouds. Brock cleared his throat to get her attention. She turned her head.

"Spin."

Brock spun in place and when he looked back at Abigale she was smiling. She stretched out her hand. Brock handed her his hiking pants. She took the old pants.

"They fit you?"

Brock looked down at his deer skin pants and ran his hands over his waist. "They feel great." He then sat down next to her. They sat in silence for a long time, watching the daytime sky turn into dusk. A crescent moon peeked over the tree line to introduce the coming night.

Brock asked, "Where are we?"

"A safe place," said Abigale.

Brock looked up towards the night sky. "The moon and stars look different."

Abigale looked towards the stars and nodded her head in agreement. "We're in the spirit world."

Brock looked at Abigale. "You mean where we go when we die?"

Abigale glanced over at Brock and smiled. "No, that would be heaven." She looked back at the stars and thought for a moment before continuing, "This place is different. In some sense we are still on Earth. In another sense we are not." She looked at Brock. "When you came through the shimmer, do you remember seeing other colors?"

Brock nodded his head. "I saw what looked like a red shimmer and moved towards it. But Sookum stopped me."

Abigale smiled, "Yes, each color is a path to a different..." she paused and then continued, "for lack of a better term, a dimension."

"Dimension?" asked Brock.

"Earth is not unique. There are many other dimensions one can visit if they know how."

Brock thought for a moment. "Is that how we can travel so far in such a short amount of time?"

"Yes and no," said Abigale. "They only use the shimmer to relocate to another forest if they are in danger. Like if one of our kind tries to shoot them. Normally, they just walk or run."

Brock chuckled. "Yes, I've been on some long hikes with Sookum."

"Here," Abigale said as she waved towards the sky, "time is slowed. In the past only the First People had access to this place. Over time the shamans learned how to see the shimmer and step through." She paused and absentmindedly drew in the dirt. "Now only those that are shown can pass through." Abigale looked at Brock. "Like you."

Brock thought for a moment. "So they come here to be safe?"

"Yes."

"Then why not live here all the time?" asked Brock.

"There is no food or sustenance here. They are still living creatures. They still need to care for their bodies." Abigale paused and smiled. "Plus, it can get boring here after a long time."

They sat quietly for a long time before either one of them

spoke. Abigale watched the stars as if she was lost in thought. Brock watched the Four Tribes of the First People. He searched out each of his tribe-mates and smiled when he saw them. Brock admitted to himself that he didn't know what love was until he met Sookum.

Abigale broke the silence and said, "The tribes of the First People meet at least once a year for the Elders to speak. Sometimes more often."

Brock nodded his head and asked, "Is that where Sookum always disappears to from time to time?"

"Yes, probably. He is in line to be one of the Elders." A moment of silenced passed. "But this time is for a burial. One of the Elders passed."

"Oh," responded Brock. "How long do they live?"

"I'm not sure, but from the stories, longer than us. Maybe a hundred and fifty years or so," Abigale guessed. "But this Elder was younger," she paused. "He was shot by one of our kind."

Brock looked at her in shock. "Shot? Why?"

Abigale shook her head. "Stupidity. Fear."

Brock had no response. He sat quietly watching the lavender sky turn dark as the night descended. "Many of the First People hate our kind. Or fear our kind," Abigale softly whispered. "But a few, like Sookum, have not given up hope." Abigale pushed a group of pebbles together and then plucked one pebble from the group and handed it to Brock. "This is you."

Brock took the pebble and examined it for something special, but found nothing remarkable. He looked at Abigale inquisitively.

Abigale looked down at the group of pebbles. "Those are our kind." She clasped Brock's hand with the single pebble. "You are the pebble. You are different. That is why Sookum brought you." She paused and looked out across the field and the dark shapes that moved through the ceremonial grounds. "We are all special. My mother's people would have called us Spirit Walkers." She looked over to the shimmering portal. "Not everyone from our kind can walk through the shimmer. Only us, because we are special." She glanced over at the Council of Elders. "The First People can tell who Spirit Walkers are. Sookum believes if the First People can communicate with the Spirit Walkers, then things can change." She shook her head and brushed away the group of pebbles. "But he is ridiculed and told he is naive like the Indians before us. That our kind only bring death and destruction."

Abigale pushed off the rock and stood. She moved to leave. Brock asked, "What makes me a Spirit Walker?"

Abigale paused and looked at the moon that hung just above the horizon. "You have Indian blood in you…" She paused. "You are open and your heart is full love." She turned and squatted down in front of him and clasped both of his hands. "In a time before, I suspect you would have been, or were, a shaman. A great one. I suspect, Sookum suspects, the One Above has returned you to continue your work."

Brock squinted his eyes at Abigale in confusion and fear. "Continue my work?"

"Yes, Brock, Sookum believes when you return you will be the bridge between our kind and the First People," said Abigale.

Brock pulled his hands away from hers. He scrambled to his feet. "When I return? Why would I return? I'm with my tribe."

Abigale's eyes showed sadness in her face more than anything else. "It is how things have always been. When a Spirit Walker leaves his tribe to become a shaman, they must return." She dropped her head in sadness. "But you will be shunned. Ridiculed for your beliefs. That is the way. But you are strong. You will find a way to bridge the gap."

Brock sat back down in disbelief. The thought of leaving Sookum and his tribe never crossed his mind. He assumed he would be with his tribe forever. He shuddered at the thought of seeing his father again. He shuddered at the thought of leaving everything he knew and loved. He looked at Abigale and whispered, "Why haven't you left?"

Abigale looked down at Brock and he could see a tear slip down her cheek. "I have done what the One Above has asked. There is no need for me to go back." She then turned and walked off into the night.

Chapter 25

The burial was at first light. The purple-tinted sun had not yet crested the top of the trees, but everyone was awake and attentive. Each tribe stood together. Skunk's tribe near the cliffs and the shimmer portal to the South. The Ancient Ones to the West. Sookum's tribe to the North, and the Dogman in the trees to the East. Brock and Abigale's kind stood as a fifth tribe to the northwest near the Ancient Ones. The Council of Elders stood in the middle of all the tribes near the Sacred Stones.

The Sacred Stones were a large semicircle of boulders in the center of the ceremonial field. This was where the Council had met since the gathering started. During the time of the gathering a large hole had been dug adjacent to the semicircle of stones. Brock estimated that approximately six more large boulders would complete the circle. But for now the Council of Elders completed the circle as the eight members of the Council waited for the ceremony to begin.

Four of the First People, one from each tribe, emerged from the shimmer portal carrying a large body upon their shoulders. The body had been wrapped in what appeared to be giant water lily pads.

They carried the body to the freshly dug hole and laid the body in the depression. A second group of First People, this time eight members, emerged from the portal and carried a large boulder. Brock was in awe when he saw the size of the boulder that the eight First People carried, as if it were made of Styrofoam. He guessed that the construction equipment he used to be fascinated with as a little boy would never be able to move such a large stone. They placed the large boulder over the hole and the body of the departed Elder. Each member of the funeral procession returned to their respective tribe.

A moment of silence fell across the entire ceremonial field. Never in his young life had Brock experienced a moment as moving as this prodigious silence. He cringed with each shallow breath he took for fear that the thundering noise of his lungs in his own ears would break the silence. The silence hung for so long Brock started to feel like he was in a dream. Then in turn, starting with the Ancient Ones, each tribe howled in unison. The sound was deafening to human ears. Some of Brock's kind fell to their knees clasping their hands over their ears. Brock felt ashamed at the disgrace they showed. He stood firm to show his respect, his people's respect, to the First People. He felt the power of each howl through the core of his body. He felt his bones shake and his nerves rattle. He felt Abigale reach out and clasp his hand. The howls continued with Sookum's tribe, then Skunk's tribe, and followed by the Dogman tribe. The council of Elders silenced all the tribes with their own mournful howls.

Then silence.

From the East Brock heard the thunder of a thousand elephants. The ground rattled under his feet. Many of his kind fell to the ground. He turned his head and watched in horror as the Dogman tribe rushed toward the humans. Many screamed in fear. Some ran away. Others fell to the ground in submission. Brock tightened his grip on Abigale's hand and stood firm. Looking back on that moment he was not sure if he clutched her hand for strength and support or to prevent her from running away. But in his heart Brock knew that Abigale would not flee.

The Dogman creatures rushed through the crowd of humans in a sporadic dash, scattering everyone. The other tribes of First People howled in anger and disgust at the action of the Dogman tribe. Many of the Ancient Ones came to the rescue for fear of any humans being hurt, killed, or snatched. In the aftermath Brock learned that some of the humans did disappear. He learned that the Elder that was buried was a member of the Dogman tribe. The Elder's death only magnified the hatred of the Dogman toward Brock's kind.

During the chaos the new Elder of the Dogman tribe came face to face with Brock. Brock stood firm. The snout of the Dogman Elder was inches from his own nose. He could feel the creature's warm breath splash over his face with each huff. Brock was unsure as to what came over him. Maybe fear. Maybe anger. But he reacted without thinking. Brock screamed, "RRRRRRRRRRAAAAAAAAAAAAAAAHHHHHHHHHHHHHHHH!" as loud and as long as he could in the face of the Elder. When he stopped the Elder closed its snout and pulled its head back. It then turned and stalked off into the tree-line. The members of his tribe followed momentarily after.

Chapter 26

Several days passed after the burial. Each day separate groupings from each tribe slowly departed the ceremonial field through the shimmer portal. Sookum's tribe was one of the last to leave. From observation, Brock could tell that Sookum was in heated debate with the Elders and suspected this was the reason for their delayed departure. He also noticed that Sookum's tribe was the only one which included a member of each tribe except for the Dogman. Brock asked Abigale why. Her only response was that Sookum was special. When Brock asked why a member of the Dogman tribe was not a part of Sookum's tribe, Abigale explained that at one time there had been. But it had gone missing shortly after he arrived with Sookum. She suspected the Dogman member of Sookum's tribe left as an act of self-imposed exile to protest Sookum's action of bringing a human into the tribe.

This conversation with Abigale was the last Brock had with her before he left. As each day passed Abigale became more distant and withdrawn. She became more difficult to find. When Brock looked for her he started to realize that he did not know which tribe she was associated with. He started to wonder if she was associated with all of the tribes based on all the interactions he witnessed during their time at the ceremonial field.

Then, abruptly, the time came for Sookum's tribe to leave. Sookum left the Council of Elders in anger. This was evident by all that were still at the ceremonial field because Sookum howled and whooped in protest before stalking off. Brock had never seen Sookum so angry and did not even know that he was capable of such hostility. Sookum gave the call to his tribe to leave. Brock watched Skunk bound off to join Sookum without hesitation. Shimmer gave a last embrace to one of Brock's kind and bounded off to the portal in a slow trot that rumbled the ground beneath him. Red gave two newlings quick hugs and strode off to join her partner. That was when Brock realized that the two newlings were Sookum's and Red's offspring. He momentarily felt guilty for not knowing that sooner.

Brock knew he needed to join his tribe immediately. There had been a time before when he did not join up with the tribe when called and was left behind. He was younger. He was scared. He felt abandoned. After a couple of days Skunk returned for him. He learned he'd been abandoned on purpose as a punishment, and the next time no one would return for him. From that moment on he promised himself to never be left behind again. But he was torn. He wanted to say good-bye to Abigale. He needed to see her before he left. He quickly scanned the ceremonial field for her, but didn't see her. He turned and raced towards his tribe. He bounded over the rocks and boulders along the cliffs edge to meet up with his tribe-mates at the portal.

Brock got to the portal before Sookum and Red. Shimmer had already opened the portal and Skunk passed through. Shimmer grunted for Brock to go next. But he hesitated. He needed to find Abigale. He needed to say goodbye to her. Shimmer grunted again.

Brock hesitated. Then he saw Abigale near where the trees and cliff met. But she was not alone. She was with Numyc. Brock took a step toward her but Shimmer placed her hand on his shoulder to stop him. In his mind he heard Shimmer's soft voice: "Partners."

Brock looked at Shimmer in surprise. "Numyc exiled," interpreted Brock from the images that Shimmer pushed into his mind.

Brock looked back towards Abigale and watched her embrace Numyc. He felt betrayed. He felt sick. Numyc had tried to kill him twice. Abigale must know.

"Numyc feared," said Shimmer. "She respected."

Sookum and Red approached. Sookum glanced over towards Numyc and Abigale and grunted. Red took Sookum's hand and they passed through the portal. Brock opened his mouth to yell out to Abigale, but he closed it without making a sound. Shimmer reached out and Brock took her hand. They passed through the portal together.

Chapter 27

Things changed when Brock returned to the forest with Sookum and his tribe. He couldn't put his finger on what exactly that change was. But everything felt different to him. He tried to figure it out. To Brock, Skunk acted the same, aloof but mischievous. Skunk would still disappear on his own and come back with some wild tale of his adventure. Brock assumed it was wild by Skunk's facial expressions and the way he used his arms and hands as he reported back to everyone. Brock never understood Skunk's chatter. It definitely sounded like a different language to Brock's ears.

Shimmer appeared to be clingier to Brock. He wondered if it was because she had gotten more comfortable around his kind while at the Gathering or if she was becoming more attracted to him. It seemed conceited to Brock to think that, but he couldn't think of any other reason. In general, Shimmer spent more time with him. During the day she took Brock on more gathering or scouting trips for food. At night, Shimmer slept closer to him. Almost as if she was protecting him. One day Shimmer showed Brock how to find a shimmer portal. He half paid attention to her because he wasn't sure what she was showing him. Once he realized, he wished he had paid better attention. Brock wanted to ask Shimmer to show him again but he had the impression that Sookum had punished her for showing him. But he wasn't sure. It was just a feeling he had.

Red appeared to be sad, almost depressed. He never really had much interaction with Red. At times he felt as if she resented him for being a part of their tribe. After the Gathering, he suspected that may have been true because of her two newlings. Brock assumed the newlings weren't allowed to be a part of the tribe because of him. Oddly, Sookum appeared to be his regular self with Brock. Sookum was attentive to all of Brock's needs and his general safety. The big difference that Brock noticed was the forest they had returned to was notably different than their normal territory.

The forest they were now in was closer to human civilization. Not a town or a city, but closer to homes. Their previous territory was a deep forest far from any home or civilization. Sookum or one of the tribe-mates could disappear in the tree line by only taking a few steps back into the brush. The forest now wasn't as thick and there was hardly any ground-level brush. From what Brock could tell, there was a lot of farm and horse land. They were still in the mountains and near a river. But at night he could pick out the houses nestled in the side of the landscape by their artificial lights.

Skunk emerged from the large oak tree that leaned across the creek and grunted at Brock. Brock looked up and smiled at his friend. Brock smelled his own armpit and then whispered, "I smelled you before I saw you."

Skunk swiped his hand over his face and shook his head no while moaning sorrowfully. Brock pushed off the rock he was sitting on to join Skunk on the other side of the stream. He gave his friend a playful shove to show he was kidding. Skunk snorted a laugh and motioned for Brock to follow him quietly. Brock followed Skunk through the creek bed, hopping from one rock to the next.

Skunk strode through the water and left a trail of oil swirling in small pools from each step. The two of them passed through a large stone tunnel and stopped abruptly when a car drove over the tunnel. Skunk continued along the creek until they reached a wooden bridge and then climbed up the steep bank to a path that connected to the bridge. Quietly the two of them walked along the dark path that cut through the woods and emerged into a small field. The trail intersected and led up a steep hill to a gravel road and three houses. Brock froze in place when he realized how close they were to the houses. Skunk grunted and motioned for Brock to join him. Brock shook his head against it and pointed to the houses. He knew they weren't supposed to be this close to homes. Skunk snorted in protest and then let out a low whoop. Brock slunk back into the dark tree line. He heard a responding whoop close to the gravel road next to one of the houses. He knew immediately it was Shimmer. Skunk turned away from Brock with a smirk and moved towards the house through the underbrush.

Brock slowly crept out of the protection of the trees and watched as Skunk and Shimmer crouched down along the tree line near the house they were watching. Brock could see several lights on in the house and three or four people moving around. Two were adults, a man and a woman. Two were children. As the night passed, Skunk and Shimmer slowly moved closer to the house until the two of them were standing a few feet from the adults' bedroom window. Brock could tell that the windows were at least six feet above the ground. Skunk and Shimmer could see in easily because of their height. Brock was amazed at how close his two friends had approached the house.

Eventually the children went to bed. One upstairs and one on the main level somewhere. The female adult in the house was already in the bedroom and Brock turned away when she changed her clothes for the evening. Brock watched as the male adult turned off the lights in the kitchen and walked in the dark to the bedroom to join his partner. When the man got in the bedroom he moved towards the window and pulled the blinds closed.

As soon as the blinds closed Skunk started to whoop and ran away from the house back into the trees. Shimmer bounded backwards towards the trees and started whooping along with Skunk. Brock dropped down in a crouch along the trail and tried not to laugh at all of the ruckus Skunk and Shimmer were making. He listened to the two of them sprint through the trees back to the creek, laughing and whooping to each other like playful teenagers about to get caught doing something bad. The lights in the house clicked on and the man ran upstairs to the boy's room and the woman ran out into the living room. Brock patiently waited as the man and woman came out on the side deck and shined a flashlight across the backyard, trying to see what made the sound. Brock slowly moved back into the tree line to remain hidden from the beam of light. He heard the man ask, "Were those coyotes?"

Brock heard the woman respond, "I don't think so."

The man continued, "If those weren't coyotes then what the hell was that?"

The woman said, "Sasquatch."

"Sasquatch?" thought Brock. "I've heard that before, but where?" He shrugged his shoulders and faded further into the trees until he found the creek. He followed the creek back to his tribe's shelter and couldn't help but smile at Skunk and Shimmer's mischievous adventure.

Chapter 28

Sookum and the tribe stayed in these new woods for a long time. Brock had counted at least four full moon cycles and Sookum gave no indication of leaving. Even though they were close to human dwellings, they never felt threatened. Occasionally they would hear gun fire, but it was always at least one mountain range over. They could hear the families that lived in the dwellings and the lawnmowers that cut the grass on the walking trails that snaked through the woods. But the people never journeyed into the woods, except for the man who lived in the house that Skunk and Shimmer had snuck up on. That man was always walking on the trails and through the woods as if he was looking for something. Occasionally, his partner would come with him. During those times they mostly stayed on the trails, though one time he led her off trail and they unknowingly passed through Sookum and Brock's territory.

Brock could tell they felt uncomfortable in their territory, even without hearing their comments of feeling like they were trespassing. Brock was also impressed that the man and woman had identified tree and stick markings that Sookum and Skunk had made to identify their territory to other tribes. At times the man seemed more jumpy in the woods than the woman. Not jumpy as in afraid; jumpy as in not being used to the forest. They never came with guns, and they always radiated a sense of peace and love about them. Almost as if they loved the forest and nature. At times Brock wondered why Sookum never scared them off. He assumed because they never posed a threat to the tribe.

One morning the man came into their territory alone and spent a good portion of the day wandering through the woods speaking out loud. Brock quietly followed him for a time to hear what he was saying. To Brock it sounded like the man was asking for forgiveness from the forest. The man seemed to be sorrowful for venturing into this part of the forest. He kept repeating over and over that he did not mean to violate the trust that the forest had given him and never intended to steal the spirit of the land.

Then it dawned on Brock: Maybe this man's actions had something to do with the confrontation that Sookum and Skunk had had a few nights back at the man's house. Skunk came back and told the story to the tribe while Sookum went off alone. Shimmer related the story to Brock. From what Brock knew from Shimmer, Sookum and Skunk had been watching the man's house for several nights after the man's last trek through their territory. Brock knew this and assumed it was because Sookum wanted to make sure the man was not a threat. According to Skunk, while the man and his woman slept a wood spirit snuck up to the house. Brock had only seen a fleeting image of a wood spirit once. Shimmer explained to Brock that the wood spirit was a black shadow of a creature. They could feel that its intent was malicious. Brock assumed that all wood spirits were peaceful, but Shimmer assured him that if something from the forest land where the wood spirit lived was taken it could turn vicious and seek out retribution.

Sookum and Skunk watched the wood spirit circle the house and stop underneath a window adjacent to where the couple slept at night. Skunk reported that the man woke in the middle of the night and stood next to the window and urinated in the house. Brock smiled because he knew this confused his tribe-mates, but he remembered bathrooms. Skunk said that when the man started urinating the wood spirit reached his three-fingered hand up through the window screen in an attempt to grab the man. Brock remembered that Skunk chuckled at that part and then said that the man must have seen the hand and screamed. Skunk watched the man run from the window. Sookum broke from the tree line and yanked the wood spirit's arm out of the window and restrained the creature. Skunk had to help his friend pull the creature back into the forest. From the way Skunk described the story it was a great battle between them to subdue the wood spirit. But in the end the wood spirit knew from that moment forward the house with the man and his woman was protected by Sookum and his tribe.

The morning Brock had watched the man wander through their forest apologizing and asking for forgiveness was the last time he or his partner came to their territory. But it wasn't the last time Brock saw them.

Chapter 29

Brock had more freedom to come and go from their camp since the Gathering. However, he knew that one or two of his tribe-mates were always near. During the day the tribe bedded down to rest, and one of the tribe mates usually stayed awake to watch over the rest of the group. A majority of the time it was Skunk. Brock believed that Skunk didn't require sleep because he was always awake or the first to be alert if he was slumbering. At night, Sookum, Red, and Skunk usually went off together to hunt. As always, Shimmer stayed near the camp and portal as a sentry. In their old forest, Brock would go on hunts with Sookum. In this new place he felt safer with Shimmer and always elected to stay near her. He knew if something went wrong, there was less chance of him being left behind if he was near Shimmer. Brock knew he was expendable because he was different than the rest of the tribe. In their old forest, when he was left behind someone always came back for him a few days later. With the tribe being so close to civilization and occupied homes, he was afraid that if he was left behind they wouldn't return for him. This thought bothered him, though he had to admit that Abigale had prepared him for that possibility. He also knew that if he was discovered in these woods it would bring unwanted attention on himself and the tribe.

Even though the safety of his tribe came before anything else, on some nights he would slip out of camp and explore the woods on his own. He was drawn to the couple that Skunk and Shimmer had spied on. The day the man was wandering through the woods talking to the trees reminded Brock of his brother. Brock was positive the man was older than his brother, but he had the same mannerisms. The man, like his brother, was muscular and gave the presence of strength. Yet, like his brother, the man also had a gentle and kind face. When he spoke his words were deliberate and precise. To Brock, the man wasn't afraid of action, but every action came after a time of thinking. Traits he remembered and knew in his heart that his brother possessed. Brock started thinking of the man as Quinn, which was his brother's middle name.

Quinn's partner, the woman, was always with him when she was home. Brock observed as the two of them moved from room to room together, went on walks together or sat on the deck together quietly talking and looking out at the night sky. Several times Brock heard their private conversations as he quietly sat under the deck waiting for them to go back inside. The few times he got trapped under the deck was not something he did on purpose. He was curious about them. Or maybe he was curious about his own kind? Meeting and talking with Abigale sparked something inside of him that he couldn't quiet. He often found himself wondering more and more about his father and brother. He was curious about this couple and their interactions. When Brock watched them, he often wondered if his mother and father were as close with each other as this couple. He doubted it.

The woman he called Hope, because he hoped his mother was as loving and fun as he had observed this woman to be. He could see why Quinn was attracted to his mate. In every sense of the word she was beautiful. Her smile and energy gave her a presence that attracted laughter and happiness to her. Often times Brock watched as the two of them sat in the dark and talked for hours or played like kittens until they couldn't breathe because they were laughing so hard. He felt drawn to Quinn and Hope.

One night, Brock left his tribe-mates after feeding and ventured down to Quinn and Hope's house. He followed the creek to mask his tracks and then followed the manicured trail to the base of the hill just below their house. One light was on in the large room and he could see Quinn sitting and Hope moving around. Brock quietly moved through the weeds and brambles to a clump of trees on the edge of their territory. He felt safe and knew he was hidden from view. If he needed to he could crawl through the brambles to make an exit or fade into the cedar and juniper trees that were off to his left. He crouched down behind the trees and watched Quinn and Hope move throughout the house.

The night passed, and as usual Quinn and Hope moved out to the deck and sat on the picnic table and looked out towards their backyard. Unknown to Quinn and Hope, they always faced the direction of the tribe's territory. Brock could hear them talking but was too far away to make out the details of their words. Anxious to hear what they were saying, he leaned forward and lost his balance. He crashed into the clump of trees in front of him and quickly pushed himself back. He popped up to a standing position, turned and took two long leaps toward the cedar trees and realized his mistake, stumbled again, and collapsed onto the ground and froze. He wanted to lay still. He knew he was supposed to lay still. But he couldn't. Everything in his mind and body screamed at him to get away. While on his hands and knees he scrambled into the thicket of cedar and juniper trees. He then stopped and listened to see if Quinn and Hope were going to give chase.

Brock heard Quinn's hushed whisper, which Hope always told him wasn't a whisper. "What the hell was that?"

"That was no animal," Hope said adamantly.

"What the hell was it? It sounded like a person crashing through the woods," said Quinn.

"Exactly!" agreed Hope. "It was like someone was watching us and got startled and tried to move away but tripped and fell. It was like an 'Aww shit I gotta get outta here' and they stumbled and fell!"

"There is no way that was a deer," said Quinn.

Hope agreed, "No way. A deer is more graceful and quiet."

"A bear, maybe?" offered Quinn.

"I don't think a bear would be so loud, and wouldn't we see it? asked Hope.

"I don't know. I'm going to get the night vision," said Quinn.

Brock watched as Quinn went back into the house, turned on a light, turned off the light and came back outside. He stood on the deck and held something up to his eyes and scanned the backyard. Brock knew Quinn wouldn't be able to see him under the cedar and juniper trees. Plus he could tell that Quinn was looking in the wrong place. He was looking at where Brock had made the noise, not his current location. Brock exhaled slowly and carefully crawled back to the manicured trail. When he got to the trail he stood up, brushed himself off, and then felt Sookum's presence. He looked down the length of the trail and saw Sookum standing just inside the dark tree line.

Brock knew that Sookum had been there the whole time. He had watched everything that had happened. Brock blinked longer than a second and Sookum was gone. Skunk grunted to Brock's right and joined him on the trail. A second later a wood knock sounded from the direction of their territory. Skunk and Brock went to join their tribe mates.

Chapter 30

The rain hadn't stopped for days. It fell day and night. The rain never bothered Sookum or the others. The water seemed to bead off of their oily hair like water beaded off of ducks. For Brock it became annoying after awhile. Red had found an old oak tree along a dry creek bed not far from their territory where the ground had been washed away from the roots years before and formed a nice cave for Brock to take shelter.

Brock's tribe-mates took advantage of the rain because it gave them more freedom to move through the day undetected. Brock's kind didn't like the rain and usually stayed inside. Brock didn't like the rain either, but it was because his tribe-mates capitalized on the solitude of the forest and he spent a lot of time alone. Unless he made the choice to go with them and endure the wetness.

This particular day he had chosen to stay back and rest in the root cave. He had thoughts of spying on Quinn and Hope but decided not to because he was under the impression that Sookum wasn't happy with him for almost getting caught a few weeks back. Sookum didn't say as much. It was just a feeling that Brock had.

When the rain had subsided Brock crawled out from under the

roots and meandered around the creek bed. He quietly played in the pools of water and mud to keep himself entertained. Occasionally he would hear some rustling of the leaves or underbrush but assumed it was the pack of coyotes that weren't too far from their territory. He knew with the break in the rain the creatures of the forest would poke their heads out of their own shelters and relieve and refresh themselves. He wondered where his tribe-mates were and what mischief they were causing.

Brock squatted down in the mud and practiced stacking rocks and pebbles like Sookum had showed him. It was a skill all of Sookum's kind learned as a form of communication and territorial markings. Brock was so engrossed in stacking the rocks he didn't hear Quinn move from the underbrush down into the muddy creek bed only ten feet from him. Brock looked up to gather another stone and saw Quinn staring at him.

Brock froze and wished he was a tree.

Quinn stared at him in shock.

Sookum quietly stepped out of the trees and stood less than ten yards behind Quinn. Brock's eyes shifted to gaze upon his friend for guidance. Sookum faded back into the trees and disappeared before Quinn looked over his shoulder and back to Brock.

Brock heard the sorrowful moan of Red off to his left and a wood knock from Shimmer to his right. Skunk rustled a branch over Quinn's head that momentarily grabbed the man's attention. And then it was quiet. At that moment Brock knew his tribe-mates were gone.

SECRETS

Chapter 31

MISSING BOY FOUND AFTER FOUR YEARS
Dustin Hollinsworth
dhollinsworth@jeffersonpost.com

Missing boy of four years has been found 3,000 miles from his home. Brock Blackwood went missing four years earlier when he was 11 years old while accompanying his father and brother on a weekend hunting trip in the Olympic Mountains of Washington State. At the time an extensive search was conducted to find the missing boy, but authorities were unable to find any trace of the boy after two weeks of intensive searching. The search gained brief national attention and ridicule when the father proclaimed that the mythical cryptozoological creature sasquatch had kidnapped his son.

The missing boy was found yesterday near Furnace Mountain and the Potomac River by a man who has yet to be identified. According to the authorities, the man found Brock in a muddy creek bed near his home while he was out looking for coyotes in the rain. At this time the authorities have no leads or theories on how Brock came to be found in the Northwestern part of Virginia. The unidentified man is not a person of interest or a suspect in this case. The local sheriff's office is hoping that Brock will be able to fill in the missing details of his disappearance four years earlier, how he came to be found in Virginia, and everything in between. Brock is currently being held at a local hospital under close supervision by the authorities and waiting to be reunited with his father and brother.

Chapter 32

The man known as Quinn to Brock sat in the corner of the hospital room and watched the boy sleeping in the bed. Quinn held the boy's deerskin leather pants on his lap and absentmindedly rubbed his fingertips on the soft fabric. When the boy was brought to the hospital the deerskin pants were removed and discarded in the trash. Quinn was able to rescue the boy's only possession and now held on to them like a talisman. Quinn assumed the boy would want the pants back at some point.

The boy's hair was long. Almost to the middle of his back. When Quinn first saw the boy in the middle of the muddy creek stacking rocks, his face was hidden behind the mane of hair. Quinn's wife, the woman known as Hope to Brock, had patiently sat on the edge of the boy's bed and brushed and picked the knots out of the boy's hair. Quinn smiled when he commented how beautiful the boy's hair was. How healthy and vibrant it looked. Hope walked back into the room and handed Quinn a cup of coffee from the hospital cafeteria. He looked up at his wife and smiled. He didn't know why they were still there. It had been three days and the boy hadn't spoken to either one of them. Hope hadn't said anything about leaving and she wouldn't. They both felt that they had a connection with the boy and he was now their responsibility. At least until his family arrived, which confused Quinn. If it was his son, he would have been by his boy's side faster than thought. His and Hope's own children had come to visit the boy also, but that seemed counter-productive. The boy shrunk away, figuratively, when his and Hope's children came to visit. Quinn's parents had agreed to watch their children until the boy's family appeared. Until then, he and Hope would remain vigilant over the boy.

Quinn stood and hugged Hope. In every aspect of their life they did everything together. It was how she liked it and what he preferred. They genuinely loved each other's company. Not only were they husband and wife, but they were best friends and lovers. When he suggested that they stay with the boy, Hope didn't even protest. It was already understood that it was their responsibility together. He leaned forward and kissed her on the lips and felt her smile. They both turned and looked at the boy. She sat on the edge of the bed and squeezed his hand.

The boy opened his eyes and turned his head to look at Hope. Hope smiled. "Hi," she whispered.

The boy grunted in response.

Quinn took a step towards the boy because it was the first sound he had made in three days. Hope placed her other hand on the boy's forearm and gently rubbed his skin. She leaned closer. "It's okay."

The boy glanced at Quinn and then the door. Quinn watched as the boy visibly squeezed Hope's hand harder and kept glancing at the door. Hope continued to rub the boy's forearm, reassuring him everything was okay.

Then the hospital room door burst open with an older gentleman crashing through the entrance with a younger man in tow. The older man had a wiry build, a crew cut, and a thick white mustache. At the sight of Quinn, the older man stopped in his tracks and blurted out, "Who the hell are you people?"

Before Quinn or Hope could answer, the younger man grabbed the man's shoulder and tried to hold him back from entering further into the room. "Dad, stop!"

The older man shot a look of anger at his son standing behind him. "Shut your mouth, boy!"

The younger man ignored his father's comment and pushed past him, extending his hand to Quinn. "Hi, I'm Darius. You must be the couple that found Brock?"

Quinn shook the man's hand and took note of the firmness of the handshake. "Brock?" Quinn questioned.

The older man pushed past his son, mumbling, "Who the hell cares who they are." He glanced down at Hope and spat out, "Little missy, you can let go of my son's hand now. He no longer needs you babying him."

Quinn could feel all of his muscle tense in response to the older man's words. He opened his mouth to respond, but Hope was always quicker with comebacks. "He doesn't need an asshole, either!"

Quinn glanced at Hope, who was still holding the boy's hand. He took note that the boy's knuckles were turning white because he was gripping Hope's hand so tightly. Quinn glanced at the boy's face and saw that his hair had fallen over his eyes. He couldn't tell if the boy's eyes were open or closed.

Either the older man didn't hear Hope's comment or he chose to ignore it. Instead, he focused on the boy's hair. "He looks like a damn girl with this damn hair." He moved to swipe at the boy's hair. Hope popped up from the edge of the bed and knocked the older man's hand away from the boy.

The older man snapped a look at Hope. "You bitch!"

Quinn and Darius moved into action. Quinn moved to stand behind his wife and Darius pushed his father away from the bed. Quinn watched as Darius moved in close to his father and whispered something in the older man's ear that seemed to calm him down for the moment. Hope glanced at Quinn, and he could see the anger in her face by evidence of the red streak popping out on her forehead. He rubbed the sides of her arms and rested his hands on her shoulders.

Darius turned to the both of them. "I'm sorry, but I think it would be best if the two of you leave now. Brock is my brother and this is his father. I," he hesitated, "we appreciate everything you have done, but you are no longer needed."

As each word was spoken Quinn could feel Hope's muscles tense, waiting for an opportunity to respond. Quinn had a feeling that something like this would happen when the boy's family appeared. He had been preparing himself for such a confrontation. When Darius stopped speaking, he and Hope didn't even have a chance to respond.

Brock sat up in the bed and screamed at the top of his lungs for longer than Quinn thought was humanly possible. The scream was so loud and piercing that Quinn's eardrums whined in protest. The pitch and tone of the scream reminded Quinn of a siren. Even if he wanted to, he couldn't even bring himself to cover his ears from the piercing sound.

When a nurse and a police officer ran into the hospital room Brock stopped. Everyone stared at the boy in silence. Hope reached her hand out to the boy and he reached up to take it. The boy made eye contact with Hope, and Quinn could see the pleading look in the boy's eyes.

The police officer was the first to break the silence. "What's going on in here?"

Quinn looked at Darius and his father and then the police officer. "Sir, these gentlemen claim to be related to this boy. But it is clear to me and my wife that this boy is not ready to see these two men and would like for them to leave."

The older man exploded past Darius, nearly knocking him to the ground, and grabbed the boy by the fabric of the hospital gown. He pulled him half way out of the bed and screamed in his face, "Those damn monsters took you like they took your mother!"

The police officer grabbed the older man and restrained him. The older man let go of the boy. The boy collapsed back on the bed and let Hope hug him. The older man stopped fighting and let the police officer pull him out of the room.

Darius looked at Quinn. "I apologize," he hesitated and then continued, looking at Brock. "Our father is not well." Darius stepped closer to the door and then turned back to everyone. "The past four years have been very hard on him." He then stepped through the door and pulled it closed behind him.

The nurse moved over to the boy that Darius called Brock and checked the monitors. Quinn indicated to the nurse that everything was okay. The nurse hesitated and then left the room. Hope brushed the hair out of the boy's eyes and asked, "Is your name Brock?"

The boy looked up at Hope and then Quinn and whispered, "Yes."

Chapter 33

Brock sensed the two men entering the hospital room before he even opened his eyes. He knew it was late in the evening. His nurse hadn't come to check on him in a while and the man he knew as Quinn had stepped out just a few minutes earlier. Brock guessed the two men that entered his room had waited for Quinn to leave. He hoped they hadn't done anything bad to him. He liked Quinn and his partner Hope. Brock could also tell by the footfalls of the two men that they were not his brother and father. Brock's eyelids gave away that he was awake when he heard the subtle click of metal.

In a hushed whisper, a gravely deep voice said, "Open your eyes, Brock. I know you smelled us when we came out of the stairwell."

Brock opened his eyes and saw a large, burly man with long shaggy black hair and a full untrimmed beard and mustache with wisps of gray leaning over his bed. The man held a knife with a blade as long Brock's forearm. The burly man's thick, meaty hand tensed and squeezed the handle of the knife. He smelled of wood smoke and soil.

The man continued in his gravely whisper, "Shhhh—not a sound."

Brock stared into the man's dark eyes. A hint of a smile stretched underneath his beard and mustache. He then sat in the chair next to the hospital bed where Hope usually sat. The man rested the long knife on his right thigh and leaned back in the chair. Brock stared at the man for a long time. He looked familiar, but he couldn't place where he had seen the woodman before.

Brock's attention was pulled away from the burly man when the second man cleared his throat. An African-American man stepped from the corner of the room and moved to the foot of the bed. The man was tall with a shiny bald head and a business suit. "We need to talk," stated the man.

Brock stared at the man in silence.

The two of them held each other's gaze for a long tense moment. The black man broke the stare first and flashed a look to the mountain man sitting in the chair. The woodman half-heartedly struck the bed with his left knee. The bed shook. Brock ignored the mountain man, knowing it was just a scare tactic to try and intimidate him. Skunk had tried the same thing to him many times.

"Please, Jake, I don't think that is necessary," said the other man with a sarcastic tone as he forced a fake smile across his lips.

Brock sensed no reaction from Jake.

"Again, I apologize for my partner," the man said. "Let's just say that his social skills are not as practiced as they should be." The man paused, adjusted his suit jacket, and then continued. "Which I'm sure you can relate to?" The man looked at Brock for some type of acknowledgement.

Brock stared at the man in silence.

The man continued, "Jake spends a lot of time in the woods. He has a skill set that is very important to us." He looked at his fingernails before continuing. "You, Brock," he paused to look at the boy, "have valuable information that would help Jake."

Brock stared at the man in silence.

The man held Brock's stare for a moment and then eventually glanced at Jake.

Jake stood from the chair and avoided bumping into the bed again. He twirled the knife in his hand as he looked down at the boy. "I told you this was a waste of time." He turned his attention to the black man. "I told you to keep me in the field. I was close."

The man ignored Jake's comments and looked back down at Brock. "As you can see, Jake has very little patience." He glanced to Jake and then back to Brock. "I can't always control his actions when he wants information."

Jake grunted, but to Brock it sounded like a grunt of annoyance that he heard from Sookum from time to time.

"So please, cooperation would be for the best," finished the man.

Brock stared at the man in silence.

Jake looked over to the closed hospital door and then quickly took a step back from the bed while twirling his knife closed and hiding it behind his forearm. The door opened and Quinn stepped into the room. He stopped in his tracks when he saw the two men standing at the foot of Brock's bed.

"Who the hell are you?" asked Quinn.

Brock watched as the black man's head slowly turned to face Quinn. His expression was one of annoyance and anger. The man softly answered, "Family."

"I don't see the resemblance," responded Quinn.

The man turned his head back towards Brock, but addressed Quinn. "You are no longer needed; please leave."

Brock watched as Quinn moved to the side of his bed and faced the two men. Brock saw Jake's hand with the knife twitch. Brock reached up and grasped Quinn's hand. He felt Quinn tense and struggle not to look down at their hands. Quinn asked again, "Who are you?"

The black man turned to look at Quinn and smiled. "How rude of me." He stuck out his hand to try and shake Quinn's hand. "I'm John Smith."

Brock watched as Quinn looked at John Smith's hand but made no move to shake it. Mr. Smith removed his hand and straightened his suit jacket.

"What do you want, Mr. Smith?" asked Quinn.

Mr. Smith looked at Quinn. "My partner and I work for the Department of Agriculture. More specifically the U.S. Forest Service."

Quinn nodded his head towards Mr. Smith's partner, Jake, and said, "Why the hell is the U.S. Forest Service sneaking around my property and the property of my neighbors?"

Mr. Smith tilted his head towards Jake. Jake grunted a response. Mr. Smith turned his body towards Quinn. "I am to understand that you have already met my partner." He paused as if looking for the right words, then continued, "That is unfortunate."

Quinn laughed. "For who? Me or you?"

Brock watched as Mr. Smith visibly twitched.

Quinn let go of Brock's hand and stepped closer to Mr. Smith. "From this whole cloak and dagger routine of sneaking into this boy's room at night and Mr. Barbarian over there sneaking around my woods, I can only guess that your government organization is trying to cover something up." Quinn paused and stepped closer. "You don't scare me. He's a boy. Do something useful with your time and catch a terrorist or something."

Brock watched as Quinn and Mr. Smith held each other's gaze. He then heard the familiar metal click of Jake's knife. He watched as Mr. Smith's right hand squeezed into a fist. Then Mr. Smith smiled.

He turned to Brock. "Brock, I am glad that you have returned safely. Hopefully you will be reunited with your biological father soon." Mr. Smith then turned and gave Quinn a curt nod. The two gentlemen left Brock's hospital room without another sound.

Chapter 34

Hope sat by Brock's head reading a book. She assumed he was asleep. It was early morning and she was used to waking early because of her job. While the nurse was checking his vitals she quickly ran down to the cafeteria to get some coffee. She was afraid to leave him alone for fear of his father or those other men returning. As a family, she was unsure what they should do. They couldn't keep vigil over this boy forever.

Hope looked at the pages of the book and realized that she was so lost in her own thoughts that she didn't even know what was going on in the book. She closed the book and looked up at Brock. He was staring back at her.

He asked in almost a whisper, "What's a sasquatch?"

Hope pursed her lips together and wiggled her nose. She felt like the witch from the television show Bewitched and momentarily wondered if she was subconsciously wishing for some magic. "Some believe it is a creature that lives in the woods and walks on two legs like we do."

Brock looked towards the window at the rising sun and then

back to Hope. "What do they look like?"

"They are supposed to be very large. I think eight to twelve feet tall. Covered in hair or fur. Very muscular." Then she smiled and added, "And elusive."

Brock smiled and asked, "Have you seen one?"

Hope closed her eyes and smiled. "Yes, I think so. It was late at night and dark."

"Tell me," whispered Brock.

"My husband and I were camping. It was pretty remote. I was staring out across this field. There was a tree line about three hundred yards away. About halfway in the field I thought I saw something crouching in the field. I assumed it was a tree stump or something. Then it moved. I thought it was my imagination." She paused and then continued, "Then it stood." Hope shook her head a little to herself. "I was scared. It was huge."

Brock asked, "Did your husband see it?"

Hope shook her head. "I'm not sure. He saw something, but it was different than what I saw. He said he saw something peeking out from the side of a tree and some movement where I indicated."

"Did it come to you or near you?" asked Brock.

"No. It crouched down again. We stayed a bit longer and then left. I was too scared to stay any longer," said Hope.

They sat in silence for a bit, and then Hope asked, "Where were you all those years?"

Brock shrugged his shoulders. "I don't know. In the forest."

"Alone that whole time?" asked Hope.

Brock shook his head no, but didn't say anything else. He simply stared out the window. He then asked, "Why are they so elusive?"

Hope shrugged her shoulders, "I don't know. Some people think it's because they have adapted to their environment. Many Native American tribes believe they are spirit creatures and can travel between worlds."

Hope watched as the word spirit caught Brock's attention, and then he tried to compose himself again. He looked down at the bed sheets. "What's a spirit creature?"

Hope pursed her lips again. "A spirit creature is an animal…" She stopped and shook her head. "…a creature that can travel between worlds." She paused and shook her head again to herself. "Hmmm, many people believe there is an afterlife. When we die our souls go somewhere." She looked at Brock. He nodded his head in agreement.

"Native Americans and other cultures throughout history also believe there are other realities or dimensions besides our own. They believe there are places on Earth that are veils, hmmm, or access points where creatures or other entities can travel back and forth between our world and theirs."

She looked at Brock's face to see if he was understanding what she was saying. To her it appeared he did, so she continued, "The Native Americans believe sasquatch is one of those creatures that can travel from their world to ours, or from what they consider their spirit world to ours. They believe sasquatch comes from their spirit world to ours in times of great change."

Brock mumbled, "A spirit walker."

Hope looked at him, puzzled, but said, "Yes, I suppose they are."

Brock opened his mouth to speak and then closed it. Hope reached out touched Brock's forearm with a gentle touch. Brock smiled and asked, "What's your name?"

The woman known as Hope to Brock smiled, "Jennifer."

Brock smiled in return, "And your partner?"

Jennifer laughed through a warm smile, "You mean my husband? His name is Jonathan."

Brock looked towards his hands and fidgeted with the seam of the blanket that covered his legs. Playing with the threads of the blanket he whispered, "My name is Brock."

Jennifer moved her hand down to Brock's hand and gave it a squeeze. He looked up at her. The smile in Jennifer's eyes matched the smile on her face. "Jonathan and I will always keep you safe."

Brock smiled and motioned for Hope to look out the window. She watched as the sun started to rise over the tops of the trees. She could feel Brock looking at her. Almost as if he were gauging whether or not he could trust her. He then whispered, "They are bedding down now."

Without looking at Brock she asked in a hushed whisper, "Who?"

"My tribe," said Brock.

Hope looked over at him and she could tell by the look in his eyes he was someplace else, remembering something important. She squeezed his hand. He returned the squeeze and said, "I miss them."

Chapter 35

The man Brock called Quinn heard the crunch of gravel from an approaching car before he saw the vehicle. He stood up from spreading black mulch around an oak tree and watched as a small blue two-door economy car rounded the corner into view. The car slowed and stopped in front of Quinn's house. The driver pulled halfway into the front lawn to keep from blocking the one-lane gravel road and parked. The car wasn't familiar to Quinn, but the driver was. Darius stepped out from the car and raised his hand in a wave. "Hey friend," Darius called out.

Quinn brushed his glove-covered hands off and walked towards Darius without saying hello. Darius reached into the passenger seat of the car and pulled out a six-pack of beer. He rounded the corner of the car to Quinn. He stuck out his hand to shake Quinn's. Quinn returned the handshake with his black-mulch-stained, gloved hand. Darius looked back at the car as he brushed his hand off on his pants. "Piece of shit. I'd never drive that back home, rent-a-car," said Darius, as if defending his pride. Darius looked back at Quinn and pulled out a beer from the six-pack. "Looks like you could use a beer."

Quinn wasn't one to turn down a free beer. He took the bottle and opened it. He took a drink before asking, "How did you know where I lived?"

Darius leaned against the hood of the car and pulled out another bottle of beer and opened it. "I didn't." He took a drink. "I'm a tracker by trade."

Quinn squinted at Darius. "You tracked me? I think some people call that stalking."

Darius laughed. "Stalking would entail me following you for the intended purpose of killing you." He paused for a moment to take a drink of his beer. Quinn wondered if the pause was intended to drive home a point. Darius continued, "I didn't do that. I simply put the facts together of where my brother was found and drove these back roads and asked kind people if they knew where you lived." He took a swig. "Took a few days."

Quinn grunted in acknowledgement and drank again from his beer. He then looked at the bottle and thought about his options concerning Darius. He shrugged to himself and looked at Darius. "Come, let's sit on the deck." Quinn turned to walk back to the deck that sat on the side of the house overlooking Furnace Mountain. Darius followed.

"You have a beautiful home with an incredible view," said Darius.

"Thank you."

"You must be rich to afford something like this," added Darius.

The hairs on the back of Quinn's neck tingled. He glanced back at Darius. "No, I'm just a teacher."

Darius swallowed the mouthful of beer and smiled. "Hell, I didn't know teachers got paid so well."

Quinn sat in one of the chairs circling a patio table and motioned his head for Darius to have a seat as well. "We don't."

Darius looked off to Furnace Mountain. "Brock and I are from a small, poor mining town. There's nothing there. No future." He looked at Quinn, waiting for a response. Quinn never gave him one. Darius looked back towards Furnace Mountain. "Why is it called Furnace Mountain?"

Quinn looked towards the mountain. "Often in the morning or after a rain storm, it appears to be smoking from hot coals or a fire."

Darius took a drink of his beer and Quinn could tell that he was lost in thought. Looking at the rim of the bottle, Darius said, "The past four years have been hard." He looked towards the mountain, quiet and pensive, before he spoke again. "When Brock disappeared, it pushed Father over the edge. He couldn't handle losing Brock and my mother also."

Quinn took a drink of beer and asked, "What happened to your mother?"

Darius closed his eyes and took a drink. "About ten years before Brock went missing, we went on a family camping trip. My father was different then." He paused and looked up at the sky. "He was happy."

Darius continued, "I was seven at the time. My father had found a remote lake in the backcountry. He parked the truck and R.V. camper about fifty yards from the lake. The first day and night were uneventful. Then I remember hearing weird sounds in the night. They started around dusk and continued until morning."

Quinn asked, "What kind of sounds?"

"Whoops mostly. But later that night it sounded like a woman screaming. My father told me it was okay. It was just a mountain lion or coyotes." Darius smiled and chuckled to himself while he took a drink of his beer. "It's funny how your father's word can make things okay when you're at that age."

"The next morning my father was adamant that I stay near the lake and the camper. I wasn't allowed to wander off in the woods.

Which was odd, because he usually never had a problem with me exploring the woods. But I was afraid of my father, so I listened. The day passed and the sun started to set. I was by the fire. My mother was down by the lake cleaning some fish. We heard the scream again from the night before. I instantly got scared." Darius opened another beer, handed it to Quinn, and then opened one for himself.

"Then we heard a crash. Then a scream and what sounded like a hundred elephants running through the forest. I remember seeing the pebbles on the ground bouncing and hopping on the ground like Mexican Jumping Beans. My father grabbed my shirt collar and pulled me towards him and screamed, 'Get in the damn camper, NOW!'"

Darius took a slow pull on his beer and Quinn could tell that he was trying to reconcile the thoughts in his head.

"My father was scared. I could see the fear in his eyes and hear it in his voice. I didn't hesitate. I picked up Brock, who was lying on a blanket near us. As I stood and turned towards the camper, I watched as this giant crashed through the tree line and slammed full force into the side of the camper. The camper shook from the stopping blocks under the tires."

"Giant?" asked Quinn.

Darius nodded his head in acknowledgement. "At the time I thought it was a giant." He paused as if he was hesitant, then continued, "It was a sasquatch." He stopped and took another drink.

Quinn leaned back in his chair. "A sasquatch?"

Darius looked at Quinn. Quinn knew enough about human behavior and body language to know that Darius believed what he'd seen and was telling the truth, from his point of view. "Do you remember what it looked like?" asked Quinn.

Darius looked out at the mountain. "He was at least ten or eleven feet tall, maybe taller. When it stood from striking the RV its head reached the top. It was gray or white, hard to tell at that time of day, but it was light colored. And massive. Bigger and thicker than any man, football player, or bodybuilder you may have ever seen. I can't even begin to describe to you how enormous this creature was." Darius slowly shook his head in awe and disbelief.

Quinn took a drink of his beer and asked, "What happened next?"

"My father grabbed me by my shirt and shoved me towards the door of the camper, screaming for me to get in. The creature had crashed into the back side of the camper so I still had access to the door. I trusted my father, so I did what he said and jumped in and closed the door. The creature struck the camper again and I fell to the floor with Brock in my arms. I could hear my father calling for my mother. Next thing I knew the camper was moving. My father had jumped into the truck and took off like a bat outta hell," said Darius as he retold the story.

He took another drink. "I lay there the whole time with Brock on my chest, staring at the massive dent in the side wall of the camper until my father stopped the truck. Even then I kept staring at the dent as I listened to my father unhooking the camper from the truck. It wasn't until he opened the camper door and told me to stay put with Brock that I stopped looking at that dent. He then disappeared and I heard the truck drive off."

"He left you?" asked Quinn.

Darius nodded his head yes. "To go back and get my mother."

"She wasn't with him? He left her?"

Darius looked at the empty beer bottle. "From what my father has told me, the creature was between the camper and my mother. He assumed she would want him to save the children before her. He said it was a judgment call. He assumed the creature would follow him. It didn't. He went back and she was gone."

"Gone?" asked Quinn.

"Gone," confirmed Darius. "Over the years Brock and I lived with our aunt on and off as our father would go out looking for her. He was convinced if he found the sasquatch that took her he could get her back."

Darius paused and shook his head. "Of course our father became the laughingstock of the town. No one believed him. Everyone thought he was a fool for believing that a sasquatch took his wife."

Quinn and Darius sat in silence for a long time, listening to the birds and watching the clouds pass over them. Darius then continued, "After that, my father never talked of my mother again. As Brock got older he would ask about her and my father would become cross. He didn't handle it well. So when Brock went missing, that sent him over the edge. Even after the authorities stopped looking for Brock, we continued. Either directly or indirectly."

Quinn asked, "What do you mean directly or indirectly?"

"Over the past four years, Father and I directly searched over a two-hundred mile radius of where Brock disappeared. Indirectly, I sold my services as a tracker to hunters and poachers just so I would have an excuse to be in the woods to look for signs of my brother. We knew he was alive. We knew he would stay alive. It was just a matter of finding him."

"So you suspected a sasquatch took him?" asked Quinn.

Darius nodded his head yes. "The signs were there. We were positive of it. But of course no one believed us…" He paused and then continued, "Well, except for a couple of people, like the government."

"The government?" asked Quinn.

Darius took a drink from his beer. "Yeah, a couple of goons have been keeping tabs on me and my dad for years."

"Let me take a guess, Mr. Smith and his partner?" asked Quinn.

Darius laughed out loud. "That'd be them. They got to you too?"

Quinn took a drink of beer. "I met them at the hospital the other night. And I saw Mr. Smith's partner in the woods near where I found Brock a few days before that."

"His name is Jake," said Darius.

"Jake?"

"Mr. Smith's partner," clarified Darius. "He's a sasquatch hunter."

Quinn leaned forward in his chair towards Darius. "A sasquatch hunter?"

"Yes. Don't let his appearance fool you, he's really an ex-Navy Seal," confirmed Darius.

Quinn sat back in his chair. "Accepting that sasquatch is real is one thing. But accepting that the United States Government is hunting them," he shook his head, "is a bit too much."

Darius shrugged, "Believe what you want. I don't care. I'm just telling you what I know."

Quinn watched Darius for a moment and then asked, "So how do you think your brother escaped?"

Darius looked at Quinn. "Escaped?" He shook his head. "No, they let him go."

"Let him go?"

Darius took a long drink of beer. "I don't know why, but one does not escape from a sasquatch."

Quinn shook his and took a drink. "So what's next?"

Darius looked at Quinn and placed the empty bottle of beer on the table. "I wanted to thank you for watching over Brock, for finding him," he paused. "Like I said, my father is not well; we got off on the wrong foot when we first met."

"I understand," said Quinn.

"As soon as we can bring him back home, we will," finished Darius.

Quinn looked out towards Furnace Mountain. When this whole thing started he knew this would be the end result. He had caught himself daydreaming that the boy would come and live with them. Be a part of his family. He never understood why he thought that or even wanted that. He pushed those thoughts from his mind. He knew the boy's family would appear and he would no longer be needed. He prepared himself for this. Still, a sense of loss washed over him. "He's fragile. Go slow with him. Protect him from your father." He then turned to look at Darius. "Gain his trust again and he'll tell you what you want to know."

Darius nodded his head in agreement and stood and extended his hand. Quinn pulled off his dirty glove as he stood and shook Darius's hand. Before Quinn let go of Darius's hand, he asked, "What about your mother?"

Darius pulled back his hand. "What about her?"

"Did your father ever find her?"

Darius shook his head. "She's dead."

Chapter 36

"SASQUATCH BOY" DISAPPEARS FROM THE HOSPITAL
Dustin Hollinsworth
dhollinsworth@jeffersonpost.com

"Sasquatch Boy," as dubbed by social media through several bigfoot research organizations and internet forums, disappeared from George Mason Memorial Hospital late Thursday night. In a bizarre turn of events, Brock Blackwood, who earned the name "Sasquatch Boy" due to his fantastical tale of living with a tribe of bigfoot creatures for the past four years, has once again vanished. Over four years ago, Brock was on a camping trip with his father and brother when he went missing. The authorities conducted a thorough search for the boy for several months but never found him. After a four-year search, the boy was found three weeks ago in Northwest Virginia, 3,000 miles from where he was reported missing. When Brock was questioned by the authorities, he told them of living with a family of creatures that can only be described as the mythical beast known as sasquatch or bigfoot. When the boy was asked if these creatures were the cryptozoological animal known as bigfoot, the boy simply said that he didn't know what a bigfoot was. When asked if he was hurt or threatened, Brock said the creatures were his friends and family.

Brock's father, Trevor Blackwood, was adamant that the creatures were sasquatch and he is thankful to have his boy back. The father then ended all interviews and announced that the full story of the boy's adventure with the group of sasquatch would be revealed at a later date. The father then refused all access to the boy for interviews by reporters. Mr. Blackwood is known to be an eccentric recluse throughout the bigfoot research community. Mr. Blackwood believes his first wife was abducted by a bigfoot almost fifteen years ago. Trevor Blackwood and his eldest son, Darius Blackwood, own a hunting and tracking company based out of Colorado.

Friday morning, George Mason Memorial Hospital contacted the authorities to report that Brock Blackwood went missing from the hospital at approximately midnight of the same day. The nurse reported that she entered the boy's room during her nightly rounds and found the boy was not in his room. She alerted security of the disappearance. Hospital administration and security conducted a thorough search of the facility and did not find the boy. At this time the authorities have no leads on where the boy could be. The couple that found Brock three weeks ago, Jonathan and Jennifer Foxhorn, have been questioned about the whereabouts of Brock. They were unable to provide any leads and are not considered persons of interest. Trevor and Darius Blackwood are unavailable for questioning.

FAMILY

Chapter 37

Approximately three years later.

B rock stood in his boxers looking out the living room windows of the house into the dark night. He watched as the hundreds of fireflies blinked through the darkness. He tried to peer past the shadows of the night that sprawled across the backyard into the trees that lined the property. He crouched down and peered harder into the darkness. He was searching, but knew he would not see what he knew was out there. Only if he was given permission.

He looked toward the sliver of the moon and knew it was not a dream. What he experienced was more than a dream. It was a visitation. No, a sighting. He exhaled and walked over to the desk and turned on the small lamp. He pulled out his journal and opened it to the next empty page.

> May 10th
> I was sitting in the kitchen of my father's house. My back was to the stove.

My father was sitting to the right of me and my mother was sitting in front of me. She sat in front of a bay window. The large bay window looked out to the backyard. In the backyard was a large Magnolia tree that towered over the house. To my left was an open doorway to the dining room and a large sliding glass door. I think we were talking. Maybe we were just sitting there. I saw a deer run across the backyard from the right to the left. Then immediately after the deer I saw a two-legged black humanoid shape run after the deer. I either leaned out of my chair or leaned into the dining room to see where the deer and black two-legged shape went. I saw the deer turned back towards the way it ran and was looking at a sasquatch that was squatting down in front of it. The sasquatch had its arm extended towards the deer and was cupping its small head in the palm of its hand as if it was going to scratch behind the deer's ear like a dog. The sasquatch was huge. No, massive. I don't think I can put in words how large this creature was. Its shoulder was the size of a bowling ball, maybe bigger. Its arms were bigger than any bodybuilder I have ever seen. Its chest and back were maybe thicker than the width of my shoulders. Its head sat atop of its shoulders and back with no neck visible. The creature was covered in brownish-red hair that covered its entire body. My mother leaned in next to me and whispered, "Oh my god, they are real." Then my father poked or touched my upper back and I awoke.

I was immediately ill. I felt sick to my stomach. I writhed on the bed in pain thinking I was going to vomit. I was so hot I felt I was burning up. I tore the covers off of me and threw my shirt across the room. I felt anxious. I feel anxious. I felt like I was being watched. I feel like I am being watched right now. I was not scared. It was not a nightmare. It was more than a dream. I feel as if I was transported to that time and place to be blessed to see that sasquatch. Or maybe it was pushed into my mind. My heart. The pain in my stomach became too much. I hurried to the bathroom and as disgusting as it sounds I had horrible diarrhea. Who's going to read this anyway? I physically felt a little bit better. But mentally I felt fuzzy. I feel fuzzy. As if my brain was thrown into a washing machine on the super high spin cycle. I still feel anxious and nervous. Rattled. I feel rattled because I experienced something special. Something important. No one is going to believe me. Oh my God, people are going to think I am crazy! I can't tell anyone! Society sucks! I have no one to tell.

Sigh.

Thank you God. Thank you sasquatch
for allowing me to see you. Thank you for
this gift.

Brock closed the journal and returned to bed. He lay in bed with
the window slightly ajar for the evening breeze to blow through the
room. As he closed his eyes and drifted off to sleep, he thought he
heard a soft wood knock outside his bedroom window.

Chapter 38

Brock lifted the hatchback to his SUV and grabbed his day pack from the back of the truck. He opened the top of the pack and glanced at the contents. He then placed his lunch on top of the contents and secured it. He pulled it over his shoulders and fastened the hip belt around his waist and clicked the chest strap closed. It was his Gopack for when he went hiking in the woods looking for sasquatch. The pack contained everything he would need to collect evidence: medical gloves, plastic bags, poncho, plaster of Paris mix, spray paint, empty jug, water, digital camera, digital recorder, binoculars, head lamp, extra batteries, and a first aid kit. He spent at least ten to twenty hours a week with his boots to the ground bushwhacking through forest undergrowth looking for signs of sasquatch.

Brock divided his time in the forest between day hikes and night hikes. During the day he walked along creeks and riverbeds looking for track signs, or bushwhacked through dense forest looking for tree markers or stick structures. If he came across any signs he would return at night and sit and wait to hear the sounds or see a sasquatch.

Over the years he had found numerous stick structures and markers and a few footprints. At night he recorded multiple howls, screams, and wood knocks from sasquatch. As far as sightings went, he had a couple to say the least. He never shared his findings with anyone. As an amateur scientist he knew the value of having his findings reviewed by his peers. However, he had no peers in the world of bigfoot research. He was known, but he was considered a loner.

Brock was okay with being a loner. He learned early on in the bigfoot research community that evidence found by one individual and peer-reviewed by another was never found to be credible. For example, if he found a footprint and knew beyond the shadow of a doubt that it was created by a sasquatch and he showed the evidence to a peer bigfoot researcher, nine times out of ten a peer would conclude it was a human print. If the same peer bigfoot researcher produced evidence they were always one hundred percent certain their evidence was the real thing. Basically, everyone was skeptical of everyone else. Brock laughed to himself and shook his head in disgust as he closed the hatchback to his SUV. He thought, sasquatch doesn't have to try and remain elusive; we'll do it for them by denying any evidence we find.

He pulled on his gloves and grabbed his walking stick. Brock never went into the woods with a gun. Just a pocket knife and a walking stick. His intention was never to harm or kill a sasquatch. His intention was to be a part of its world. As most creatures in the wild, Brock suspected that sasquatch would sense his intention as soon as he reached the forest's edge. He paused at the tree line and closed his eyes and reflected on his intention before entering the forest. He wasn't a fool to think all sasquatch were peaceful, loving forest creatures as portrayed in the movie Harry and the Hendersons. He knew their personalities varied as greatly as humans. He knew the dangers of the teenagers or the rogue males. He accepted those dangers and trusted his intentions. He trusted his sixth sense and the warning signs when he needed to leave an area.

Brock opened his eyes and stepped through the tree line and entered the forest. He knew immediately he was in the right place. If he had to explain his feeling to someone else he wouldn't be able too. It was a feeling. He could feel that he wasn't alone. He could feel he was already being watched. He took a deep breath and followed the abandoned gravel road that eventually turned into a foot path.

Brock had looked for this stretch of woods for months based on a hunch. Months prior he had found a set of tracks in a creek bed that emptied into a large river. Upon closer inspection he found three differently sized prints. He suspected a family unit, or tribe as he liked to call them. By the size of the prints he suspected a young male and female, and one newling. He cast the print of the newling because it was the most clear and distinct. The prints of the suspected male and female were in mud and sand that were not conducive to leaving prints. Brock wondered if that was deliberate in that the older sasquatch may have known where to step, whereas the young one did not. It was possible, he concluded.

Brock never shared the casts or the photographs with anyone. There was no point. He wouldn't be believed, and besides it was for him, not the world. Once when he was out West he found a set of sasquatch tribe prints near the skeletal remains of an elk. When he shared the information with another bigfoot researcher, he was told that the "prints" were made from free-ranging cattle stepping in their own prints. Was it possible? Sure, Brock concluded. Anything is possible in nature. It was the perfect catch-all for anything and everything unexplainable.

He went back several more times to the area where he found the prints by the river. Once in a while he had the feeling he was being watched. Once he heard a loud noise crash down from the tree top to the ground, as if something jumped or fell. When he investigated there was no evidence of anything falling from the top of the tree. It may have been nothing, but it was still curious. Brock found that he used that term a lot, curious.

Brock hopped across a scattering of rocks to sit on a larger rock in the middle of the river to eat his lunch. He pulled off his shirt, reclined on the rock, and ate. He looked across the river to a mountain range he was unfamiliar with. He made a mental note to himself to figure out what mountain it was. He knew it was almost directly across Windhill Heights. Then a thought struck him. The creatures who made the prints by the river came from the mountain he was staring at. He stood up and hopped along the rocks and realized the river was relatively shallow. If he waded across it may have been hip deep. To a sasquatch, it would be knee deep. Looking at the unknown mountain in front of him, Brock hypothesized that after a heavy rainfall the creatures would wade across the river to the creek that emptied into the river to retrieve any fish caught in the pond they had created by damming up the end of the creek with railroad ties. After gathering the fish they would return across the river and to the safety of the mountain in front of Brock.

He went home that night and searched the internet and a collection of maps until he was able to pinpoint the exact location. The creek with the dammed-up pond was called Israel Creek, which was a curious name for that region of the country, which had been settled by Germans and Dutch. He made a note to check with a friend from the local Historical Society on the origins of the name. The river was the Patawaemac, an old Native American Indian word that meant death.

The River of Death. Made sense to Brock. The river was known to be dangerous to kayakers for its deadly undertow. The mountain in question, directly across from Israel Creek, was Niki's Hill.

According to the map, Route 528 led to the base of Niki's Hill. It was the closest he would get to the river. Brock assumed there would be a deer trail to the river he could bushwhack through. According to a map, which was now two years old, a swath of land, or ridge, cut through the local county from Niki's Hill to join with the Devil's Mist mountain range. The Devil's Mist range connected with a larger chain of mountains that transverse North and South along the Eastern Seaboard. Again this made sense to Brock in the respect that if a tribe of sasquatch lived on Niki's Hill they would be able to access Devil's Mist and the larger mountain range for seasonal migration purposes. Brock also suspected the name, Devil's Mist, was in large part due to unexplained strange happenings and disappearances in those mountains caused by migrating sasquatch tribes.

Today was the third time he had come to Niki's Hill in the past week. The first was a short visit. More to scout where Route 528 ended, which to his surprise ended about a half mile from the river. More to his surprise, it ended at the entrance to an abandoned National Park. Route 528 ended at the park gate and the collapsing Ranger building. From there the road turned into a footpath. That day he had followed the footpath down to the river and found the skeletal remains of a water mill built in the early nineteenth century. Upon further research he found the mill was known as George's Mill. But what was more curious was the lack of information he could find about the abandoned national park associated with the mill.

That day Brock also discovered the path into the park cut through two pieces of private property. On the right it appeared to be an estate of some kind. On the left was Niki's Hill. Both properties had numerous no trespassing signs posted on the trees. The property associated with Niki's Hill periodically had a wire fencing stretched across the trees. For urban explorers, a no trespassing sign meant "please proceed." Brock wasn't ready to cross that line yet. If he had good reason and hard evidence to cross that line he would, but for now he was content with exploring the river's edge.

On this day, Brock was both surprised and delighted to find a well-worn path along the river's edge leading north. He found it curious that the path was so worn for an area that was clearly devoid of human habitation. Meaning, there was no evidence of camp fires, tree stands for hunting, or trash. He also found it curious that several parts of the path that were covered with fern or grass appeared to be matted down in certain areas. The most curious thing was there were no spider webs across the path. Usually when he walked trails early in the morning, like he was now, or on paths devoid of human traffic, the path was netted with spider-webs. This path had none. Lastly, he didn't have to duck under any low branches or brush. This, in other words, was a well-worn path.

After about forty-five minutes of hiking along the river's edge, Brock spied curious stick structures and tree breaks that appeared unnatural. He pulled out his binoculars and confirmed that he was almost directly across the Patawaemac River and Israel Creek. He looked behind him towards Niki's Hill and didn't see anything that suggested a game trail or path. He continued along the path and the river's edge for another fifteen minutes before his way was blocked by fallen trees. He surveyed the scene and there appeared to be a small path around the fallen trees. Before taking the path, he climbed on top of the trunk of the tree to see if the trail continued. It did. It was still used. Brock encountered at least three more fallen trees blocking the path before he saw the deer skull.

The skull sat on a branch in a tree about seven feet off the ground. It instantly reminded him of the countless stories he had read about where a group of people would place skulls around their territory to scare off would be invaders. Brock spent some time documenting the deer skull in the tree. He admitted that it was possible for the deer skull to have been "placed" there by the river flooding or swelling. But that would mean the river would have to have risen at least thirty feet in depth to deposit the skull on the thin branch where it now rested.

Brock's heart told him it wasn't the river. It was a warning sign. Despite the bright sun and cloudless sky, the path ahead looked dark and ominous. Brock had the distinct feeling that if he continued along the path he would be trespassing. And not trespassing on Niki's Hill property, but on sasquatch territory. The feeling of being watched never left him as he hiked along the river path. The feeling was even more intense now. He wondered if it was his imagination at finding the deer skull or if he was really being watched.

Brock turned back south along the trail and headed back to George's Mill and his truck. It always amazed him that the hike back along the same trail always went quicker. It took him about an hour to reach the deer skull, but only thirty minutes to reach the mill. A few times he thought he caught a glimpse of something moving in the corner of his eye. When he looked he never saw anything. Just trees, bushes, and rocks.

He crossed over the service road used by the park, now a small creek from erosion and climbed the small but steep incline to his truck. He suspected he was about two hundred yards away from the park entrance and his truck when he heard, "WHHOOOOOOOOOOOOO," from the direction of the river path he had just hiked.

Brock froze and smiled. He knew no human was on the river. He knew no human was along that same path or in that part of the woods. Brock knew that was a sasquatch howl. He was being watched. The sentry of the tribe had been watching him and tracking his movements. Now that Brock was at the edge of their territory the sentry was signaling that the coast was clear and they were alone again. Brock smiled and walked off to his truck.

Chapter 39

Mama Boobs was a large woman in every sense of the word. Brock would never call her Mama Boobs to her face. But to him, that was her name. To his few friends and co-workers he referred to her as Mama Boobs. To her, he called her Shelly, her real name. Brock never asked, but he assumed Mama Boobs was in her late fifties. She was a large woman. So large, in fact, she had to use a cane to move around, or a chair with wheels. He suspected she didn't want to be that big, but her body just ran its own course. Her boobs were impressively large. The biggest he had ever seen. There was no doubt in his mind that she could compete for the Guinness Book of World Records in that department.

Brock suspected that she was lonely. Shelly, Mama Boobs, talked a lot. It was almost as if once she got your attention she didn't want to lose it for a second. Whenever he went to her home, Brock always resigned himself to being there for at least two hours, if not longer. He admitted, he liked her. She was a good friend. Mama Boobs always wanted to see his pictures of sasquatch trail markers and footprints. He could tell that if she could, she would be right alongside him in the woods looking. Mama Boobs wanted to see the evidence for herself, but she also knew it was physically impossible for her to get to those locations.

By trade, Mama Boobs was an energy healer. She worked out of her home selling crystals conducting energy healing sessions for her clients. Brock had happened upon her one Saturday afternoon when he was out driving the back roads looking for trails to hike. He drove past her house and saw her struggling to carry groceries. He didn't know why, but he stopped and offered to help. He did that sometimes. He also occasionally picked up hitchhikers, even though he knew that presented its own dangers. It was a feeling he had. Almost like God tapping him on the shoulder and saying, "They need your help." Who's one to argue with God?

So that day he pulled into her driveway, actually her yard, which was already cluttered with six other cars, and offered to help. Mama Boobs accepted. They were friends ever since. He visited her weekly. Helped her bring in groceries, took her trash to the dump, and helped in any other way that he could. In exchange, they talked. According to Mama Boobs, she had lived in this part of the country her entire life. Her parents owned the land where she now lived. Interestingly, she didn't know any of the local folklore or history. She had plenty of stories, though, there was little doubt about that. But they were stories she heard from her clients. Nothing from things she had experienced directly. Maybe that's why Brock liked being around her; she was a story collector.

Brock pulled into her grassy dirt driveway and saw her sitting in her garage rummaging through her crystals. He smiled to himself because she didn't even look up. That was her way. To play coy and not excited that she had a visitor. "Hey, Shelly," called out Brock as he got out of his truck and walked towards her.

Shelly smiled. "It's been a while," she said without looking up from her rocks.

"Been busy," he said, knowing it had only been a week. He saw the ten or so grocery bags on the garage floor. He gathered them up and took them into her house and placed them on the kitchen table. She never wanted help putting the food away, just bringing them in. He gathered the trash and went back down to the garage.

Shelly glanced up at him and mumbled her thanks as he moved past her to collect the other trash bags. Brock nodded his head. He knew she was prideful and respected that. As he came back from his truck, Shelly asked, "Anything new?"

Brock pulled out his cell phone and moved next to her as he scrolled to his pictures. He showed her the tree markers and the deer skull in the tree. She took the phone from him and examined the deer skull closer. She handed the phone back to Brock and said, "That wasn't the river's doing. That's a territory marking."

Brock slid the phone into his back pocket. "I was thinking the same thing."

"Did you examine it?" asked Mama Boobs.

Brock shook his head. "I examined it on the tree, but did not move it."

"How high off the ground was it?" asked Mama Boobs.

"Seven feet."

"Any teeth marks?" asked Mama Boobs.

Brock shrugged his shoulders. "Maybe, but it was hard to tell," he paused. "I didn't want to touch it. Not my place."

"Smart."

"I heard a howl right before I got to my truck," said Brock.

Mama Boobs looked up at him from polishing the crystal in her hand. "You did?"

Brock nodded his head in acknowledgement. "It was almost like the sentry was saying, 'All clear, he's gone.'"

Mama Boobs smiled. "It's a good thing you didn't move that skull; yours might have been next to it later that night."

Brock smiled. "Oh, I'm sure I would have pissed him off. But I think they know I don't mean any harm."

Mama Boobs went back to polishing the crystal in her hands. "You may have good intentions, but they are still wild animals."

Brock nodded his head in agreement and absentmindedly picked up a handful of stones and shifted them through his fingers. Without looking at her, he asked, "Check the mail lately?"

Mama Boobs nodded her head. "Nothing."

Brock exhaled deeply, maybe too deeply, because Mama Boobs looked at him with sympathetic eyes. "Sweetie, people around here don't talk about these things."

He looked at her. "They talk to you," Brock countered.

She nodded her head in agreement. "Sure, but my name wasn't on the flier."

Brock remembered. He had made the flier. It was his idea. He sensed that she wanted to help him search for sasquatch in the area. Since she couldn't bushwhack through the forest with him, he thought of something else to capitalize on her strength of story collection. He created a flier with a classic drawing of a sasquatch and underneath the drawing wrote the words, "Have you seen or heard them?" At the bottom of the flier he listed an email address that he had created for people to contact him, or Mama Boobs to report any sightings. Once a week he walked or drove along sparsely populated dirt roads and left the fliers in people's mailboxes. It was Mama Boobs's job to check the email account periodically and notify him of any correspondence. In reality, they got more hate mail and ridicule than anything else. To say the least, it was disappointing.

Mama Boobs broke into his thoughts. "Maybe the next batch put my name on the flier?"

Brock shook his head. "No, no need to open you up to ridicule."

Mama Boobs laughed. "Sweetie, everyone around here already thinks I'm the crazy crystal lady who beats Indian drums at night."

Brock smiled; it was true, she did have a reputation as being an odd bird. Still, he wasn't ready to make his efforts a circus side show. He had a purpose and that purpose was to find them. He had no intention of exploiting them.

Mama Boobs's telephone rang and she looked at the caller ID. "I have to take this," she stated and started to turn her back to him in her rollie chair.

"I'll see you next week," Brock said with a smile and moved off to his truck.

Chapter 40

"Professor Foxhorn?" asked the man who was standing in the doorway of his office.

Professor Foxhorn looked up at the stranger and stood from his desk to greet the man. "Yes? And you are?" asked the Professor as he extended his hand towards the man.

The man eagerly took his hand and shook it. "My name is David White the Third, but my friends call me Buzzy."

Professor Foxhorn motioned for Buzzy to have a seat and asked, "Why is that?"

"Why is what?" asked Buzzy with a confused look on his face.

Professor Foxhorn smiled. "Why do your friends call you Buzzy?"

"Oh," said Buzzy as he leaned back in the chair and smiled. He then looked perplexed and said, "I don't know really."

The Professor smiled and nodded his head as if he'd received a better answer, and then said, "Nicknames are a form of endearment. It's curious that you introduce yourself with your nickname. It's as if you expect us to be close friends." Professor Foxhorn paused and looked as if he could retract his words and then continued. "I didn't mean for that to sound rude," he said apologetically.

Buzzy almost seemed to ignore the comment as he reached into his carrying bag and pulled out a notebook and pen. "Not at all," he said, and then added, "but I do hope we can be friends."

Professor Foxhorn smiled and leaned forward on his desk. "What can I help you with?"

Buzzy opened up his notebook and pulled out a piece of paper and handed it to the Professor. "I'm the founder of an organization that looks for evidence of elusive hominid creatures in North America."

Professor Foxhorn leaned back in his chair and flatly asked, "You mean sasquatch?"

Buzzy tilted his head towards the Professor. "Yes. But can I ask why you use that particular term?"

Professor Foxhorn knitted his eyebrows together and responded, "Isn't that their name?"

"No doubt it is," said Buzzy. "However, the more common term in society is bigfoot."

"Hmmm, I see," said the Professor. "I would argue the common media name is bigfoot," he said. "For true believers, I would argue the name sasquatch is more respectful to the species. I feel the term bigfoot carries a derogatory connotation."

Buzzy opened his mouth to respond, but the Professor continued, "Just as an individual referring to sasquatch as a hominid is trying to mask their true intentions."

Buzzy momentarily squinted at the Professor as if he was trying to discern what the gentleman had just said. By his actions, the Professor assumed Mr. David "Buzzy" White was at a loss for words and was trying to figure out a way to recover the conversation for the direction he intended it to go. Professor Foxhorn offered his help by saying with a slight nod of his head, "I apologize; again I mean no disrespect. It's a matter of semantics to say the least."

Buzzy visibly exhaled.

Professor Foxhorn looked down at the piece of paper Buzzy had given him and asked, "How can I help you?"

"I want you to join me on an expedition to the Pacific Northwest to look for sasquatch," said Buzzy in a slightly faster manner of speech, as if he was afraid the opportunity to ask would slip away.

Without looking at Buzzy, Professor Foxhorn asked, "Why me? I am a sociologist and professor by trade. I would add no value to the expedition."

"Sir, I think you underestimate your value," said Buzzy.

Professor Foxhorn looked up at Buzzy with a quizzical look.

Buzzy asked, "If I may be honest?"

"Please," said the Professor.

Buzzy continued, "Three years ago, you found the boy Brock, who lived among a family of sasquatch for over four years, near your home. Your wife Jennifer and you watched over and protected that young man until his family came to get him. Since that time, you have continued your own research into finding proof in the existence of sasquatch and have documented significant evidence supporting the creatures' existence. I believe the reason why you are so successful is because the boy Brock provided you with insight into the creatures' habits."

Professor Foxhorn raised his hand to quiet the man. He then waited a considerably long time before he started talking. "Mr. White, your facts are not completely accurate."

Buzzy exhaled in frustration and leaned back in the chair.

"Please let me finish," said Professor Foxhorn, "The movie about Brock's life was highly fictionalized. There is no proof that Brock lived with a family of sasquatch. That's what the boy's father believed. Yes, I found him. Yes, my wife and I watched over him until his father and brother came for him in the hospital. But in that short amount of time the boy never spoke to us. In the end, the boy disappeared. I am afraid the movie where you got your facts has misled you."

"With all respect, Professor Foxhorn, I was a friend of the Blackwood family for years." Buzzy paused as if he contemplated his next thought. "I was there the day Brock went missing."

"Then why not ask the Blackwoods for help?" asked the Professor.

Buzzy held the man's gaze for a long moment before answering. "Trevor is dead. Darius and I had a falling out."

"That's unfortunate," stated Professor Foxhorn. He continued before Buzzy could interject. "I still don't think I could be of any help to you on your expedition."

"But aren't you an active researcher in the subject of sasquatch?"

"Yes, I am, and I would never deny that part of my life," said the Professor.

Buzzy continued to press. "And haven't you documented some significant finds?"

Professor Foxhorn nodded his head in agreement. "Sure, if you agree with my theories and supporting evidence. But you have to remember something; I'm a trained scientist. I am obligated by my training and mindset to offer my evidence and theories up for peer review. For every person, like yourself, that agrees with my findings and theories, I can provide you with at least ten individuals that disagree with my findings and theories." The Professor shook his head in disappointment. "The field of bigfoot research is a joke."

Buzzy asked quietly, "Why do you do it?"

"Hmmm, good question," said the Professor as he contemplated his answer. "I want to be a part of their world. If it's true that Brock lived with a tribe of sasquatch for all of those years, I envy him. I want that experience."

The two men sat silent for a moment, and then Professor Foxhorn asked, "Why do you do it?"

"To make amends," said Buzzy without hesitation.

"Amends for what?" asked the Professor.

"When I was younger my grandfather told me he shot one," said Buzzy as his eyes glossed over remembering the story. "He regretted what he did. I've always felt like it was my responsibility to make amends for his actions."

Professor Foxhorn glanced at his bookshelf of treasures, pictures, and books for a long moment before he asked, "What is your intention for this expedition you are organizing?"

"To make contact," said Buzzy without hesitation.

Professor Foxhorn regarded the man for a moment and then sat quietly for a long time thinking about their conversation. He could tell by Buzzy's body language that he was uncomfortable with the silence but knew their conversation had come to a critical moment. The Professor broke the silence and said, "I'll attend, but on two conditions."

Buzzy's smile spread from ear to ear with excitement. "Yes?"

"No guns," stated the Professor.

"No guns," repeated Buzzy.

"And I get to bring a couple people along," stated the Professor.

"Of course," said Buzzy.

Professor Foxhorn smiled. "Then count me in." He stuck his hand out to shake Buzzy's.

Buzzy eagerly shook his hand and said, "That is wonderful, Dr. Foxhorn."

Professor Foxhorn smiled and said, "Please, call me Jonathan."

Chapter 41

Brock bounded from rock to rock until he was approximately in the middle of the Patawaemac River. He dropped his pack on a rock and stretched his arms over his head. He looked off to the west, at the setting sun, then dug through his pack until he found his water bottle and journal. He took a long drink of his water and then sat on the rock. He pulled his journal from the plastic freezer bag and opened it to the next blank page.

> July 11th
>
> I waited a week before I went back. I brought my digital recorder to try and capture any howls or wood knocks. I checked the battery before I left my house. Fully charged. However, once I arrived at George's Mill to set up the recorder the battery immediately died. I guess the universe was working against me. I hiked on anyway. I went earlier in the morning this time. The forest was quiet again and the trail lacked cobwebs. When I first entered the

tree line I did hear several bird whistles and a chattering squirrel. The further I walked along the trail the more the sense of being watched intensified. My goal was to hike to the deer skull and leave a gift. My gift of choice was a large crystal that I had acquired from Mama Boobs. I am forced to scramble across several rocks along the river's edge to meet up with the trail again. I found a muddy footprint on one of the rocks. I could clearly see the toes and heel. The print was approximately the same size as my foot. The curious thing was I don't recall seeing any mud. But then again I hadn't been walking along the river's edge until I started scrambling across those rocks. Near the footprint I also found a large spider that appeared to be stepped on and squished. I also found small bits of a turtle shell and then the full empty turtle shell about twenty yards further along the river. I documented all of these findings. I climbed back on the trail to travel the last of the distance to the deer skull.

The deer skull was gone. In its place at the base of the tree were the skeletal remains of what appeared to be a small animal. I should also note that at the time of finding the muddy footprint, something jumped or fell into the water, getting my attention. I am unaware of the Patawaemac River having jumping or flying fish. Could have been a thrown rock, but I have no way to prove it. The rest of the hike to the spot of the deer skull I noticed an abundance of leaves falling. As I examined the skeletal remains of the small animal several acorns fell around me. I pulled out my gift, the crystal, and placed it at the base of the tree. From the corner of my eye, up the slope of Niki's Hill, something moved. I scanned the hillside for a long time, but never saw anything. I climbed on top of a large fallen tree that blocked the path leading towards the Route 430 Bridge and debated if I should continue a little further. But I had the same foreboding feeling as last time I contemplated the same thing. I checked the time and decided I should head back to my truck. I walked approximately ten yards past the deer skull tree when a large rock the size of a softball smashed into a tree directly in front of me. I froze in place.

And then he stepped out from behind a tree directly onto the path. His hair was completely black and smooth. He was maybe a head taller than me. In my heart I knew he was the one that left the muddy footprint on the rock by the river. He stood there glaring at me. Watching me. I could see its chest and shoulders rise and fall with each breath it took. The fingers on both of its hands twitched and curled as if it was nervous and waited for me to do something. I could feel my own breathing and heart rate increase. I could feel time slowing down almost to a halt.

I sat. I simply sat on the ground cross-legged. This is what I wanted. This is what I had been looking for. I didn't need proof. I knew they existed. I wanted contact.

He screamed at me. He screamed loud and long. The pitch and depth of his voice reverberated through me. I could literally feel the vibration of his scream penetrate my body. I closed my eyes and waited. He stopped screaming. I opened my eyes. He was gone. He didn't know me.

I think...

Brock looked up from his journal when he heard the splash of water behind him. He turned and saw his friend, Jonathan, hopping from rock to rock towards him. Brock put his journal back in the plastic freezer bag and laid it next to him. He stood and waited for Jonathan to join him. When Jonathan reached the large rock that Brock stood on they embraced in a hug.

"Thought I'd find you out here," said Jonathan. He glanced down at Brock's journal. "Writing?"

"Yeah," said Brock as he sat back down on the rock.

Jonathan joined him and pointed to the Route 430 Bridge. "It's a long walk to that bridge from here."

Brock looked at the older man. "It is," he confirmed.

"Did I ever tell you that story?" asked Jonathan.

"I don't think," said Brock smiling. He liked Jonathan's stories. He imagined that was how Jonathan taught his classes, through stories. Brock always wanted to go watch his friend teach, but never seemed to find the time. He made a mental note to try harder in the future.

"I was on the river trail back behind us that runs parallel with the canal trail," said Jonathan as he pointed back towards the way he had come. Brock noted it was not far from the mouth of Israel Creek.

"I wasn't really looking for anything. Just hiking and exploring. Jennifer was at work. I had some time to kill. It was a beautiful day, almost noon time. The entire time I was walking on the trail I felt like I was being watched. I didn't think much of it. I just figured I was being hypersensitive that day. Then out of nowhere a rock crashed down on the path in front of me, followed by a large trunk of a dead tree blocking my path. I froze. Maybe five seconds passed. But it felt more like five minutes. I heard movement off to my right in the woods." Jonathan paused. He picked up a stone and tossed it in the water and shook his head. "I figured it was some teenagers messing with me. The canal trail was only about a hundred yards through the woods. I found some courage and turned to look. As soon as I turned my head to look a rock the size of a football came rocketing out of the trees and just missed me. The rock shattered against the tree. I realized at that moment it wasn't teenagers. I was instantly scared for my life. Whoever or whatever threw that rock had some strength. It was clear whatever threw the rock and pushed down the tree did not want me there. I honestly felt trapped."

Brock looked at his friend and asked, "What did you do?"

Jonathan laughed. "I ran for the river! I crashed through the undergrowth along the river's edge. Jumped on a few rocks and then into the water." Jonathan visibly shivered as he remembered and retold the story. "The water was colder than I expected. It took my breath away! I stumbled and fell, fully submerged. I kept moving. Luckily, the river was only waist deep. I thought I heard some crashing behind me. Maybe more rocks being thrown at me? I thought I heard a deep growl or maybe a scream? But I can't be sure. I was making too much noise running and falling in the water. I never looked back. I clearly wasn't wanted there and I wasn't going to push my luck."

Brock couldn't help but smile. "How'd you get back to your truck?"

Jonathan chuckled to himself like he told a funny a joke. "I did what any sane grown man would do." He paused. "I waded upstream through the river all the way to the Route 430 Bridge."

Brock laughed. "Shut up!" He pushed his friend. "You did not?"

Jonathan nodded his head in acknowledgement. "I sure the hell did. There was no way in hell I was getting back on that trail and looping around to my truck. I was going to give whatever threw those rocks at me enough time and space to calm down before I stepped foot in those woods again."

"Seriously, it had to take you hours to get to the bridge and back to your truck?" asked Brock.

"It did. I missed my class that night. But I didn't care," said Jonathan. "Once I got to the bridge I was able to hitch a ride back to my truck. The gentleman that picked me up wanted to know why I was wet. I told him I fell in. I figured that was more believable than telling the truth."

Brock nodded his head in agreement. The two men sat in silence for a little while. Brock contemplated telling Jonathan about his encounter. He decided not to. He rarely shared any of his encounters with Jonathan. Brock looked at his friend and asked, "Is that when you started searching?"

Jonathan nodded his head. "Pretty much." He paused as if to collect his thoughts and looked towards the setting sun. "Jennifer and I have always believed sasquatch was—is real. We had read stories and watched documentaries on television. We had our own experiences while camping and hiking to convince us that it was possible for a creature to elude the detection of man. But we never believed it was possible for such a large elusive creature to live so close to our home. So close to a major metropolitan city."

"The capital is over an hour away," stated Brock.

"It is," confirmed Jonathan. "Still, I grew up in that city. To me it's not that far away in the scheme of things."

"This is actually a prime habitat spot," stated Brock.

"Yes, with the river, the mountain range, the hiking trails, and the canal system, they do have many access points," agreed Jonathan.

"Plus this place is special," said Brock in almost a whisper.

"There is an energy about this place. I think that attracts them more than the habitat," offered Jonathan.

"The ley lines. The energy portals," said Brock.

"Yes," said Jonathan. "Same reason why there are reports of large cats, like black panthers and such, spotted in these mountains, when they aren't supposed to exist in this part of North America."

"I'm kind of glad no one believes us," said Brock. "Keeps people away."

Jonathan pursed his lips. "From a scientist point of view, it's frustrating that my theories are ridiculed by the bigfoot research community." He paused, "But yes, I agree it does keep the glory hunters away."

Brock knew if he shared with Jonathan his experiences and findings of the sasquatch on Niki's Hill, it would help validate his friend's theories. At the same time his findings were his. His stories. His memories. His experiences. Brock wasn't ready to let them go yet. It was almost as if when he told his friend what he had experienced, the experience would disappear. It would no longer be real. Brock wasn't ready to lose the realness yet.

Secretly, Brock felt guilty withholding any sasquatch findings from Jonathan because the man had done so much for him in the past four years. Both Jonathan and Jennifer had provided him with food, shelter, and safety as he transitioned back to society. Brock considered them family, like an older brother and sister. However, Brock had made such an effort over the past four years to keep his time in the woods a secret that he often felt like what he experienced was a dream. It was Jennifer who suggested he write his memories in a journal. At times he would tell Jonathan and Jennifer a few things that happened to him. What he appreciated the most was that they never asked what happened in the woods or demanded details. They would simply listen and accept what he had to say as the truth.

Jonathan interrupted Brock's train of thought by asking, "Want to go to the Olympics with me?"

"What?" asked Brock.

"I was approached earlier today by a gentleman who is putting together a sasquatch expedition in the Olympic National Forest. He asked me to attend," reported Jonathan.

Brock laughed. "And you agreed?"

"Yes I did," said Jonathan. "Under two conditions."

"Which were?"

"No guns, and if I could bring my own team along," answered Jonathan.

"You have a team?" asked Brock.

Jonathan smiled. "Kinda."

"Who? Me and Jennifer?" asked Brock.

Jonathan looked away. "Jennifer can't make it because of work."

"Just me?"

"Yes," confirmed Jonathan.

Brock shook his head. "I don't think it's a good idea."

Even as the words left Brock's lips he knew he was lying. He wasn't sure if it was a shift in the wind, the fresh chirp of the bird that flew over, or the immediate racing of his heart, but he knew this was his opportunity to find his tribe. Abigale was right in the sense that he didn't fit in with his own kind anymore. But she was wrong that he was something special. Or even a spirit walker. He was just a young man misplaced in a world he didn't belong. If he was a true spirit walker he would have found a shimmering portal long ago and gone back to the world where he belonged.

Jonathan exhaled deeply and looked across the river towards George's Mill and Niki's Hill. "Look, Brock, you spend a lot of time alone in these woods. I know you have seen and experienced more related to these creatures than you are willing to share with me." He paused. "I don't ask. I won't ask. You have your reasons for keeping your experiences to yourself. I respect that." He paused again and threw a rock out into the water. "I'll be honest. I want you there for selfish reasons. I want you there for support."

The two men sat quietly for some time before Jonathan spoke again. "Plus, Jennifer doesn't want me to go alone."

Brock laughed and relented. "Okay, I'll go. But only under one condition."

Jonathan narrowed his eyes at his friend. "What?"

"We bring Mama Boobs."

"Are you serious?" asked Jonathan, not knowing if he should laugh or take his friend seriously. "What the hell for?"

Brock looked out across the river in the direction of Mama Boobs's house. "I owe it to her."

"I don't know," said Jonathan as he shook his head.

Brock looked at his friend. "I'm sure there will be a base camp. She can secure camp and manage the meals."

Jonathan thought about it and agreed. The two men chatted for a bit longer about nothing in general until the last rays of the day's sun disappeared. Once the sun had set and the first stars of the night started to twinkle above the river, Brock stood to leave. He pulled on his backpack and heard two distinct wood knocks echoing from Niki's Hill. He squatted down next to Jonathan and froze.

Jonathan asked in a whisper, "Did you hear that?"

Brock nodded his head yes.

A few second passed before the two men heard two more wood knocks. Brock stared into the dark forest across from the river and whispered, "They want to feed. We have to go."

Quietly the two men scrambled across the river rocks to the canal trail. They hiked back to their trucks in silence.

Chapter 42

Jonathan walked up to his house in the dark and could see Jennifer through the kitchen window doing the dishes. He could smell dinner cooking. He smiled. She used the same spices every time, and he could honestly say that he loved her cooking. He also loved that she cleaned up the dishes as she prepared and cooked the meal. He had never experienced that before. It made sense and he picked up the practice. He stopped on the path leading to the house and smiled. He loved his home. He loved his wife. He loved his family. He loved his life.

He walked through the front door and kicked off his shoes. He placed his bag in the office and walked into the kitchen to give Jennifer a hug and a kiss. She greedily took in his kisses and hugged him with an intensity that never faded. When she pulled away she handed him a glass of red wine and picked up one herself. She took a sip and asked, "Did you talk to him?"

Jonathan nodded. "He agreed to go."

"Oh good!" said Jennifer with true excitement in her voice. She turned and shuffled the chicken around in the skillet.

Jonathan watched her move and smiled. He took a drink of wine and said, "There is more to him than we know."

Without looking at him, she said, "Of course there is. We've always known that."

Jonathan took another sip. "He has experienced more than we have," he added.

"Yes, he has. He spends at least twenty hours a week alone in the woods," said Jennifer. "In some ways he's antisocial."

Jonathan smiled. "It does take a lot to convince him to join us for a game of cards or dinner." He paused. "We heard wood knocks tonight. Twice."

Jennifer turned and looked at him. "Really?"

Jonathan took a drink of wine. "Hmm. But it was more than that." He paused looking for the words. "He knew what they meant. It's hard to explain. But something inside of me told me that he knew what those wood knocks meant."

"I could see that about him," said Jennifer. "He does have an ease about him when he is in the woods."

"He does," confirmed Jonathan. "His movements are fluid."

Jennifer corrected, "It's more than just his movements. He has a sixth sense about the forest. He's at home there."

Jonathan grabbed the two plates and walked them over to Jennifer. "He does."

Jennifer kissed him on the cheek. "I'm glad he's going with you to the Olympics." She paused and then added, "It'll be good for the both of you."

Chapter 43

Mama Boobs sat in her rollie chair with her big arms crossed over her body, resting on her boobs. "And how the hell do you think I am going to be able to get to this base camp?"

Brock shrugged his shoulders. "I don't know. A truck? A jeep? A four-wheeler?"

"Pft, a four-wheeler? Are you crazy? This body hasn't been on a four-wheeler since I was your age," spat out Mama Boobs.

Brock smiled.

"Stop your smiling, boy," snapped Mama Boobs. "This is a mean joke you're pullin'."

"It's no joke. I'm being serious," said Brock. "We fly out next month. I'll figure out some way to get you to base camp." He paused and smiled. "Trust me."

"Pft, trust you to get me killed," said Mama Boobs as she looked away towards her parakeet.

Brock leaned back against the couch cushion and waited. Without looking at him, Mama Boobs said, "Fine, I'll go."

Brock smiled. "I promise it will be an amazing experience. The

Olympics are unbelievable."

"Hmpf," grunted Mama Boobs as she pinched some bird feed into the cage.

Brock pushed off the couch and moved towards the front door to finish the chores he came to complete. Mama Boobs called out his name, "Brock."

He turned back to face her.

"Thank you."

Chapter 44

Jennifer was antsy whenever she and Jonathan were apart. It wasn't right. It didn't feel right. They were supposed to be together at all times, doing all things together. She felt perhaps it got on his nerves that she always wanted to be together. But he was a good sport about it. He never complained. He always accepted her. Even if it was work-related events or him peeing when he got up in the morning. She wanted to be by his side. Until Jonathan was by her side again she would walk. Other than Jonathan, walking was the only thing that gave her solace or quieted her soul.

The sun had already set, but there was still enough light for her to see the walking paths through their community. As she walked, she got lost in her thoughts about Jonathan and their life together and found herself on top of the large hill behind their house. She stopped and admired their home and smiled at the thought of how perfect it was for them and their family. She then turned and watched the moon peek over Furnace Mountain. The moon was going to be bright and full. It was one of those nights that she wouldn't need a flashlight to find her way home. She wished for Jonathan to be as lucky in the Olympic National Forest, but she suspected he would have a lot of rain.

A rustling sound caught her attention off to the right in the tall grass. She swept her gaze over the tall grass and the few trees but didn't see anything. She turned back to the moon and then heard a low grunt. The skin on the back of her neck bristled. Maybe it was a deer, she thought. It grunted again. She slowly turned to face the tall grass. Whatever was grunting, she was going to face it head on. To her right she saw a flash of something bound across the trail into the thicket of grass. It was a deer, she told herself. She heard a third and louder grunt just a few feet in front of her in the grass. The grass rustled as if something was moving and then it stood up.

In the moon's light, Jennifer watched as a red-haired sasquatch stood up in front of her just ten feet away. The creature stared her down and huffed loudly. Wrapped around one leg was a smaller sasquatch, peering out at Jennifer like a small kid. Though her heart raced, her breathing quickened, and her muscles tensed—she was ready, in fact, to run in absolute terror! She instead, incredibly, found herself smiling. Almost on the verge of laughing.

The red-haired sasquatch turned its upper body and head towards the moon and grunted at it, then turned back to face Jennifer. Jennifer watched the creature in amazement and the younger sasquatch watched her just as intently. When the sasquatch grunted, Jennifer felt the force of the grunt ripple through her. She quickly glanced at the moon and then the creature and she suddenly understood. They knew she was alone. They knew that Jonathan left for the expedition.

The sasquatch looked down at the younger one and then back to Jennifer. Jennifer knew that universal look. The sasquatch wanted to be with her mate, just like Jennifer wanted to be with Jonathan. Just like her, the sasquatch had obligations. Then the moment passed and the sasquatch whooped twice. Two more sasquatches emerged from a clump of trees to join the red-haired one and together they moved off towards the adjoining forest.

Jennifer was never one to participate in anything. It was a running joke between her and Jonathan that she was not a participatory individual. For reasons beyond her comprehension, she whooped one time. The red-haired sasquatch turned her entire upper body to look back at Jennifer and she swore that she saw a slight smile spread across the sasquatch's lips in the moonlight.

Chapter 45

Brock sat at the small table with Jonathan as they waited for Buzzy White and the rest of the expedition team to join them. Buzzy had made reservations for everyone at a European-style hotel in the heart of Seattle as a jumping off point. Brock and Jonathan were unaware of what a European-style hotel was, but they quickly figured it out when they opened the door to their room that was no bigger than a two-man tent. Jonathan laughed and said, "Well, I guess he's getting us prepped." There was no bathroom. That was down the hall for everyone to share. Mama Boobs was having the hardest time with it because of the stairs and lack of elevator.

Buzzy insisted that everyone meet in the common room on the fourth floor before venturing off into the deep forest for the next few weeks. He was a little put off when Mama Boobs refused because of the four flights of stairs she could not climb. Instead, she slowly made her way down to the two vans where the equipment and supplies were being packed. Jonathan and Brock made their way to the common room and found a small breakfast of coffee and bagels spread out on one of the tables. They helped themselves to the food and drinks and sat by a window that overlooked one of the many city streets. Brock pushed open the window to let a blast of chilled air into the stuffy converted attic. He stared out the window and watched as young college-age students hurried to classes at the nearby university.

Jonathan put his coffee cup down when he heard the creak of the stairs as someone ascended them. Buzzy walked through the door first, followed by one other man. Jonathan immediately shot to his feet, almost knocking over the table, and practically yelled, "What the hell is this?"

Brock instantly knew both men. Buzzy was a friend of his father and Jake was the mountain man who had visited him in the hospital. He stared in shock as the two men moved further into the room. They were the last two men he suspected to be joining them on the expedition. Brock watched as the two men glanced at them but it appeared that they didn't recognize him.

Jake stepped forward past Buzzy to get a coffee cup, waved his hand in dismissal at Jonathan, and said, "Chill, brother, I have no bad blood towards you."

Brock watched as the anger seethed through Jonathan. His friend clenched and unclenched his fists in rage. Buzzy moved towards Jonathan with both hands up in defense. "I didn't tell you beforehand because I didn't think you would agree to join us."

"You're damn right," shot Jonathan.

"I needed a tracker and he's the best there is," defended Buzzy.

"He's a killer," argued Jonathan.

The man smirked and grunted. "Prove it, Professor."

Buzzy reached out and touched the man's arm. "Jake, please." He then turned to Jonathan, "I apologize for not being upfront with you. But I need him and I need you."

Brock looked up at his friend and watched as he reluctantly sat down. Brock knew what he was feeling. He was stuck. Buzzy had paid for all of their expenses and gear to be on this expedition, so they couldn't just leave now. Well, they could, thought Brock. But on the flight out to Seattle, Jonathan and Brock both confirmed what the other was feeling: this trip was important. They didn't know why, it was just something they felt deep inside of them.

Brock glanced over to Jake and caught the burly man staring at him. It unnerved him because he knew that Jake recognized him. He turned to Jonathan and said, "It'll be okay; let it go."

Jake piped in, "Yeah, Professor, let it go; we're on the same side now."

Jonathan glared at Jake. Brock could tell by the look on his friend's face that a half dozen words and comments were flying through his head in response to Jake, but Jonathan didn't say a word. Instead he looked at Buzzy and asked, "What time do we leave?"

Buzzy glanced at Jake and then Jonathan. "We just need to check out of the hotel."

Jonathan pushed up from the table and glared down at Jake. "We'll never be on the same side."

"Suit yourself," answered Jake.

Jonathan then turned to Buzzy. "I expect you at least held up your end of the bargain in regards to there being no guns."

"As promised, no guns," said Buzzy proudly.

"Pft," replied Jake.

Jonathan glanced at Jake and then addressed Brock. "I'll be downstairs with Shelly, waiting." Jonathan turned and walked out of the common room into the stairwell.

Buzzy exhaled audibly and shook his head. "That went better than expected," said Buzzy.

"Whatever; I don't care," said Jake. He then looked at Brock. "He's the magnet, not Dr. Professor."

Brock instantly felt uncomfortable being alone with the two men. Jake smiled at him; that confirmed that he recognized him. "Good to see you again kid," said Jake.

Brock knitted his eyebrows together and gave his head a quick shake. "Sorry, never seen you before."

Jake stood from the table with a chuckle. "If you say so, kid." He walked out of the room.

Recognition swept over Buzzy's face, and he asked, "Brock Blackwood?"

Brock made eye contact with the man and said nothing.

"I knew your father and brother." Buzzy leaned closer to Brock and, in a whisper, said, "I wanted Darius for this expedition but I couldn't find him. Do you know where he is?"

"I haven't seen either of them in years," said Brock.

Buzzy leaned back in his chair and stared at Brock for a moment, nodded his head, and then asked, "You ready?" No, thought Brock, but instead he nodded his head yes and stood from the table. Together they walked down to the lobby.

Chapter 46

Brock carried his pack down to the two waiting vans by the hotel entrance and saw Mama Boobs fussing over her own cooking gear that she insisted on bringing. A larger man that Brock had never seen before tossed Mama Boobs's bag of pots and pans into the back of the black van and grunted a response to her as he walked away to the second van. Mama Boobs saw Brock and turned to him for support. "Did you see that lug toss my stuff around like it wasn't important? That is no way to treat the chef."

Brock tried not to smile, but it did strike him funny. He asked, "Who is he?"

"Pft, I don't know that other man," said Mama Boobs as she nodded her head towards Jake. "Said his friend's name was Butch, short for Butcher."

Brock glanced over to the man known as Butcher. He was tall, at least over six feet, with a shaved head and face with a lean build. Brock saw several military-style black and grey tattoos on the man's arms and legs as he continued to pack the second van. That was when Brock noticed that Butcher and Jake were both wearing shorts in near freezing, wet rainy weather. Mama Boobs broke into his thoughts and said, "I told them it was a stupid name. His friend Jake said he earned the nickname."

Brock nodded his head in acknowledgement but didn't continue the conversation. Instead, he reached into the van and rearranged Mama Boobs's bag of cooking pans and packed his own gear. He helped Mama Boobs into the front passenger seat and took a seat in the back. Jonathan jumped in the driver's seat and fiddled with a stack of papers and a map. Brock assumed his friend was trying to avoid any form of communication because he was still fuming over Jake joining the expedition. Brock knew there was history between the two men and didn't want to intensify his friend's anger by bringing the subject up. He leaned back in his seat and stared out the van window at the passing college students and waited for the trip to begin.

Brock didn't mind the three-and-half-hour van ride to the expedition spot until they reached the last thirty miles of curvy gravel road they had to cross. In all honesty, he preferred to walk. Planes, trains, boats, and automobiles made him sick. Granted, it probably would have taken him a few days to walk the almost two hundred miles they had traveled in the past few hours. But at least he wouldn't have been nauseous and could have taken his time to admire the waterfalls and lakes they passed as opposed to the two-second glimpse he got through a dirty window.

Jonathan slowed the van as they turned into a single lane gravel road and passed through a gated archway. Scrolled across the archway in cursive writing were the words "Hoyt's Ranch." Mama Boobs spoke up first. "Where the hell are we?"

"I don't know," answered Jonathan. "This trip just keeps turning into a big mystery."

"It'll be okay," whispered Brock.

Mama Boobs glanced back at him and Jonathan simply nodded his head. After a short drive on the property they pulled the van up to a log cabin of a house. Through the front windshield Brock watched as a man of Native American descent walked out of the house toward their van. Jonathan climbed out of the van and Brock slid the side door open and stepped out in time to see the Indian's hand outstretched in front of him. Brock quickly glanced at it and then shook it. The man had a firm handshake and a broad smile on his face.

"Welcome to my grandfather's ranch; my name is Wynn," said the man.

"My name's Brock." He then turned to Jonathan as his friend rounded the corner of the van, "This is Jonathan." The two men shook hands. "And our friend, Shelly," said Brock.

Mama Boobs had opened the van door and was slowly swinging her first leg out the door. "Let me help you," Wynn said quickly and turned to run off to the porch of the house. He quickly returned with a small stepstool for Mama Boobs to step down on. She thanked him as he held her hand as she slid more than climbed out of the van. Jonathan asked, "I didn't know there were ranches on the Olympic Peninsula?"

Wynn nodded his head yes and said, in a slight accent, "There are a few, mostly owned by my people. My grandfather Hoyt was one of the first to purchase land on the Peninsula."

"Interesting; I would love to meet your grandfather," said Jonathan.

Wynn laughed and glanced at Jonathan and Brock. "Only if you are a spirit walker." He paused, held his gaze at Brock for a moment, and then finished, "He travels with the Great Spirit now."

"I'm sorry to hear of your loss," said Jonathan.

Wynn laughed and slapped Jonathan on the shoulder. "No loss."

He then patted his chest over his heart twice with his open palm and said, "His spirit is with me always."

Buzzy broke up the conversation by grabbing Wynn on the shoulder and turning him around. Wynn laughed and embraced Buzzy in a bear hug and said, "Old friend, it has been too long."

Buzzy laughed and agreed, "It has been."

Wynn pushed his friend out at arm's length, still holding his shoulders, and said, "At least our hairy friends give you cause to visit me."

Buzzy smiled and nodded his head in agreement. Wynn then turned to the gathered group and said, "My land is your land. The lady will stay in the cabin over there." He pointed to a rustic wooden building that couldn't be larger than a one-bedroom apartment. "The rest of you I assume have tents?"

The men in the group all nodded their head in agreement. Wynn turned to Mama Boobs. "I'm thankful you have agreed to be the chef. I do not envy the task of feeding this motley crew."

"As long as there is a full kitchen in that building, and Lugnuts over there..." she motioned towards Butch, "stays away from my stuff, I'll be fine."

Butch and Jake both grunted at the same time as if one brain controlled both mouths. Wynn laughed and gave Mama Boobs a sidewise hug and let his arm linger on her shoulder. Brock thought he saw her blush. Wynn continued, "Get set up and let's talk over a fire." He nodded his head towards a ring of rocks and log stumps halfway between Mama Boobs's cabin and what looked like a fenced corral with a spiked roof.

Chapter 47

Jonathan sat on the stump of a log by the fire and stared into the flames. The heat felt good on his chilled body. He wore a thin waterproof jacket in anticipation of rain. In the three days that he had been in the Pacific Northwest it had not actually rained, but there was a mist in constant swirl. He heard movement off to his left and turned to see Brock walking towards him. He smiled and waited for his friend to sit.

Brock sat on the log next to Jonathan and said, "It gets dark out here quick."

Jonathan nodded his head in agreement and said, "It's like God flicks a switch and turns out the sun. Is Shelly all situated?"

Brock smiled. "I think so." He paused. "She complains a lot, but I think it's more just to hear herself talk."

Jonathan chuckled. "I'm sure. I bet her birds are happy for the break."

Soon Buzzy, Jake, and Butch joined Jonathan and Brock by the fire. Wynn helped Mama Boobs and brought her a special chair. Jonathan looked around the fire at the faces staring into the red and orange flames and agreed it was a motley crew of individuals. He didn't know what to expect over the next few weeks. From his conversations with Buzzy, Jonathan got the impression that the man had good intentions, but poor choice in companions if he excluded himself and Brock. Then again sometimes leaders needed shady characters in order to do the messy work. Jonathan just didn't want there to be messy work to begin with. He knew from experience that the man known as Jake was a killer and a hunter. He still remembered his confrontation with the man in the woods on Furnace Mountain and in the hospital room with Brock. Jake may have shaved his bushy beard to a goatee, but Jonathan was sure that the man was still guilty of unimaginable things. Jonathan remembered his conversation with Darius also. Darius had warned him about Jake and his intentions. Jonathan wouldn't be surprised that if Jake was confronted by a sasquatch he would try to kill it. In Jonathan's eyes, that compromised the purpose of this expedition.

Jake's companion, Butch, almost seemed dimwitted, but Jonathan was sure that was a ruse. The man hadn't said more than two words to Jonathan since the start of the trip. Jonathan was already irritated with Butch because of his stupid soul patch of a goatee on his shaved face, not to mention his association with Jake. He then realized that he wasn't being fair to the man and shook his head to try and remove the negative thoughts. But when he looked at Butch again he still didn't like him.

Wynn seemed genuine and smitten with Mama Boobs, which cracked him up. Then again, like his father used to say, "There is always someone for everyone." Jonathan watched as Wynn threw a log on the fire and asked Buzzy, "Why bring us here?"

Buzzy glanced at Wynn. Wynn smiled and stared into the fire and said, "They are watching us right now."

Jonathan restrained himself from looking into the darkness and noticed that everyone else did the same except for Mama Boobs. She turned in her chair and eagerly looked around as if she was looking for a sasquatch to shake her hand and introduce himself. Jake and Butch exchanged a glance. Jonathan made eye contact with Buzzy.

Brock broke the silence and asked, "What kind of ranch is this?"

"Goats," answered Wynn.

"Goats?" asked Shelly.

Wynn threw another stick on the fire and nodded his head. "Well, I try, but our hairy friends like the taste of goats." He paused with a smile. "At night I corral the goats to keep them safe, but during the day I occasionally lose one."

Buzzy asked, "Is that why you have spikes on the roof of the corral?"

"Yes. At night our hairy friends would reach over the fence of the corral and pick them out and carry them off." He prodded the fire with a stick to readjust the logs. "The spiked roof helps prevent me from losing my goats at night. But during the day I have to let them graze. I can't watch them all at all times. From time to time one goes missing."

Jonathan asked, "How do you know it's a sasquatch stealing them?"

Wynn shot Jonathan a look at hearing the word sasquatch. "I find their remains. Their legs are snapped in half. Their heads smashed as if slammed against a tree or rock. No other animal kills in that way."

Butch spoke up for the first time with his deep resonate voice. "Have you seen one?"

Wynn stared into the fire. "I have."

The group sat in silence for a long time before Mama Boobs asked, "What happened?"

Wynn looked at her and said, "I've seen them several times since I was a young boy living here with my grandfather. He taught me how to listen to my heart to know when they are near." He reached out and touched Mama Boobs's chest just above her heart and then pointed to her stomach. "If you silence the noise inside of you, you will feel them in your heart and stomach. When I was younger I would not pay attention to what I felt. I ignored my heart and therefore wouldn't encounter one."

Butch asked almost impatiently, "So it's been years since you saw one?"

Wynn looked at Butch. "I am human. I don't always listen to my heart. Just as you." He paused and stared into the fire as he told the group about his most recent encounter. "I was repairing my fence a few weeks back. I was alone. My assistant had gone into town to get some supplies. I was using a small sledgehammer to bang a new post into the ground. I wasn't paying attention. When I finished I looked up, and about twenty or so yards away from me stood one of our hairy friends."

Mama Boobs asked, "What did it look like?"

Wynn chuckled more to himself than anything else. "Scary."

"Pft," said Butch.

Wynn shot the man a look. "Maybe you don't respect them?"

Butch countered, "What's there to respect? They're just wild animals."

Wynn shook his head in disagreement. "No, they are spirit creatures."

Butch waved his hand at Wynn and pulled out a knife to carve on a piece of wood that he held in his hands. Wynn turned back to Mama Boobs. "He was the biggest one I have ever seen. He had to be at least twelve feet tall and easily six feet wide across the shoulders and pure white."

At the sound of hearing that the sasquatch was pure white, Jonathan noticed Butch and Jake exchanging a look of recognition.

Brock asked, "Pure white?"

Wynn nodded his head yes. Mama Boobs asked, "What happened?"

Wynn looked at her. "It screamed. I ran." He looked away from her and into the fire. "I haven't been back since."

Buzzy broke the silence. "Tell them about the woman."

"Hmmm, the woman," said Wynn as he nodded his head in agreement while staring into the fire.

"What woman?" asked Jonathan.

Buzzy waited for Wynn to answer the question and then answered it himself. "About two months ago Wynn contacted me about his encounter at the fence post. He's been hearing wood knocks and calls for almost a year now. During that time he has had glimpses of a woman in the woods."

Brock asked, "A human woman?"

Wynn nodded his head in acknowledgement.

Buzzy continued, "Because of the amount of secluded and secure land and the recent sustained activity on Wynn's property, that's why I picked this location."

Mama Boobs asked, "How much land is on this ranch?"

"Hundred plus," answered Wynn.

"That was how much land my Pa owned back east before he sold it all off in parcels," said Mama Boobs.

Wynn looked towards the night sky. "The Great Spirit owns this land. I am just a caretaker. It is not my right to sell it. My right is to oversee it. To protect it."

Mama Boobs reached out and rubbed Wynn's back.

"What about this woman?" asked Jake, bringing the subject back to Wynn's encounter.

Wynn did not move to answer the question. Buzzy looked to Wynn, and Jonathan caught the slightest nod of Wynn's head as if granting Buzzy permission to tell them. Buzzy turned towards Jake. "Wynn has seen a half-naked woman darting in and out of the trees at dusk or early morning. He thought she was a wood nymph until the day he had the encounter with the White One."

Jonathan asked, "You mean at the fence post?"

Wynn nodded his head. "As I turned and ran I saw her standing not far from the hairy one, watching me."

Butch grunted, "A beast hag."

"What?" asked Jonathan as he turned to face Butch and Jake.

Butch answered, "A beast hag is a woman who thinks bigfoot is a big, gentle, hairy beast, like Harry from the movie Harry and the Hendersons. They run around in the woods leaving gifts and food for bigfoot like they are a pet. Hoping to catch a glimpse or take a picture. They don't think bigfoot is dangerous and deadly."

Brock spoke up first. "Neither do I."

Jonathan followed, "Nor I."

Butch stared at the two of them before answering, "Then you both are beast hags."

Brock sat in silence, staring at the man. Jonathan's blood started to boil and he had visions of shoving a red hot flaming log into the man's face. Buzzy's voice broke into his thoughts before he reached down to find a log to club the man with.

"Gentleman, please," pleaded Buzzy.

"Pft," grunted Butch and shook his head in disgust.

Jake asked, "What was she wearing?"

Again Buzzy looked to Wynn and then answered the question. "Wynn said her dark hair hung past her breasts and she wore what appeared to be a deerskin skirt, and she was barefoot."

Butch and Jake exchanged looks again as if they were having their own private telepathic conversation. Jonathan saw the exchange and asked Jake, "Is that significant to you?"

Jake scrunched his lips together as if in thought and then shook his head. "Honestly it's probably some stupid hippy woman runnin' around the back woods playin' Injun and teasing poor Wynn," laughed Jake in a mocking tone of voice as he nodded his head toward Wynn.

Wynn threw a log on the fire that caused the flames to momentarily explode and silence everyone. He then spoke, "Elders from tribes under the great sky of the Great Spirit have spoken for generations of our hairy brothers kidnapping our kind, especially women. Sometimes men. Sometimes woman go with the hairy brother because they are better hunters. Better providers." He stopped and glared right at Jake. "It is no stupid hippy woman playin' Injun tryin' to tease me. She is the White One's mate."

The image of Abigale hugging Numyc flashed through his mind. As if on cue, everyone sitting around the fire heard a loud, high-pitched wail of a scream that lasted for several seconds and ended with a low-pitched raspy grunt from the nearby tree line. Jonathan quickly scanned the faces of everyone sitting around the fire. Jake and Butch systematically turned their backs to the fire and peered into the darkness of the tree line. Buzzy nervously glanced from Jake and Butch to Wynn. Wynn stared into the fire, and Mama Boobs rested her hand on Wynn's back and stared into the darkness. Brock immediately stood and stared into the darkness of the forest. He was visibly rigid and tense as if ready to react to a crisis. Jonathan quickly stood next to his friend and asked, "Are you okay?"

At first Brock didn't respond. Jonathan shook his friend's shoulder harder and stepped in front of his vision. Brock's eyes focused on Jonathan's face. He stood still for a moment longer before answering in a whisper, "I wasn't expecting that."

When Jonathan stood he saw that Butch was gone. Before he could ask where he went, Wynn stood and looked at Jonathan. "They want us to go." He then turned and offered his hand to help Mama

Boobs.

Jonathan nodded his head in agreement.

Chapter 48

Two days later Brock approached the one-room cabin that had become Mama Boobs's domain and could hear her and Wynn laughing on the other side of the wooden door. He smiled at the sound. It made him feel good that she found someone to bring her a moment of joy. He raised his fist to knock and heard Wynn's voice call out, "Come in, friend, we know you are there."

Brock dropped his fist to the door handle and pushed it open to see Wynn and Mama Boobs sitting at the small table near the fire place. A black cauldron hung above the fire in the fireplace and a delicious smell filled the small cabin. Brock smiled and nodded his head at Wynn and said, "Good morning, Shelly."

Mama Boobs looked at Brock and smiled. "Good morning, hon. Sit." She patted the seat next to her.

Brock pushed the door closed and dropped his daypack on the ground by his chair. He sat. As he did, Mama Boobs reached down and picked up a medium-size sack from the wooden floor. From the sack she pulled out a small leather pouch. She glanced at Wynn and then Brock. Brock smiled to let her know it was okay to continue.

Mama Boobs asked, "Do you have the large quartz crystal?"

"I do; it's in my bag wrapped in cloth," said Brock.

"Good," said Mama Boobs. She then pulled out several stones from the small leather pouch and laid them on the table. She handled each stone with delicate care and took a moment to admire each one of them.

Wynn quietly asked, as if not to disturb Mama Boobs as she examined each stone, "What is your intention, Brock?"

At hearing his name he broke away from the trance he'd fallen into watching Mama Boobs place each stone on the table. He looked up at Wynn. "I plan to find a quiet, secluded spot to create a crystal grid."

"To summon our hairy friends?" asked Wynn.

"Hmm, not necessarily summon them." Brock scrunched his lips together in thought. "More as a place of safety. A way to show my good intention."

Wynn pressed his fingers from his right hand to his heart and said, "They feel your good intention here when you step into their domain." He then squinted his eyes as if he was peering deeper into Brock's soul. He then pulled back his head and smiled. "But you know this already."

Brock held the gaze with Wynn for a moment longer and looked away when Mama Boobs said, "I picked stones and crystals based on courage and protection, focus, and communication." She picked up two stones and placed them in front of Brock. "These are petrified wood and crazy lace agate. They will provide courage, protection, and focus." She then picked up a blue stone and moved it closer to Brock. "This is a blue lace agate. This will help open your throat chakra," she said as she motioned to her throat, "to enhance your communication abilities." She then moved a greenish, moss-covered-looking stone towards Brock. "This is moss agate. This will help with communicating with nature spirits."

Wynn reached out, rubbed Mama Boobs's shoulder, and said, "Hmm, good choice. Our hairy friends are spirits of our Great Mother Earth." Brock watched as the smile on Mama Boobs's face stretched from ear to ear. He thought she blushed, but it was hard to tell in the dim light of the cabin.

Mama Boobs then moved another stone closer to him that looked almost like a petrified eye. "This is apatite, or cat's eye. This also will help you communicate with nature." She then moved two more stones to him and said, "And these are Brecciated Jasper and Leopardskin Jasper. They will help you communicate with the animal kingdom in both the physical and spiritual planes."

"Thank you for helping me with this, Shelly," said Brock as he started to drop each stone into the leather pouch.

Mama Boobs reached into the other sack and pulled out a quartz wand and bundle of sage and handed it to him. "Remember to cleanse the site first, and I want my wand back," she said with a smile.

"I promise to bring it back," reassured Brock.

Wynn stood from the table and moved to the back corner of the cabin and removed something from a high shelf. He returned to the table and extended an open palm to Brock. In his palm was a rough-looking black and white stone. Wynn motioned his hand forward for Brock to take the stone. He did and examined it more closely. "That is the Day and Night stone. It attracts strong magic and is often carried by our shamans." Wynn paused and then continued, "It was my grandfather's."

Brock offered it back to Wynn. "It's beautiful."

Wynn sat down, making no effort to retrieve the stone from Brock's hand. "It has waited here for your arrival. I have only been a keeper until the Great Spirit has brought the true owner, which is you."

Brock offered his hand again. "I can't; it was your grandfather's."

Wynn shook his head slightly and said, "You, my friend, are a shaman." He leaned closer across the table and whispered, "You have walked with the spirits of our hairy friends." He then leaned back in his chair.

Brock glanced at Mama Boobs to gauge her reaction but she almost appeared to be in a trance staring at Wynn. Brock guessed that either Wynn had some magical powers and froze time to prevent Mama Boobs from hearing their conversation, or she was so enamored with Wynn and his knowledge of the spirit world that she just fell deeper in love with him and didn't care who was witness to the event.

A sharp knock on the cabin door made Mama Boobs jump and Brock relax. Brock dropped the Day and Night stone in the leather pouch and pulled the strings closed as Jonathan walked into the cabin. He greeted everyone and sat down next to Brock. Brock watched as his friend looked over the quartz wand and sage.

"Want me to go with you?" Jonathan asked.

Brock shook his head. "I got this."

"What if those goons bother you?" asked Jonathan, referring to Jake and Butch.

Wynn laughed. "Oh, I sent them on a goose chase elsewhere."

Mama Boobs asked, "Do you need paper?"

Brock shook his head no and pulled out a copy of the famous picture of Patty, the sasquatch that Patterson and Gimlin had captured on film so many years ago, to show everyone gathered. Wynn grunted in approval. Jonathan nodded his head in agreement. Mama Boobs reached out and squeezed Brock's hand. "Be patient, it may take time."

"I know," Brock said as he stood to leave.

Chapter 49

Butch sat in the tree, leaning against the thick trunk about sixty feet off the ground. He had a direct line of sight to the fence post that Wynn had talked about a few nights back at the fire. Before climbing the tree he had scouted the area around the fence post and found Wynn's discarded sledgehammer, fence wire, and spun-out tire tracks from his all-terrain four-by-four. Surrounding the fence post was a small circular area of about thirty yards free of trees. The ground was covered in moss and dead wood, which Butch thought was perfect if the need arose to sneak up on the boy.

Jake suspected that Brock was the key to this expedition. And Butch knew from experience that whenever Jake had a suspicion he was always right. He and Jake knew that Wynn had sent them on a wild goose chase on the other side of his property, but they went along with the game. It took them some extra time to double back around to the fence post. But with their training it didn't take them long and Butch still had time to spur-climb the tree to have a vantage point. Now it was just a matter of waiting. And waiting was as easy to Butch as it was to breathe.

After Butch had gotten into position, Jake disappeared. Jake did that a lot. It never bothered Butch. It bothered others. But never him. He smiled at the thought of how much it irritated Mr. Smith. The smile faded from his cheeks when he remembered what happened to Mr. Smith. He slowly shook his head at the thought and said out loud to the trees, "It was a damn shame what happened to him." Then again, Mr. Smith was never comfortable with field work. He preferred his suit and ties. His clothes were always pressed and his shoes always shined. Butch would never admit that Mr. Smith was a people person. But compared to himself, Jake, and the rest of their Unit, Mr. Smith was their public face. The few times he came out in the field with them, Mr. Smith was always on edge. The man admitted hating bugs and grass. Butch assumed it was because he was an inner-city boy, not a redneck like the majority of the Unit. Rumor in the Unit was that Mr. Smith used his athletic ability to get himself an education and escape the poverty he was spawned from. Butch didn't know, nor care. Mr. Smith was a good man and it was a shame how he died. According to the autopsy report, Mr. Smith died from a toxic poison known as corpse dust: a poison that causes the tongue to swell and turn black, which leads to convulsions and death. What was left out of the report was how Mr. Smith's body was mutilated by the removal of his skin.

Butch readjusted his position and used the bark of the tree to scratch his right shoulder blade. He looked up to the canopy of the tree and smiled. This is where he belonged, he thought to himself. In the heart of the forest. He always told his little sister that he was born in the wrong time period. He should have been a "mountain man" or a fur trader when America was first discovered. His little sister suspected he had been in a past life. But he didn't believe in that nonsense. Just like he didn't think bigfoot was a benevolent spirit creature that walked between two worlds as a messenger like the Indians preached. He knew bigfoot was a monster. He supposed that was why he had been invited to join the Unit. He shrugged his shoulders and frowned. It wasn't his job to think. His job was to act and follow orders. His job was to do the dirty work that no one else wanted to do. That was what he did and he knew he was good at it. He smiled at the silly thought that always kept him going, that he was like Wolverine from Marvel Comics: "He was the best at what he did, and what he did was not very nice." He almost chuckled out loud to himself as he thought about it. Giddy at the thought he reached into his backpack and pulled out the plastic bag that protected the one comic book he brought with him on every mission: Incredible Hulk, Issue 181. The first real appearance of Wolverine. Any true comic book collector would be appalled at the idea of bringing such a priceless comic book out into the field. But this comic book was his inspiration.

As a young boy he found the comic in his grandfather's attic. He couldn't read at the time. That came later when he was in middle school. But he loved the pictures. A mere man battled two monsters: The Hulk and at the time what Butch thought was a bigfoot. He learned later that what he thought was a white bigfoot in the comic was a Wendigo, which was a fur-covered creature that was once a man, turned into a monster because the man ate human flesh. But to Butch it was the closest thing that represented a bigfoot. Therefore, in his mind, it would always be a bigfoot. Which for him meant that he was the equivalent to Wolverine. A superhero. Which was what he always wanted to be when he was growing up.

Movement to Butch's left caught his attention. He lifted his rifle to his shoulder and peered through the scope and scanned the area. He and Jake both knew they weren't supposed to have guns on the expedition. But there was no way Butch was going into the forest unarmed. He had seen firsthand what these monsters were capable of and he wasn't about to become another statistic in a missing persons report. Butch took sight of Brock through his scope and watched him step out of the tree line into the small clearing near the unfinished fence that Wynn had vacated after his last bigfoot sighting. The crosshairs of the scope rested center mass on Brock's chest. He momentarily felt bad for pointing his rifle at Brock, so he checked the safety. It was engaged. Butch knew it took less than a second to release the safety and take the shot, if necessary. However, killing Brock was not an option at this time. Butch lowered the rifle to his lap and picked up a pair of range-finding binoculars. He peered down at the kid through the binoculars and his features snapped into focus.

Butch watched as Brock stood in the tree line and slowly scanned the meadow. Butch could tell by the kid's body language that he was being cautious. After a few minutes Brock slowly walked out into the center of the meadow near the fence post and removed his backpack. Through the binoculars, Butch watched as Brock removed what looked like a clump of weeds tied together no bigger than a hand. Brock ignited a match and held it to the tied weeds. He then walked the perimeter of the small meadow wafting the smoking weeds. Once he completed the circle of the meadow Brock walked back to his backpack in the center. He snuffed out the smoking weeds after he encircled his body with the smoke. He then pulled out a piece of paper that looked like a photograph and a small leather pouch. Brock squatted down, brushed away the debris on the ground, and laid the photograph on the moss. He then placed a large crystal on top of the picture.

"What the hell is he doing?" Butch mumbled out loud in his tree perch.

Brock reached into the pouch and pulled something out into his closed fist. He opened his fist and peered down at whatever was in the pouch. Then from the crystal in the moss he traced a path that resembled the infinity symbol. Every few feet Brock would bend down and place something on the ground. The infinity symbol pattern stretched from one end of the meadow to the other with the crystal and photograph in the middle at the intersection of the symbol. Brock then removed what appeared to be a crystal wand and followed the same path a second time. When he completed the second circuit of the infinity symbol Brock sat on the ground cross-legged.

Butch adjusted the binoculars and watched as the kid sat there with his eyes closed. For a moment Butch was glad that he had put down the rifle because the thought of pulling the trigger and sending a bullet through the kid's head flashed through his mind. He lowered the binoculars and just watched the kid sit in the grass. He pulled out a PowerBar and quietly chewed on it as the sun descended lower through the trees to the west. When Brock moved again Butch dropped the PowerBar in his lap, pulled the binoculars to his eyes, and peered through the scope. Brock stood and slung on his backpack and moved towards the tree line. Before he reached the tree line, Brock turned around and looked across the meadow into the tree where Butch was perched. He made direct eye contact with Butch through the lens of the binoculars.

"Sonofabitch," muttered Butch as he lowered the binoculars. He watched as Brock melted into the trees.

Brock couldn't help but smile to himself as he walked into the trees. He knew the man named Butch was in the tree the moment he entered the meadow. The man's presence was unmistakable. It took Brock a moment to find him. The man's malicious intention was what gave his position way. Brock had to admit the rifle was a bit unnerving. At the same time he counted on the fact that it would be hard for Butch to explain how he died if they weren't supposed to have guns on this expedition. Brock also suspected that Butch didn't realize they were being watched the entire time. He guessed that Butch was so hyper-focused on him that he didn't pick up that a sasquatch was watching the both of them.

Chapter 50

There was nothing that Jonathan liked about Jake. He disliked the man the first time he saw him in Brock's hospital room all those years ago. He was pissed that Buzzy had tricked him into attending this expedition. He'd given Buzzy an earful to make himself feel better. It didn't do any good. Jake and his friend were still a part of the expedition.

Jonathan stood from the fire and brushed off the bottom of his jeans before he walked over to Jake's tent. Jake sat outside of his tent on a log by a small fire sharpening a large knife. The man didn't bother to look up when Jonathan approached. Jonathan cleared his throat, more out of nerves than announcing himself. Jake continued sharpening the knife.

"Where's your friend?" asked Jonathan.

"Takin' a dump," muttered Jake without looking up.

Jonathan shook his head at the crass comment and muttered, "Nice. I meant Mr. Smith."

Jake stopped and looked up at Jonathan. They held each other's gaze for a moment.

Jonathan asked, "That was his name, right?"

"He retired."

Jonathan countered, "I thought you retired?"

"So did I."

The silence between the two men was thick enough to be felt. Jake returned to sharpening his knife. The screech of metal on stone cut through Jonathan. He was about to turn on his heels and leave. Then Jake said, "I always knew the boy was with you and Jennifer."

Hearing Jennifer's name come out of Jake's mouth unnerved Jonathan. Looking down at the man he shrugged and asked, "What does it matter?"

Jake stopped sharpening the knife and pushed on his knees as he stood. He let out a small grunt as if it was difficult to stand. Jonathan suspected the man was faking it. Jake squared his shoulders to Jonathan. "It doesn't. As far as the world knows, the boy disappeared from the hospital."

Jonathan held the other man's gaze.

Jake looked at the ground and shook his head with a smile. He looked back at Jonathan. "I just wanted you to know that I knew. Like you said, I'm a killer." The words hung in the night air for much too long. "I don't do snatch and grabs like you," Jake said at last. He then sheathed his knife and walked off.

Jonathan looked down at the small fire and then up at the moon and sighed aloud. He missed Jennifer.

Chapter 51

The disjointed group sat by the communal fire and quietly ate the late breakfast that Mama Boobs had prepared. Brock watched as Buzzy and Wynn stepped out of the cabin and walked toward the fire. Butch elbowed Jake. Jonathan and Mama Boobs stopped their side conversation when the two men sat. Brock thought Buzzy looked tired and drained. Wynn appeared giddy and excited like he did every morning. Mama Boobs offered Buzzy a plate of fried eggs and potatoes, which he reluctantly took.

Jake spoke up first: "Who pissed in your cereal?"

Brock watched as Buzzy looked down at his fried eggs and tried to reconcile Jake's statement with the food he was holding. He then shook his head and spoke to the plate. "It's been three weeks and nothing."

Butch grunted.

Jonathan looked at Jake and then spoke up, "I don't think that is entirely true. Jake and Butch found some tracks. We've all heard the howls and screams at night."

Buzzy nodded his head in agreement. "Yes, but no visual sighting.

The individual financing this expedition isn't going to let us play in the woods for endless weeks without hard proof."

Jonathan glanced at Brock. Brock knew from the glance what Jonathan was thinking. They both had suspected and wondered how Buzzy was paying for the expedition. Now it made sense. He had a financial backer. Whoever this individual or group was would want hard evidence. Not just recordings and casting of footprints.

Jake spoke up. "What about you, boy?"

Everyone in the group turned to face Brock, except Jonathan. Brock looked at Jake. "What about me?"

"You see anything on your lil' walkabouts alone?" asked Jake.

"No."

Butch spat in the fire.

Wynn stared into the fire as he spoke. "They need time."

Buzzy asked, "Time for what?"

Wynn poked at the fire with a stick. "To measure your intentions."

Buzzy took a quick bite of his cold eggs. "I believe we have made that clear over the past few weeks."

Wynn looked at Jake and Butch, and then back at the fire. "Maybe not everyone."

Butch grunted and spat into the fire again.

Buzzy quickly spoke up, "We are all here to find proof. Each of our intentions may be different, but each of our end purpose is the same."

Wynn looked at Buzzy and shook his head in disagreement. "Everyone around this circle believes. Everyone's end purpose is different. This is why our hairy friends have remained hidden." The Indian paused, glanced at Jonathan, and then continued, "If you want your proof, stay here and wait."

"Why here?" asked Jake.

Wynn poked at the fire with his stick. "This is one of their reservations."

"What?" asked Butch. "Are we talking about Indians or bigfoot?"

Wynn glared at Butch. "Sasquatch."

"Then what the hell are you talking about?" asked Butch.

"Just as the white man has segregated my people to reservations, they tried the same thing with our hairy friends," answered Wynn.

Butch laughed out loud. "Who told you that bullshit?"

Wynn looked into the fire. "The story has been passed down through our tribal leaders. After your great white father Teddy Roosevelt experienced our hairy friends in the deep wilds, he started the National Parks to give them land to roam, feed, and breed."

"You are flippin' crazy!" countered Butch.

Wynn shrugged his shoulders. "Believe what you will, but I only speak the truth."

Jonathan countered, "I've never heard that before."

Wynn looked at Jake. Jonathan followed his gaze. Wynn said, "There are certain people who keep the information quiet to protect the masses."

Brock asked, "The masses?"

Wynn looked at Brock. "The public. The businesses."

"Why?" Brock asked.

"Tourism to the parks would drop if the public knew monsters that have been known as cannibals to some tribes live in woods. Your government wouldn't want that," answered Wynn.

Jonathan shook his head, not understanding. "Wait. Why create a park system that allowed tourists to endanger themselves?"

Before Wynn could answer, Jake cut in with an irritable tone. "You're missing the point, Professor. President Grant's attempt at Indian Reservations was a failure. Presidents don't like to fail. President Roosevelt improved that failure. He created the National Parks. He never envisioned they would become as popular as they have."

Jonathan stared at Jake as he realized what the man had just divulged and confirmed what he had suspected. Jake shook his head in slight disgust and looked down at the fire. For a moment Jonathan suspected that Jake regretted what he just revealed. He looked over at Wynn, who was nodding his head in agreement. Jake stood and walked away. Jonathan suspected there was more to the man than he had ever given him credit for.

Wynn pulled a long stick out of the fire that almost looked like a pole. At the red hot tip a wisp of smoke ascended into the morning sky. Smiling, he looked at Butch and said, "I too have a smoke pole."

Butch spat in the fire and walked off.

Chapter 52

There more days passed with no incident. Buzzy kept near the camp with Mama Boobs. After Wynn's story about the National Parks, Buzzy made no indication that he wanted to journey deeper into the woods than a hundred feet. Wynn went about his business of maintaining his ranch. Jake and Butch frequently disappeared into the forest at odd hours of the day and night. They never reported where they were going or when they were leaving, which irritated Buzzy because it was against the protocol he had instituted at the beginning of the expedition. Jonathan and Brock continued their daily hikes at dusk and late into the night. In the early mornings before most of the team was awake, Brock would go to the meadow where he had laid the crystal grid. He would sit quietly and write or meditate for a time before returning to camp for breakfast.

One morning in the early sunlight, Jonathan stood at the edge of the tree line watching his friend write in his journal. He didn't want to disturb him. Brock looked up and smiled. He closed his journal, grabbed his backpack, and walked over to Jonathan. As Jonathan watched Brock move towards him he saw movement over his friend's right shoulder. Jonathan focused past his friend and watched as a woman with long dark hair and a brown leather skirt walked between the trees. As he continued to watch, something large and hairy stepped away from a tree and moved deeper into the forest.

Brock stopped in front of Jonathan and said, "I was hoping you would see them."

Jonathan looked at his friend.

Brock smiled and walked off.

Butch lowered the scope of the rifle and watched as the woman and the bigfoot disappeared into the forest. He glanced down at the base of the tree and instinctually knew that Jonathan and Brock were gone. Jake was right. Brock was the magnet. He leaned back against the trunk of the tree and settled in for a long wait. He closed his eyes and waited for Jake.

Chapter 53

Jonathan was giddy. It was the only way he could describe how he felt the entire day. He called Jennifer before breakfast, waking her, and shared with her what he witnessed. He could hear in her sleepy voice that she was excited for him. Of course, she teased him about the woman he saw. It wasn't that she didn't believe him; she always believed him. Jennifer just didn't want him running off into the woods falling in love with some other woman. He assured his wife that she was the only half-naked mountain woman he wanted. He finished the conversation by telling her their plan for the evening and promised her the expedition would be ending soon. He guessed maybe two or three more days. Or a week. Jennifer told him to take as much time as they needed. Their work was important. Jonathan knew she supported the purpose of the expedition. He also could hear in her voice that she was anxious for him to be home with her.

The conversation ended, and he joined the rest of the group for breakfast. Jake and Butch were absent. No one seemed to care. In a short time, Buzzy left, making an excuse that he needed to contact their financial support about securing more time at Wynn's ranch. After hearing Wynn's theory about National Parks being reservations for sasquatch, Jonathan had the impression that Buzzy was ready to end the expedition. That was when it hit Jonathan that Buzzy was just an armchair researcher. He was fascinated by the subject but terrified to witness a sasquatch face to face. Jonathan watched as the man walked off to his tent and sympathized with him that it would be terrifying to stand toe to toe with a sasquatch.

Looking into the fire, Brock said, "Tonight at dusk I'm going to the grid."

Jonathan looked at his friend. "Why?"

Brock poked at the fire and looked up at Wynn. "Just a feeling I have."

Wynn nodded his head in agreement. "Hmmm, the magic of the stones has spoken to our hairy friends."

Brock nodded. "Jonathan saw them this morning."

Excitedly, Shelly spoke up. "You did?"

Jonathan almost felt like he was blushing when Wynn and Mama Boobs looked at him. He sheepishly nodded his head.

Wynn asked, "Did you see the woman?"

Brock answered for Jonathan. "Yes." He paused. "And a sasquatch."

"The white one?" asked Wynn.

Jonathan looked at Brock and then Wynn. "No. It was a deep, dark brown, or black color."

"Hmmm, I have not seen that one," commented Wynn.

Shelly asked, "Are you sure it was a woman? Or maybe a juvenile sasquatch?"

Jonathan smiled, "Oh, I'm pretty sure I know what a half-naked woman looks like."

"Half-naked?" asked Shelly.

Brock answered, "She wore some type of tannish-brown leather skirt with no shirt."

Shelly looked over at Brock. "What? That's it?"

"She had long black hair almost to her waist that covered her breasts," added Jonathan.

Wynn asked Brock, "What will you do?"

"Hope they approach," answered Brock.

Wynn looked at Jonathan and asked, "Will you go with him?"

Jonathan looked at Brock for an answer.

"Yes."

Chapter 54

At dusk Brock stood at the edge of the clearing and dropped his backpack to the ground. Almost absentmindedly he squatted down to unbuckle the clips on his pack and pulled out his journal. He stood and looked over at Jonathan. "Make yourself comfortable; it may take a while."

Jonathan asked, "Are you sure this is going to work with me here?"

Brock smiled. "They let you see them. It'll be okay."

Jonathan picked up Brock's backpack and backed away into the tree line. Brock turned to face the clearing again and took several slow deep breaths to calm his nerves. Gripping his journal, he confidently walked to the center crystal of the grid. He sat cross-legged on the ground and waited.

Butch heard Brock and Jonathan walking through the forest before he spotted them with his binoculars. He rested on a thick tree branch, dropped the binoculars and picked up his rifle. He half-grinned when the two men emerged from the woods directly in line with his rifle scope. It would all be too easy, he thought to himself as he imagined pulling the trigger twice. Instead he lowered the rifle and again picked up the binoculars. Butch watched the two men talk and then split apart. Jonathan backed into the tree line. Butch followed him with the binoculars to ensure he knew the man's position. Jonathan sat under a moss-covered hardwood that had fallen before either of them had been born. He swung the binoculars around and found Brock in his usual cross-legged position in the middle of the clearing. Butch slowly swiveled his head with the binoculars to confirm that Jake was still in position.

Butch confirmed that Jake was about twenty-five yards from Brock's position in the meadow. He watched his partner for some time and was amazed at how slow the man could move. Butch had helped Jake piece together the ghillie suit he now used for camouflage during this expedition. Shortly after this morning's sightings of the bigfoot, Jake dressed in the ghillie suit and relocated over two hundred yards deep into the forest. Jake had a feeling that Brock would attempt contact later that evening. Therefore, he ordered Butch to remain in the tree. Jake moved into his position and gave himself all day to move to the intended target, which would be Brock at the center of the clearing by nightfall. Their plan was devised from experience. Jake and Butch both knew that to be successful in getting close to a bigfoot they had to become a part of the environment. Hence the reason Butch had been in the tree for over a day and Jake was starting from a position of distance. Jake had the more difficult task of covering a large section of ground as slowly as possible in a finite amount of time.

Butch lowered the binoculars and smiled. His partner was the best. He could watch him move all day long. But he needed to prepare.

Brock felt the movement before he saw it. He glanced up to

the night sky and peered at the full moon directly over him. The clearing of the meadow was almost as bright as day. A few times he could see the crystals of the grid sparkle in the moonlight. He wanted to stand up and call out to them. The anxiety of seeing them had built up so much inside of him that he felt like he was about to explode. He knew they could feel his anxiety. He also knew that they felt the intention in his heart. He suspected his intention was what made them apprehensive. He reached down and palmed the Day and Night Stone in his hand and whispered out loud, "Please."

Something snorted. Brock's eyes popped open and standing directly in front of him on the edge of the crystal grid was a massive sasquatch. The creature's jet-black hair made it appear to be a shadow in the night. Brock closed his eyes and silently prayed to himself that he wasn't dreaming. He could feel a hot boil of warmth rush through him as his body accepted the truth before his mind could. He heard the snort again and opened his eyes a second time. The creature was closer. Brock could feel the blood draining from his face. His heart dropped to his stomach. His stomach threatened to release everything he had eaten that day. Tightening his grip on the Day and Night stone, he stood. As he stood, the sasquatch took one more step closer to Brock.

Brock stood frozen in front of the creature. With his head titled slightly back, he noticed every detail on the sasquatch's face. He noticed the streak of gray hair that ran from the creature's forehead across its right eye at an angle. He watched as the creature's breath escaped through its flat nostrils with each exhale. He looked closely at its upper lip, which began to curl upwards in a kind of sneer before lowering back down. He watched as its yellow eyes squinted as it peered down at him, then went wide in recognition.

The creature leaned forward toward Brock and sniffed the air. Its massive chest and shoulders hunched slightly forward to get closer to Brock without taking a step. It grunted at Brock. Almost as if it was asking a question.

Brock smiled and whispered, "Sookum."

Brock felt the hairs on the back of his neck rise at the same time he saw Sookum's own hair bristle in agitation. For a moment Brock feared that Sookum didn't recognize him. The sasquatch rose to his full height and towered over Brock. The creature peered past him and Brock watched as its eyes grew large in fear. Sookum opened his mouth to scream.

The crack of the gunshot broke the silence of the forest before Sookum could make a sound. Brock felt the whiz of the bullet fly past his head. He watched in horror as Sookum was struck in the right side of his chest. The massive creature stumbled backwards. A second shot struck Sookum in the right shoulder. The force of the second shot knocked Sookum to his back. The creature struck the ground as hard as a falling redwood tree.

Brock felt the ground shake under him as Sookum hit the ground. He dropped next to the sasquatch and quickly grabbed the creature's head. He peered down into Sookum's eyes to make sure he was still alive. The creature looked at him and then behind him in fear. Someone forcefully hit Brock in the head with something hard. He looked up and saw Jake standing over Sookum, lowering the point of the rife at the creature's eye.

Jake could feel the hint of a smile stretch across his lips as the giant sasquatch stepped into the clearing. His patience of so many years had finally paid off, he thought. He forced himself to focus and suppressed the joy he felt until the job was done. Until the damn bigfoot creature was dead. He tightened his grip on the rifle as the creature took a step closer to Brock.

Jake looked through the scope and had a clear shot of the

creature. But he waited. The boy was the magnet. The boy was not expendable. Jake waited. He needed the creature to be closer to get a kill shot. He knew Butch would have a clear shot. But he gave explicit orders to not engage. This was his kill. His trigger finger itched. Then the boy stood in front of the creature, blocking his shot.

Jake stood from his position behind Brock in his custom-made ghillie suit. He needed to reveal his position in order to take down the creature. He knew Butch covered his back. As Jake stood, he watched as the bigfoot creature saw him. He watched as the creature rose to its full height in a form of intimidation. He watched as the hairs on the bigfoot's back, shoulder, and head bristled in an attempt to frighten him. Jake wasn't frightened. He was used to this display of intimidation by the bigfoot creatures. He held his ground and pulled the trigger. The first bullet struck just right of the sternum. The second bullet penetrated in the creature's right shoulder just above the pectoral muscle.

Jake felt the ground shake as the bigfoot hit the earth. He knew Butch would be rapidly descending his tree perch to provide backup. Butch's job was to dispose of Jonathan and provide support until the creature's body could be extracted. When the body was secure in their possession, then he would activate the extraction beacon. He advanced on Brock and struck him in the head with the butt of the rifle. First he would finish the kill and then secure the boy. He spun his rifle around and lowered the barrel for a direct shot into the creature's brain through the eye.

Through the scope of his rifle Butch watched as the bigfoot appeared on the edge of the clearing. He watched as Jake compromised his position and delivered two shots to the creature's upper torso. They weren't kill shots. But the caliber of the shots were designed to take the creature down in order to finish the job. Butch dropped from his tree perch in a rapid descent. He quickly unhooked his harness from the self-belay and moved into the clearing. His first priority was to secure the area from any additional bigfoots attempting to retrieve their dead counterpart, in order to successfully extract the specimen. His second priority was to dispose of Professor Jonathan Foxhorn. Securing the area from the other bigfoots was always ugly work. Disposing of Jonathan Foxhorn would be a pleasure.

As Butch entered the clearing he froze in his tracks as he watched three more bigfoot creatures and Jonathan emerge from the tree line. One bigfoot appeared to his right almost directly behind Jonathan and was covered in what appeared to be blondeish hair. A second bigfoot with jet-black hair dropped out of the trees behind the bigfoot that had been shot. The third bigfoot was the giant white one. The one that he and Jake had been hunting for years. The massive white bigfoot advanced on Jake faster than Butch could react. Butch opened his mouth to warn his partner but fell silent at what he witnessed.

Jonathan heard the gunshots before he saw anything. He wasn't sure if he had fallen asleep or simply zoned out. When he heard the first shot he jumped to his feet and ran to the clearing. He watched as the second gunshot knocked the sasquatch to the ground. He was momentarily confused at what he saw. To him it appeared that a smaller sasquatch creature was holding a gun. The scene didn't make sense to him until he saw Butch break through the tree line in a dead run. That was when Jonathan realized the smaller sasquatch holding the gun was Jake in camouflage.

Jonathan watched as Jake struck Brock in the head with the butt of his rifle. He took a step forward to rush to his friend's side but froze when he felt something move next to him. He glanced over and saw a blondee-hair-covered sasquatch standing next to him watching the events. Movement in the corner of his eye caught his attention. He turned back to the meadow and watched as a massive white-hair-covered sasquatch sprinted into the meadow toward Jake.

Jake heard the scream of the sasquatch behind him. He whirled around and brought his rifle to his shoulder to fire. The massive white bigfoot knocked the rifle from his hands with a single swipe. Standing vulnerable in front of the massive creature he felt fear for the first time. He stood nose to nipple to the monster he had been hunting for his entire adult life. Jake felt his bowels release. His knees shook and all he could think about was calling out for his mother.

The white bigfoot reached out with its massive hand and palmed Jake's head. Jake felt the immense strength in the creature's hand as it squeezed his cranium. He vaguely felt his feet lift off the ground. He thought he heard the tendons and ligaments in his neck snap. The last thing he saw was the pure hatred in the creature's dark red eyes.

Butch stood frozen in shock as the massive white bigfoot charged into the meadow toward Jake. He watched as his partner spun around and brought his rifle up to shoot. The creature smacked the rifle away as if it was a stick. It then palmed Jake's head like a basketball. Butch started moving at that point in a dead run to his partner. Instinctually, he pulled out a gun from his chest holster under his jacket.

The bigfoot tore Jake's head from his body. Butch watched as his friend's body crumpled to the ground. The bigfoot tossed the head away as if it was a piece of trash. Butch aimed the pistol at the monster's back and pulled the trigger. A single flare shot out of the barrel of the pistol and struck the massive bigfoot in the back. It howled in pain.

Jonathan stood in shock and horror as he watched the white sasquatch rip Jake's head from his body. Blood exploded from the man's neck as it burst apart. The body crumpled to the ground near Brock. The head bounced and rolled away. The screams from Butch caused the blondee-hair-covered sasquatch to react. The flare momentarily blinded Jonathan as it left the chamber of the gun.

The blondee-haired sasquatch was on top of Butch in a matter of seconds. A third, black-haired sasquatch appeared at the sides of the two injured sasquatch creatures and Brock. The blondee sasquatch grabbed Butch's outstretched arm. It tore it from his body. Butch crumbled to the ground. The blonde sasquatch looked over at Jonathan and he swore it smiled at him.

Brock watched as Numyc lifted Jake off the ground by his head. He instantly remembered the immense pain he had felt as a kid when the same sasquatch had lifted him off the ground so many years ago. He watched as the man's neck exploded and the body crumbled to the ground. Brock felt the blood and tissue splatter against his face but he didn't care. The bastard had shot his best friend.

The light from the flare momentarily blinded Brock. When he was able to see shapes again he could discern that Numyc was on his knees in pain. Brock reacted by smothering the flames on the sasquatch's back with his own body. When his full vision returned, he saw Skunk cradling Sookum and Abigale rushing towards Numyc.

Abigale slid on her knees and embraced Numyc around the neck. She looked at Brock and whispered, "Thank you."

The stench of Skunk struck Brock as he scrambled to Sookum's side. Skunk reached out and palmed Brock's face in a gesture of love. Brock smiled and grabbed his friend's wrist. He then looked down at Sookum and was relieved to tears to see Sookum's eyes open. The creature grunted at him and lifted his giant hand to Brock's chest.

Brock grabbed his best friend's wrist and said, "Next time be a damn tree!"

Chapter 55

The blonde sasquatch, Shimmer, joined the group still carrying Butch's arm. Jonathan followed close behind her. She grunted at the night sky. Skunk and Abigale looked towards the stars and listened. Skunk grunted in agreement. Abigale touched Brock on the shoulder and said, "Brock, we have to go."

Brock looked at Jonathan and then Abigale with apprehension. "It's time for you to come with us again," Abigale clarified. She reached out and placed the palm of her hand over his heart and said, "The spirit of sasquatch lives within you. Your home is with us again."

Brock looked into Sookum's eyes and images of the forest from his time with the tribe flashed through his mind. He knew Sookum wanted him to return to the tribe. That was why his friend had risked coming back for him. He stood and attempted to help Sookum stand. Sookum stood and rested a majority of his weight on Skunk. Abigale touched Brock's arm. "They are coming. We have to go," she said with a bit more urgency.

In the distance Brock could hear the rapid approach of a

helicopter. Jake or Butch must have activated a homing beacon before the confrontation started. He knew there was no time to make a decision. He had to react to his heart's intention. He turned and handed Jonathan his journal. "Thank you, Quinn. Tell Hope I will miss her." He then embraced his friend with a tight hug.

When he released his hug, Shimmer grunted and shoved Butch's bloody arm into Jonathan's chest. He reluctantly took it. Shimmer helped Skunk and Sookum move off toward the tree line and disappeared into the foliage. Abigale reached out and took Brock's hand. He looked down at their hands clasped together and smiled. He didn't realize until that moment how much he had missed his tribe and Abigale. He squeezed her hand tight to make sure she didn't disappear on him.

The sound of the helicopter grew louder. It was a matter of moments before it would appear above the meadow. Numyc stood in a fluid motion. Brock took an instinctual step backwards away from the massive sasquatch. He was tempted to let go of Abigale's hand. She squeezed his hand tighter. The massive sasquatch peered down at him and then whooped out loud. Within the tree line Brock heard a second whoop. Numyc motioned with his head toward the second whoop. Abigale turned and ran towards the tree line pulling Brock with her. Brock ran along beside her but stopped when they got to the trees.

Brock looked back and watched as a single black helicopter rose above the trees on the far side of the clearing. Numyc turned to face the helicopter and screamed at the top of his lungs. Jonathan dropped the journal and Butch's arm to the ground and clamped his hands over his ears. He dropped to his knees and crumbled into a ball. Numyc then ran in the opposite direction of Abigale and Brock into the forest. Numyc sounded like a freight train running through the trees. Brock watched as trees shook and crashed to the ground as

Numyc diverted the attention of the helicopter. The black helicopter turned in the air and pursued the sasquatch.

Silence descended into the forest once again. Abigale and Brock heard a soft whoop off to their left. They both saw Shimmer's head poke out from the side of a tree. Brock couldn't help but smile. Abigale tugged on his hand to start moving again. Brock glanced back at Jonathan, who was looking around in bewilderment. "More are coming. He'll be fine," reassured Abigale.

Without looking at Abigale, Brock asked, "Are you my mother?"

Abigale squeezed his hand and pulled him deeper into the forest.

Chapter 56

O nly a day had passed since Jonathan had returned from the Olympic National Forest. After the incident on Wynn's ranch he was forced to stay an extra week in Seattle, answering questions for the local police and park rangers. During that time, he was anxious to return home to Jennifer and his family. Upon returning home he felt drawn to Brock's cabin in the mountains. After sharing what happened to Brock, Jennifer quickly agreed to hike up to Brock's cabin with him. Now as he stood in front of the A-frame structure on the mountain ridge, all he could do was smile. He flicked at the lock on the latch of the cabin door and shook his head. It wouldn't take much for a person to break the lock. Then again, Brock...

He stopped himself and closed his eyes. He and Jennifer hadn't helped the boy escape the hospital three years ago. At the same time, they didn't turn the boy away when they found him sleeping under their deck. Instead, he and Jennifer made up a story that he was their nephew. To make it official, he contacted an individual he had met while doing research on inner-city gangs to have a fake social security card and birth certificate made to hide his identity. It worked.

Jennifer moved behind Jonathan. He turned around and watched as she picked up a wooden table that had tipped over at some point. They sat on a fallen tree together and looked out over the river below them. Jennifer leaned her head against Jonathan's shoulder and snuggled close to him. He opened the journal and cleared his throat.

September 27th

Hi, Quinn. Hi, Hope. I never explained to the both of you why I picked those names for you. At the time I had been with my tribe for almost four years, I think. You two were the first regular people we saw. Looking back I think this was on purpose. Sookum, our tribe leader, always kept us in the deep forest and never around civilization. But after the meeting with the Tribes, everything changed. I think everything changed because of Abigale. She was the first person I had contact with after I "disappeared" with Sookum. She explained a lot to me on the dynamics of the Tribes. I also learned that she was Numyc's familiar, or partner. Sookum always protected me from Numyc. I could see in the creature's eyes that Numyc hated me. Or maybe hated my presence. I may never know why.

After the meeting of the Tribes, Sookum brought us to Furnace Mountain. Skunk and Shimmer took a liking to the two of you. They used to watch you two sit on the deck at night. I started watching the both of you as well. Jonathan, you reminded me of my brother, Darius. I remember I thought you had the same mannerisms as him. You had a gentle and kind face. Your actions were precise and fueled by thought. So I started referring to you by my brother's middle name, Quinn. Jennifer, I started calling you Hope, because I hoped that my own mother was as loving and fun as you.

Growing up, Darius told me that my mother was dead. My father believed she was kidnapped by a sasquatch. My father was angry. He wanted his partner back. Not necessarily because he loved her. I suspect more because he wanted her to take care of his two boys. Darius tried to protect me from his wrath. But he wasn't always there.

Find Darius. If you do, tell him everything.

Jonathan, Jennifer, thank you for your love. Thank you for your support. And thank you for your family.

EPILOGUE

Caven stepped from the tree line into the meadow holding the lead rope to his horse. His horse pawed at the ground and refused to move forward. Caven turned and looked at the animal. "Stubborn cuss," he said. The horse snorted at him. Caven dropped the lead rope and moved toward the center of the meadow. He wasn't worried about his horse wandering away. They had an understanding relationship.

In the center of the meadow Caven squatted down to pick up a crystal rock. It lay on top of faded white paper that had partially dissolved from the continuous mist of the mountains. There was an image on the paper, but it was so faded he couldn't make out what it was. Off to his right he saw what appeared to be a white tree branch. As he moved closer, he noticed it was a human arm. He picked it up by the wrist and examined it at arm's length. Hundreds of maggots and bugs crawled all over the rotting flesh. He looked up towards the sky and the circling birds. He understood why they circled. He shook the decaying arm to try and shake off the bugs.

Caven moved back towards his horse and strapped the decaying arm to the outside of the saddle bag. Without looking up he said, "Wynn."

The Indian stepped from the side of the tree towards the horse. "Caven."

Caven made eye contact with Wynn and thought how much the man reminded him of his old friend Little Otter.

Wynn said, "It's been a while. You look good."

Caven looked down at his lean frame. He scratched at his beard and ran his hand through his thick hair. He smiled. "I miss the Rendezvous."

Wynn knew the man was referring to meetings the mountain

men and fur trappers had in the Rocky Mountains over a century ago. "Need anything?"

Caven frowned and shook his head no. He turned and looked out over the meadow. He tossed the crystal rock in the air and caught it. Without looking at Wynn, he asked, "Did you see what happened?"

Wynn shook his head no.

Caven nodded his head in acknowledgement. He turned back to his horse and grabbed the lead line. The horse willingly lifted its head from eating the grass and started to move towards the tree line. Caven glanced at Wynn. "Be seein' you."

Wynn watched as the mountain man disappeared into the thicket of trees. When he no longer heard the man or the horse, he left the meadow. He strolled through the forest to his cabin on the ranch. As he stepped through the trees he saw his love, Shelly, sitting on the porch waiting for him. He raised one hand to wave to her and smiled when she waved back.

As Wynn reached the porch he climbed the three short steps and sat next to Shelly in one of the wooden rockers. Shelly reached out and clasped his hand in hers. "Everything okay?" she asked.

Wynn smiled and nodded his head. "Yes."

Shelly leaned back in the rocking chair and looked out towards the mountain peaks in the distance. "I feel safe here." She then turned and kissed Wynn on the cheek. "And I feel loved."

Wynn leaned in towards Shelly and whispered, "You are safe and loved here."

ACKNOWLEDGEMENTS

My dad was from a small town in West Virginia, called Mallory. As a child growing up we spent many summer weeks and Thanksgiving weekends near Mallory at my Uncle Steve's house. During the summer, it was usually just my dad and I and occasionally one of my friends. We would spend a week or two at my Uncle's house and I was free to run through the West Virginia "hills" that buffered my Uncle's property. I ran through the forest unsupervised with a machete and BB gun, swinging on vines, rocking climbing, and exploring the thick forest.

As a child, my dad wanted to hike to the top of "Mallory Hill" and carve his name and birth date on a rock the locals called Devil's Table. The summer I was 12-years-old, my dad, my friend Jeff and I bushwhacked our way to the top of Mallory Hill to Devil's Table. My dad insisted that we bring a .22 rifle and a Remington 3.06 rifle for protection. We cleared a space on the ridge, made a fire, and pitched our tent. My dad grabbed his hammer and chisel and started banging away on the rock carving his inscription. Jeff and I explored the surrounding area until evening came. We ate hot dogs, Vienna sausages, and craved gallons of water! As the dark night descended my dad built the fire to a roaring blaze. The hours passed, and we sat talking about nothing and everything. Late in the evening, something screamed. My dad described it as a blood-curdling scream from a mad, crazed woman. According to my dad, Jeff's eyes bugged out of his head and it took all of his own self-control to not panic. He warned Jeff he was going to shoot the .22 to scare off whatever was screaming. He shot into the air and then put down the .22 rifle to pick up the Remington 3.06. He turned his back to the fire to let his eyes adjust to the blackness of the night. Over his shoulder he instructed Jeff to place some more wood on the fire. They sat in silence for several minutes before they heard the blood-curdling

259

scream again. My dad thought it sounded further away. Not wanting to fire the 3.06 (because it has never been fired) by dad picked up the .22 and shot towards the sky a second time. The rest of the evening past in silence.

Unfortunately, I missed the entire event because I was asleep in the tent. Upon returning to my Uncle's house the following day my dad shared the story with his brother. Uncle Steve dismissed it as a bobcat, cougar, or mountain lion. Which it may have been. However, through the years as I heard the story again and again I started to wonder if maybe it wasn't a mountain lion, but a sasquatch. Maybe, just maybe, that night my dad and Jeff heard a bigfoot by Devil's Table in Mallory, West Virginia.

As always, thank you to my parents, Carol and Ernest, and my sisters Robin and Retha, for their continued love and support in my hobby as a writer. Thank you to my children, Christian, Cassandra, Alyvia, and Tahlia for thinking that it is "really cool" to have a dad as an author. A special thank-you to Cassandra for coming up with the title for this book. Your questions and thoughts helped to shape the foundation of the story. To my friend Wes Bowman, thank you for your company on the trails and rivers while we talked, discussed, bantered, and joked about science fiction, fantasy, literature, friendship, love, family, and life. Your thoughts, ideas, and insight helped me tell a better, more believable story. Your scientific brain kept me grounded in reality. I know for you, seeing is believing, I am confident one day you will see the truth. To my life-long friend, Bruce Panneton, for knowledge related to hunting, rifles, and the military. I can always count on you for an answer. I hope one day you see one. A special thank-you to Ellen and Brandon Wick and Lori Popovich for reading the first draft of this story and finding the beauty of the story through the rough edges. A special thank you to Rob Speiden from Natural Awareness Tracking School (www.

trackingschool.com) for spending the day with me and answering all of my questions related to tracking humans and animals. I still think your casts of animal prints should be displayed as artwork. To my friend Karen Keyes, your wealth of knowledge on crystals has been invaluable. More importantly so has your friendship and our many conversations. And to my friend Doug Cook, my trusted personal editor for all things written.

To my editors at Zharmae, Keri Phillips and Chris Hassett, thank you for making me feel like an accomplished writer and finding the unique qualities that make this story different than every other bigfoot tale. Thank you, Anna Kowalczewska for bringing Sookum to life with your amazing art work. Thank you to the entire Zharmae crew for their eye to detail and professionalism.

And most importantly, thank you to my Muse, Christine. You are my wife and my best friend, and I cherish every moment with you. God has blessed me with your love, energy, and inspiration. Thank you for always believing that I can do anything and everything, even when I doubt myself. Together, we know they exist. Together we are strong. STS.

NOTE FROM THE AUTHOR

Thank you for reading!

What did you think of *Spirit of Sasquatch*?

I would be grateful if you could leave a rating or review for this book at your favorite review site

(i.e., Goodreads, Amazon).

Reviews are a great way for indie authors to gain readers.

Thank you for your support!

Follow My Work...

Twitter: @ErnestSolar
Instagram: @Ernestsolar
Facebook.com/spiritofsasquatch

ABOUT THE AUTHOR

ERNEST SOLAR has been a writer, storyteller, and explorer of one kind or another for his entire life. He grew up devouring comic books, novels, any other type of book along with movies, which allowed him to explore a multitude of universes packed with mystery and adventure. A professor at Mount St. Mary's University in Maryland, he lives with his family in Lovettsville, Virginia.

www.ingramcontent.com/pod-product-compliance
Lightning Source LLC
Chambersburg PA
CBHW021417110726
47901CB00008B/2192

* 9 7 8 0 6 9 2 8 9 2 1 9 0 *